TIME NOVA

DERRICK BLISS

That's My Client

This book is a work of fiction. Any references to historical events,
real people, or real places are used fictitiously. Other names, characters, places and events are products of the author's imagination, and
any resemblance to actual events, places or persons, living or dead,
is entirely coincidental.

For Devin and Dylan

I love you more than can be expressed
with words. Live happily and be good to
each other.

1

Brooklyn, New York

Current Day

June 9, 2052

"Damn it," he huffed when his right shoulder swing attempt failed, and he was suctioned back into his pillow top.

Just getting out of bed was a remarkable feat for Wellington Brackford. Certainly, the lack of neither energy nor desire was the obstacle. The damn chronic lower back pain battled Welly with great vigor and the ensuing frustration weighed down his shoulders like a wet blanket since the pain had arrived six years earlier.

Dull beeps persisted inside his head.

He lay staring at the darkness for a moment before mentally requesting, "Time."

The beeping stopped.

A soft voice replied, "Six o' three a.m."

The in-house mind's eye concierge program was uploaded by his only child, sixteen year old Kyle, and Welly used it more now out of habit. His company developed the program and while he appreciated the enormous sales and cash flow it generated, he wanted nothing more than having nothing but old in his home. It was his sanctuary. He was engulfed in modernity all day and the contrast of his home kept him sane, or at least somewhat sane. For thirty one years since he started his technology company, he's awoken between 5:50 and 6:10 without the aid of an alarm.

He appreciated Kyle's effort, but just wished the whole of Kyle's focus was on kicking his bad habits. His few good deeds had been even fewer and more far between lately, since he brought around that crude Daisy girl. Or was it Lily? It was some kind of flower.

Welly called her the Impatient because she messaged Kyle nonstop. In fairness, she wasn't alone. Young women were crawling all over Kyle like ivy. He was a good-looking kid and one of the richest people in the world and in this world, all that had meaning of far too high an order.

Welly knew the back pain was perpetuated by his frustration *about* the back pain and round and round he went. He was in an age where he didn't need to suffer through the pain, but he instead chose to suffer which added to his frustration. Medicine was not an option for him. In the twenty-fifties, the average life expectancy of a male reached ninety-six and was rising rapidly. He should be in his prime.

This particular morning arrived as any day did for Welly, with those all too brief fleeting moments of wonderful amnesia and then - he remembers the pain. He tries to get up and fails. Then he feels as helpless as a belly-up turtle as he contemplates how to best rise and face the day. It was a process.

He tried going for it again.

He heaved his feet over the side of the bed and they dropped to the floor, his legs following closely behind. He stood up. He was hunched like a lowercase r for a few seconds. He raised his back ever so slowly to forty five degrees and shambled across the bedroom floor.

Welly liked to attribute his back pain to stress caused by Kyle. It was less painful than other attributions. He knew it was unfair, but if Kyle was to continue to do what he was doing then Welly can attribute pain unapologetically if he so desires. This mental practice helped to increase the rate of speed of the daggers entering his lower back.

Yes, of course Welly knew that Kyle's trauma was real enough and contributed to his vices, but he'd be damned if he ever fed into any excuse, reasonable or otherwise, for the decisions one makes in one's life.

The moment Welly stepped foot on the creaky wooden floor in the hall he was dazed by a dream-worldly déjà vu rush. The feeling was overwhelming, as powerful as booze.

He shrugged it off and shuffled a few steps over to the bathroom. As he urinated, he stared down at his growing gut. The weight he could cope with, but the annoying part was not being able to view his manhood. He sucked in his gut to peek at his out of work friend. Somehow that made him feel better - momentarily. He moved over to the antique ivory mirror perched above the sink.

Life is hard.

He looked at his face. The older he gets the more in the morning he feels that he looks as if he was in a barroom brawl the evening before. His nose all puffy, sand bags under his eyes.

Wow, Welly, he thought. *Never will you find a woman willing to invest her energy in your feelings looking like this. She'd be gone the second she notices the way your stupid hand balls into a fist uncontrollably and unconsciously when you think of Christine. Why wouldn't she? Look at you. You're starting to look like a damn fuddy duddy.*

Welly found himself pondering more and more about life lately. Life is hard and it gets harder the further one goes. More and more debris and weight is collected and it takes more and more discipline to keep moving forward but we must - so we do. Life's difficulties being attached like a variety of fishing sinkers, each amount of weight in direct relation to the level of heartache or tragedy, until you are dragging hundreds behind you like a bride's train comprised of marred jewelry growing heavier by the day, but you pull it because you've built up the strength with each piece of lead added, some three ounce round pebble weights, some twenty thousand pounds worth of thick galvanized steel chain and barnacle encrusted anchor soldered for a cruise liner of grief, and you pull it day in and day out until you can pull no longer. Welly hoped that some great event might shed some of his sinkers and he may live out some number of years in a lighter fashion.

No such event transpired yet.

So, his spirit carried him. His spirit and discipline to control his thoughts.

Yes. It's discipline that we need more of with each passing day, he reminded himself. *The discipline to train our thoughts away from the miniscule, the microscopic, the should-be-non-existent thoughts that invade the human mind on a constant basis. It's discipline that we need and strength of spirit is what we need to refuel that discipline. And what I need right now more than anything - coffee.*

He eyed his aging face morosely. Christine had always remarked how different he could appear to her at times. "The many faces of Wellington Brackford," she would say ominously. You had your Yard Work Welly with frantic hair and grass stained blue jeans, your Astronaut Welly in that skin tight derma suit and neatly parted hair, and of course your boardroom Mr. Brackford with slicked back hair and three piece suit a.k.a., your Gordon Gecko Welly. This look appeared most when world leaders were in town. "You have to look a certain way to be taken seriously," Welly said then in defense of himself. "They react as much to your appearance as to your tone. Sad but true."

If those diplomats could only see him now. I guess you could call this look, your Shitbag Welly.

It was upsetting because it meant something. Appearance meant something. That fact alone was upsetting, but it was additionally troubling that his appearance was in decline and even worse than that; he cared.

His mind was a finely tuned machine. He exercised it more frequently than the world's leading bodybuilder worked out their traps. It bothered him that as enlightened as the world was slowly becoming, most still viewed him simply as some pasty, puffy, out of touch middle-aged white guy. He looked forward to the day that the external appearance mattered not, but he feared he may not live long enough to witness it.

In a flash, that waking dream feeling washed over him again. Images and voices and text whizzing through his mind created a schizophrenic feeling. The feeling was foreign and then all too familiar. This was not a drill. It was not practice. It was a mod - a history modification.

A mod was simply when someone travelled into the past and altered something, anything. At the moment of awakening, all people's minds living at any point after the modification, begin to consciously center and experience this intense psy-chotic feeling as the new memory washes away the previous reality. Most people realize not what the feeling actually is, as once the previous reality dissipates, it disappears forever. It's a fleeting thought. It's a dream that went from vivid to hazy to gone. Welly knew exactly what he was experiencing. He led the research and training initiative on this very topic at his company for the past three years.

Part of the training he provided to each member of the travel certified staff was a four week Data Stay workshop. It was intense hypno training the purpose being when a history mod is recognized, your brain, if trained properly can hone in on the streaming data, the soon to be lost history, and re-re-member it before it is gone. The trickiest part is recognizing a mod when it's happening as most scrambled thoughts when one first awakes are credited to the haze of the mind getting adjusted to the world. Most scrambled thoughts *are* exactly that so even the Data Stay workshop graduates will fail to rec-ognize the experience and soon forget an experience has oc-curred.

It's not an exact science like some would have you believe. One may wake and vividly remember a dream that is so real that it *must* have been real. Then a short time passes and the dream cannot be retrieved. It is gone. Sometimes, this is the re-sult of a history mod. Other times it is not.

He covered his forehead with his palm instinctively and foolishly, attempting to ensure the data remained inside. He stomped onto the auto shoe soles placed next to his door. Counterfeit leather emerged from slits around the top edges of the soles and enwrapped his feet, clasping together securely with magnets. These were loved by the youth and old timers like Welly with lower back daggers.

Pacing hurriedly through the rickety hallway, he tried ignor-ing his discomfort.

Slab, where's the slab?

Among other things, the slab was a physical object to store thoughts and memories and data that is designed to withstand the changes of time in this era where everything is saved and accessed and happening virtually and in thought.

He checked the kitchen table. No. The counter. No.

Snores ricocheted off the walls from the living room.

Kyle!

Welly stomped with the grace of a primate to the living room where he found Kyle asleep on the couch without a blanket, wearing his blue jeans and black t-shirt from the day before. Sure enough, the slab lay on the nightstand beside the couch. Welly reprimanded him numerous times about all present activities; sleeping on the couch, sleeping in his day clothes and using *his* slab. Kyle owned his own slab until he mysteriously lost it and Welly refused to buy, well, technically, bring home another one, to teach him the value of a dollar or sixty four hundred, which was the current cost. He was out of tricks or carrots or new ideas to break through to his son.

He picked up the slab having the dimensions of an old-fashioned plastic credit card - those still in use as late as the 2020's - and ran his finger along the top. The microscopic lighting mechanisms framing the face of the slab generated the adjustable four dimensional image hovering a pinky's length above the slab. It was currently set to the commonest default, and immediately projected a nearly full sized, scantily clad young lady dancing.

The accompanying music thumped loudly.

Doof doof doof-doof tss tss juwwwehhh. Doof doof doof-doof tss tss juwwwehh.

Welly shook his head and scoffed at the ridiculousness of this new music.

The voice of the beautiful girl dancing in her underwear said, *"Uh-huh. Yeah. You like that."*

Welly hastily swiped his pointer from top right to bottom left closing out the screen, but not before the image of the par-tially nude woman produced one last fading orgasmic moan.

He needed to download his thoughts onto a physical object - right this second.

Kyle let loose a baritone grunt of a snore, unaware that his father was looking over him censoriously. Welly shook his head as he ran his finger over the section of the floating screen that enabled him to change the frequency to his setting which he simply named Welly. Once on his brainwave setting, he can se-lect programs, psype - or mentally type - and save information without touching the screen. He just has to think of the proper commands and the machine acts just the same as voice command just without actually verbalizing thoughts.

He prompted the pad and began pouring his thoughts onto the screen. A person really concentrating can put up to seven hundred rational words per minute on the air-pad produced by their slab. Welly's thoughts were fragmented but at least they would be saved to reference later.

Battle of Lexington and Concord...battle that marked start of American Revolution - Paul Revere and William Dawes rode to warn patriots of secret raid of Concord by British on the command of patriot leader Joseph Warren...Samuel Prescott joined Revere and Dawes along the ride and the three men successfully stirred the minutemen...700 British led by Francis Smith marched to Concord on the night of April 18th 1776...morning of April 19th 1776 British encountered 70 minutemen Captain John Parker Lexington on way to Concord...mysterious first shot...battle...British move on to Lexington...find nothing...militiamen attack British road back to Boston...cover by trees and houses...1,000 British reinforcements sent to Lexington save Smith's troops...worried General Thomas Gage further reinforces Boston...

Stop stop, Welly thought as this was the phrase he selected as his prompt to switch off the brainwave writer.

But Lexington and Concord didn't happen. No!

A newer, more vivid memory streamed through Welly's mind as he read the words he had just transmitted to his air-pad.

Revere and Dawes never made it to Lexington, never warned the minutemen. Samuel Adams and John Hancock were captured at Concord along with a stockpile of munitions. Shortly thereafter they both died imprisoned on a British ship in Boston harbor.

Psype Psype.

Welly began pouring as much American Revolution data as he could remember onto his air-pad fearing that something or someone affected history and soon new data will forever replace the pure history. He produced every bit of information he was capable of, prior to inhaling his first cup of coffee.

"Kyle, wake up."

Kyle groaned and rolled onto his side.

"Kyle! Up! Now!"

Kyle slowly muscled his eyelids open and uttered, "What Dad? There's no school today."

"I know. I need you to get up now and put your shoes on. Grab the reader with school books. Don't question me. Now!"

Sensing a tone in his father's voice, Kyle rotated his body and slid on his bright white and red sneakers on the floor beside the couch. "I didn't do anything," he said.

"You're not in trouble, but there's no time to explain. Get the reader. Meet me in the car."

Welly stomped back to his room and lifted his secret floorboard. He put his thumb on the space on top of the narrow safe and the top opened. He snatched the small black pouch and hurried it into his pants pocket.

"Keys," he shouted inside his mind.

For a tech tycoon, Welly was in love with the old school. He somehow relished a nostalgic comfort in referring to them as keys, but they were actually fobs housed in a chicklet sized device. A gentle rub on any particular location sends a small jut out that opened his home, office, car or anything else locked with encryption. Even the gentle rub was technically speaking old school as all was more easily operated with mental prompts communicating with the device.

No one was a bigger advocate for moving the planet forward than the guy who founded the Forward Facility, but as much as he embraced evolution, he embraced choice. Having options.

Having the ability to choose, even the little things, was akin to freedom.

A high pitched, steady tone sounded and Welly walked towards the noise. The keys crawled out from under some old legal documents atop his desk and zipped through the air to Welly's palm and stuck there.

When he was a boy, he would undoubtedly be searching for the string or the trapped door or something to figure out how that trick worked. Now, ironically, this tech was child's play and a simple combination of grounded sensors commanded through use of brain waves and objects guided with GPS, and pulled along with magnetic currents.

"Found," he said. The piercing tone inside his head stopped. He grabbed the key square and walked briskly out of the room.

The door shut and locked behind him as mentally commanded.

2

Welly boarded the Jeep and placed his thumb and pointer on the screen in the center of the steering wheel. He spun his two fingers as if twisting a soda bottle cap and the car started. Two minutes passed and still no Kyle. Welly's blood pressure climbed with every passing second. It was as if Kyle was purposely taking his time. Beeping the horn may attract unwanted attention from anyone seeking to stop Welly. The only productive actions were biting a fingernail, shaking his head and waiting.

Just after four minutes of time wasted, Kyle came strolling out empty-handed. Reader, where's the damn reader?

"Kyle," Welly said as Kyle opened the truck's door. "Where's the damn reader?"

"Oh man," Kyle said.

"Damn it, Kyle," said Welly. "Just forget it. I give up. You can't handle one thing."

Kyle slammed the door and reached into his navy blue windbreaker. He pulled out the paper thin reader and put it atop the center console.

Welly looked at it and said, "But you—

"I was just messing with you. You're such a spore."

"Hey, I told you not to call me that."

The anger in Welly's voice was harsh. It now felt like it was derived more from necessity than defeat. The feeling steeply dropped off, landing him in a pit of guilt.

"Look, Kyle, I—"

"Just save it and drive."

Staring at Kyle made it difficult not to notice the black Mercedes sedan accelerating rapidly down the block, getting larger and larger in the passenger side mirror.

"Good idea," Welly said and pulled out of the spot, swiping the Audi parked in front of him. "Sorry fella, no time."

"Jesus!" Kyle said. "Ya know everyone has accident avoidance except you. The guy whose company invented it." Kyle shook his head and stared out his window.

"Don't take the lord's name in vain," Welly said.

Kyle shook his head again. "Really? Oh my God."

Welly gave him a brief scowl and then looked in his mirror. In the rearview he witnessed the Mercedes screeching dead in front of his detached home. It was the latest model Mercedes, Welly knew, as it slid sideways into a parking spot as if the ground was greased, and strong men pushed it into the spot from the driver's side. The pocket doors slid open and two impeccably suited men jogged towards the house.

The clock was ticking.

"Dad!" Kyle yelled.

Welly realized he was caught up too long in the rearview cinema and looked forward. A kid no more than seven was flapping his way right into the Jeep's path on one of those new toys - Tera-Zip. It's basically a pool noodle that floats. The child can flap his or her arms to make it go slightly higher, forward and backward, and into oncoming traffic.

Parked cars on the right. An oncoming truck up left. Only one option remained. Welly reached behind the steering wheel and ran his finger down then up. The front of the car up-ended and jerked off the ground and into flight, the front right tire grazing a tuft of the little boy's brown hair. Either the force of the wind gust from the Jeep or the shock of this maneuver, sent the boy flopping off his Tera-Zip and onto the concrete.

Kyle looked out the back window and down at the boy crying on the ground. "Real nice, Pop."

"That kid will think twice before playing in the street again. I'll tell you that," Welly said as he guided the car back down to the ground.

This area was not permitted for auto aviation and the last thing Welly could afford was being stopped by the Artificial Intelligence Police (AIP) or the Apes as they were called by most.

"Pretty excellent how it up-ended and shot up like that, huh? You don't see these other new techie cars taking off like that. No you don't. This baby is-"

"Custom," Kyle cut off. "I know it's custom, but they left out a bunch of *helpful* technology."

"This baby has more technology than you can shake a stick at."

"Shake a stick? I can't deal. Whatev."

Wellington and Kyle raced toward the Forward Facility. Flatbush Avenue on the ground floor was surprisingly backed up with traffic. Welly exited to the second tier to avoid further delay.

Overall, traffic is much lighter in volume then it was even back in the 2040s. Now that the generation was fine-tuning the in-mind experiences they can have without leaving their homes, the need to travel around was becoming a lot less vital.

With the addition of the product piping system or PPS, the need to go to the store was a lot less important too. Sahara retailing had taken on the initiative to run the pressurized piping from warehouses to homes in many neighborhoods across the United States and in a few European countries as well. A consumer sits on his or her couch in his or her potato chip encrusted clothing and selects an item, adds it to their shopping cart, makes the purchase with encrypted payment technology and within minutes it is being piped into the designated entry point at their home. For some this is a chute outside of their home perhaps opposite their mailbox that looks like a steam exhaust pipe on a cruise ship. While others have a sliding door that opens allowing the package to enter right into their foyer or living room and then closes again once the package has arrived. Returning something? Not a problem. Scan the package with your installed scanner and re-enter it into the chute. It works both ways.

Welly's future agency reporting team, FAR for short, which is precisely where Welly used to want to be in relation to them, predicted another nearly twenty percent decline in traffic over the next decade to come. Driver-less taxis were increasingly gaining popularity as well, and more and more young people were opting to not learn how to drive at all.

Welly began to shift on into the right lane as a car came flying through the lane at a fast speed, relative to the speed limit. The vehicle was travelling at well over one hundred miles an hour and Welly swerved back onto the shoulder just avoiding ending up sitting on the hood of this hooligan's car. Welly and Kyle whirled with the Jeep from the force and proximity of the passing car.

"Jesus," Welly said. "Believe this guy?" He shook his head.

"Lord's name," Kyle said.

Welly huffed. "He could kill someone not to mention you're guaranteed a fine with all the sensors. Some people just don't care about anything." Welly shifted into the parkway's upper stack right hand lane and accelerated. "Still the most dangerous way to travel if you ask me."

The over crowdedness was something Welly always complained about, but deep down knew he could never leave. It irritated him immensely, but invigorated him as well.

Kyle rolled his eyes.

Welly wove his green Cherokee from lane to lane through the air.

"Thank God for these stacks," Welly remarked.

He received no reaction from Kyle which he had learned to live with over the last few years. The truth was that Welly was quite proud of this modernized road system. He was the single largest donor and part of the design team.

Without the stacks, considering the ever-growing population, it would take the average driving Long Island commuter upwards of 4 hours to get to New York City. But since it was only finalized within the past two years, many drivers were still nervous jumping up a level and especially up two levels. Despite the technology being sound and the altitude monitoring system keeping every vehicle at the exact proper altitude, some folks were just slower to adapt. It worked out so that the three levels were generally considered as the slow to fast lanes, bottom to top.

The Jeep glided off the parkway before the Flatbush Avenue exit and well out of the bounds of the upper stack exit air ramp.

"What are you doing?" said Kyle, clutching the door handle.

"We have no time," Welly offered. This maneuver was highly illegal, but something told him time was of the essence. Besides, he figured, after having a few more clarifying minutes on the road, running into a police officer would not be the worst thing.

"You're going to get arrested," Kyle pointed out.

Welly raised his eyebrows and lowered into the half empty Forward Facility parking lot on Flatbush Avenue. He pulled the Jeep into a spot next to Stewart's immaculate 2035 gold Honda Civic.

"I swear that guy sleeps here."

Kyle looked left and right. "Stewart?"

"Huh," Welly said as he reached underneath his steering wheel to a secret compartment for his security card. The card was the third and final step in gaining access to the vessel named Christine II after Welly's late wife and Kyle's late mother.

The first access step for getting to Christine II was a fingerprint scan using a device that randomly shuffled to request any one of the five fingers. The second step is a retina scan and the third is the security card featuring a bar code similar to that of a quick response code used in marketing. This code was generated by a new computer operating on a new server and both were destroyed seconds after the code's creation by personnel with the highest security clearance.

"Got it, let's boogie," Welly said, gripping the two square inch metallic card, ignoring Kyle's question.

Kyle rolled his eyes, opened his door and sprang out of the door. Welly was still easing his stiff abdomen off his seat as Kyle was already over by the driver's side door.

Welly looked up at his son then grabbed hold of the half-opened door panel and the door jam and pushed himself onto the pavement, wincing internally.

"This damn dank cold air. I thought summer was here."

The two opened the astronomically priced, unlocked, and disabled security door and walked hurriedly into the lobby of the building across the cold steel floors to the elevator bank. The ceilings were somewhere up by the edge of the Milky Way and crafted of heavy white metal and solar glass.

"No one listens to me," Welly said, thinking about the door being unlocked again. "I hate this place. I don't know why I let them talk me into this design."

Most of all he hated the corridor leading to the elevators featuring those agoraphobic-high ceilings and the ridiculously oversized framed photos of himself in any one of the many monumental moments of his life. It was uncomfortable for everyone. It was embarrassing. He wanted to put his head down and scurry through the corridor but had an image to uphold or so he was told. There was a mega picture of him cutting the ribbon in front of the building when the one hundred and ninety-four million dollar renovations were complete.

There was another picture of Welly in his interstellar gear standing beside his first vessel composed of Mauvite, the metallic rock-like resource found on the planet Mauve by the edge of the Milky Way - not far from the top of the ceiling of the Forward Facility's rotunda.

The Mauvite was discovered by Welly and his crew. It's not hard when you know where to look. Without Mauvite, the vessels that travel as far as Time Nova, the grid, are not possible. The grid is two hundred forty eight times the distance traveled by any vessel pre-Mauvite extraction.

The photo of Welly shaking hands with the United States President, Dennis "Denny" Neuhas, was snapped right after they inked the deal allowing Welly's company to offer to the ultra-wealthy, visits to the grid and a peek into actual history at a rate that would bankrupt the average tycoon. The government was agreeable as the courts proved constitutionally they were obligated to be and also, perhaps more importantly, it created a healthy revenue stream for them. Government sponsored space exploration was defunded decades earlier, and all space travel was privatized. Welly's Forward company led the private sector charge in this industry, going away. The government's role was to pass legislation to punish severely those that commit crimes using the day's modern technologies and advancements. A major concern of Uncle Sam's was history tampering, which officially became a law that if broken, was punishable by life in prison.

The ultra-wealthy could purchase tickets to travel aboard the vessel with Welly, or one of the few other certified operators, and take a guided tour through deep space to Time Nova and through to a specific destination in the past. Hovering at a safe distance, they observed a certain historical event taking place live, before their very eyes and telescopic viewing equipment.

Wellington ran his barcode under the scanner embedded on the wall of the elevator beneath the floor selection buttons. He pressed LAB9 for the cavernous floor that housed the vessel and launch pad. The hard click that followed indicated that the doors were sealed. Five seconds later the door clicked again and then opened.

Wellington and Kyle jumped back when the doors separated. The imposing presence of Stewart, Head of Janitorial, was enough to startle anyone.

Welly said, "Oh boy Stew, we weren't expecting anyone down here."

"Sorry sir," Stewart said in his slow northern New York droll. His khaki one-zee uniform was always unusually neat and clean. "You know me. I always work my way up from the bottom."

"Yes of course," Wellington said, doing his best to not seem in a tizzy. "Kyle, you know Stewart."

"What's it Stew?" Kyle asked.

"It is fluid, K. See I know the lingo. Sammy's graduating high school this year. Keeps me in tune."

"Yes I know," Welly said. "Speaking of which, we're kind of in a rush because I have to grab something and go somewhere so I can stay in tune too, you know?"

Stewart looked over Kyle and Wellington. "Okay," he said. "Don't let me stand in your way. L.O.L."

Kyle blew out a gust. "You were doing so good," he told Stewart.

Stewart entered the elevator and removed his Comm4, much improved from the Comm3, and began psype texting on his device. The youth referred to it as braining though it still meant the same; text messaging by way of acquiring the text from the thoughts in the mind presented through waves put out by a dedicated individual frequency.

Welly said, "Close," the moment Kyle's foot passed over the red metallic track on the floor and the tank-proof lead doors instantly sealed behind him.

Kyle looked back at the sealed entryway and then forward, seeing his dad padding quickly toward the platform Christine II rested atop. "Dad," he said.

Welly heard nothing. He was in hyper-focus mode. Welly's mind had a way of becoming so wrapped up in plans and outcomes and effects that it bordered on entrancement. He started solving the puzzles presented on the air-screen to unlock the barrier of indestructible glass. After fifteen seconds of convulsing and conducting with his swollen finger, the glass walls fell through the floor like water through a drain.

"Dad!" Kyle said, jarring loose Welly's attention.

"Jesus, what do you want?"

"I've been calling you for ten minutes," Kyle said.

"I didn't hear you. What is it?"

"Can you tell me now what we're doing here?"

Welly glanced at the secure door the two entered moments earlier. "Yes," he said. "We're taking this vessel."

"We? How can *we* take the vessel? You tell me every day I'm not old enough."

"You're not, nor are you mature enough or sober enough, but I have no other options."

Kyle's jaw nervously shifted left then right. "I am so sick of this shit," he told his father. "I told you I haven't done anything and that was not my stuff."

"Yeah and I'm the Easter Bunny."

"You never believed me about anything before. I shouldn't expect you to start now."

"Don't worry I won't," Welly said. "But this is no time for that. What do you recall about the American Revolution?"

Kyle shrugged his shoulders. "I don't know. America won."

Welly waved his hand at the air.

Why bother?

The black Mercedes was now threading its needle on the Belt nearing the Flatbush Avenue exit. It took little time for the two stoic agents to clear Welly's house. For one of the wealthiest men on earth, Welly lived barely to middle class standards.

Inside the car was silence. No talk, no music. The two men were stone serious, both knowing exactly what had to be done. The ambassador delivered very specific instructions.

The Mercedes parked directly in front of the front entrance at the Forward Facility. The pocket doors slid open, the two stoic men exited, car doors slid shut.

Stewart suction the last mound of smudge from the corner of the front door with his squeegee-vacuum instrument. The reflective surface showed the two men briskly marching toward him. He rose to his feet, spun around.

"Morning gentlemen."

3

Welly studied two projected images and frantically slid select bits of information into a third. The third image was a sophisticated program that mapped out the bulk of the mission based on weather, activity in space, destination and many other factors. It was the GPS for the multiple million mile journeys.

"Look," Kyle said. "I appreciate this effort to try and connect with me and spend some time together, or whatever this is, but I gotta pass Pop."

Welly focused on the task before him. It's not that he chose to ignore Kyle, he just ceased hearing anything when he locked into something. His ability to concentrate on occupational assignments was one reason for his incredible professional success.

"I'm not going," Kyle shouted loud enough to break the Welly barrier.

"It's not an option Kyle," Welly calmly explained, still fixed on his screens.

"Well, I don't care. I'm not going," Kyle said.

Welly made a circular, counterclockwise, applying wax-on type motion with his right hand, making all three images in front of him disappear. He turned around to face his son. "In case you couldn't figure it out by my obvious duress, this is an emergency, not a trip to your Grandma's house."

"Yeah cause this is the first time you've been frenzied about something. No, I've never seen you worked up about nonsense before."

"Kyle, this is different. Our country is at stake. You are going."

"Thanks anyway."

Kyle stepped toward the room's entrance and the elevator door opened. Welly's head spun like an owl. Something was wrong.

The two suited men from the Mercedes accompanied Stewart at gunpoint into the room.

"Wellington Brackford, you are required to come with us," the shorter man of the two said with a British accent. He changed the aim of his weapon from Stewart to Welly. Kyle's mouth dried completely.

"Who are you?" Welly asked. He then thought, *P164...CHRISTINE%2001#...Act G Block 14 to 22*. He accessed his main control with his mind and activated a gaseous shield between him and Kyle, and the armed men and Stewart.

The shorter man spoke again. "You are to come or this man and then your son perish."

"Thanks anyway," Welly said.

Kyle looked at his father in disbelief. "Dad?"

"Kyle, I will not tell you again. Let's go. *Get into the vessel!*"

The man changed his aim from Welly to Kyle and said, "Your loss." He fired his silent gun and Kyle hit the floor. He looked up only to see the toothpick thin bullet lodged in the air, stopped, levitating. The man fired again and then again. Now three bullets hovered, fixed in the air.

"*Now* Kyle!" Welly said with a higher level of sternness.

This time Kyle sprung to his feet and entered the vessel. Welly entered behind him. "Sit," he told Kyle.

"Chamber!" Welly said. They both stepped inside the over-sized test tube and a clear, almost imperceptible suit, composed of more than a billion particles, energetically swarmed around them sticking to every nook and cranny of each of their bodies. It looked like clear coat spray paint covering them. Now they would be safe on this ride of rides.

"What about Stewart?" Kyle asked.

"We'll try to take care of that later."

"Try? Why not take care of it earlier? You *can* do that. "

"Not now. Quiet Kyle."

Kyle rolled his eyes and kept quiet.

Welly sat next to him and slid his finger around on the jelly like screen to his left. The vessel's entrance sealed shut, fourteen straps wrapped Kyle's and Welly's chest, abdomen, legs and forehead. A perfect oval in the ceiling of the laboratory opened and the vessel vanished.

Stewart and the two suited men stared up at the vacant opening in the incredibly high ceiling. The taller suited man raised his hand. The tip of his index finger glowed dimly. He raised the glowing finger to Stewart's neck and pressed. Stewart's eyes rolled back and he dropped to the ground.

4

West Babylon, New York

June 2, 2012

Skies were clear with an inspiring under glowing blue that fateful day on 14th Street in West Babylon. Visibility was good. Winds were gentle. A perfect day for flying craft.

Welly looked around at the sky for a while as he often did. He felt something electric, a presence or perhaps a calling by the air itself, or, perhaps it was pollen. Something about this day felt more vivid than others. It was ultra-real. It felt richer, more vibrant, like a day that would stay with him - and it certainly did.

He was ten years old and he had few friends. In fact, he had no friends that he spent much time with apart from school. He and his dad were buds, but he put in a lot of hours at work. It was okay though. He had so much passion for exploring the unknown that he felt he didn't have much time for friends anyway.

On this spring day he was in the yard playing with the drone that he had received as a Christmas gift six months earlier. He'd wanted this piece of equipment so bad it was all that he thought about for the months leading up to Christmas morning. But he felt deep down it would never happen. As much as his parents loved him he knew they could just barely afford to live in their Long Island neighborhood and pay the "ridiculous taxes" as his father often called them. When he tore open the wrapping paper he was overwhelmed with joy and possibility. He thought the feeling likely similar to an explorer discovering a new land hundreds of years ago.

Wonder. Intrigue. The future will never be the same.

.The magic and curiosity and limitless potential were held in his pudgy palms that morning. Little did he know about what laid ahead.

The drone touched down in his yard - the Brackford's modest eighth of an acre property and Welly dashed over to inspect his equipment. The flight would go down in the record books he thought, based on the mere fact of how incredibly crystal clear the skies were overhead. The eye of the drone undoubtedly saw for miles.

As he sat with his legs crossed on the deck, facing the house, he poured over his drone and excitedly found that everything was in tip-top shape. He turned on the small screen to get a sneak preview of the footage he captured from above his and the neighbor's houses. Oddly, there was no new thumbnail to play.

Nothing recorded?

Impossible.

Suddenly he felt an energy scrabble up his neck and it was so prevalent that he jerked his head up and then somehow felt with every fiber of his being - something was behind him. He turned and faced the wooded area behind his house. The wooded area being the one still undeveloped lot in a five mile radius which backed up on the Brackford property.

He saw light beaming a jagged line through the wall of Leyland Cypress trees. These evergreen trees created the tall natural fence in the far back perimeter of Welly's backyard.

He rose as if someone or something was lifting him by the fabric in the back of his crew neck tee.

Strangely enough, as he would always remember, he was without fear and absent the question of whether he should go into the woods, alone, to investigate. He was a young boy weighing in at less than a hundred pounds, even with his telescope strapped to his back like the machine gun of Rambo.

He was a moth drawn to the light without deep thought or questioning why; just a lucid, primal feeling that everything was going to be alright. There would only be one other time in his life when that intense calm and ecstasy filled the place inside him where fear should have been.

Yet he can still remember every step he took, every blade of grass he bent and flattened beneath his Skechers, every twig crack and every breath as he walked into the wooded section through the line of Leyland Cypresses. He was feeling and absorbing with every bit of his flesh. It was as if time slowed down, processing every molecule of information.

Only much later would he decide that it was more likely that the world did not slow down, but rather his brain sped up.

After five steps and unconsciously brushing the big green Cypress feathers aside from the first line of trees, he saw what looked like an object on the floor.

He glanced back at his house. It seemed so far. It was a few steps away, but *he* was far. The humble ranch was now a foreign domicile - a castle on a hill in a painting. The energy he neared was encompassing and somehow he was light years away, although his house was still right there. He turned his head forward again and walked through the brushy tree branches toward the object.

5

Boston, Massachusetts

March 5, 1770

An extremely recognizable face in Welly and Kyle's era was among the few bundled up Bostonians crunching swiftly down the snowy street. His drawn, pale face carved by the cutting edges of vigor and grit, contrasted that jovial, easy going character the public was used to viewing in press conferences. His attire was also quite outside of his norm, but the ragged clothes he donned aroused no suspicion in this city, fitting the description of so many poor citizens of this time. His emaciated frame was one of the signs of wealth in his home time, but here and now he was a dead-ringer for a lower class citizen.

Lord Francis Walton, England's Prime Minister as he was known in 2052, fixed his icy blue eyes straight ahead. His eyes seemed to glow, almost white, like the snow on the cobblestones, against his black hair.

He was determined not to get lost in the majesty of the moment or to think for even a second about how truly incredible it is that he made it against all odds and that he is padding through the streets of Boston, Massachusetts on this historic day in 1770. He stomped with purpose as did his wing men, one on his right and left.

On Walton's left, John Livingston, the balding, much taller, brick built Royal Marine Commando with lifeless black eyes was renowned in modern day for leading the small force that infiltrated the South Gate of Zhongnanhai, headquarters of the Chinese Government, which proved a turning point in the American-Chinese conflict of 2029.

On his right wing, the heavier set, former British SBS (Special Boat Service) military expert and historian and now, consultant to the Prime Minister, Timothy Mayweather. Mayweather's expertise in another life was amphibious craft operation. There were few craft he could not figure out as he was armed with vast technical expertise and incredible problem solving capabilities.

Mayweather possessed a unique data stay talent and developed his mind's eye ability and strength greater than anyone known or unknown, besides Wellington Brackford of course. Mayweather knew why his talent was so advanced, and he knew he would carry that answer to the afterlife with him.

His appearance was as unpleasant to Walton as his strategic reasoning was impressive. Mayweather placed no interest in the advances of dental technology, nor skin or hair care, though it never hindered his political career. Walton, as most were, was more interested in what lay behind the yellowed teeth, bulging gut and dry derma.

The faint jeers echoing in the cold Boston night grew louder. The mob was now visible as the three men reached the intersection of Cornhill and King Street. They peered down a jagged block at a small crowd marching with great ferocity. Rapidly approaching was Crispus Attucks and the others as they passed.

Walton said, "Gentleman," without looking at either wing man. Fixed were his narrow eyes on the trudging young men, now within a few steps. It was one thing witnessing history from the great distance of the hovering tour (regardless of how clear and accurate the zoom), but it was quite another being planted on the actual street, smelling the musk of the filthy rabble. Walton knew this experience was meant for no one else. He knew he was in the right place and was struck by a strange ecstatic surge as a confirmation.

The three men fell in with the crowd and began stomping along with the group. This was the commencement of the friction. Walton now saw the small sentry of British regulars and the station house setting the background. Snowballs were being formed as a new history was about to be, Walton knew. The cacophony of argumentative shouting ensued.

At fifteen yards from the soldiers, the frustrated crowd sent some snowballs into flight. The jeers became louder and the regulars' patience grew thinner as time went on. The red faces of the young sentry men grew redder and redder.

Walton, Livingston and Mayweather made sure to enter a few emotionless "Yeah" shouts after the colonial youths shouted something. It didn't really matter, they realized. They were not being paid any attention by the mob or the onlookers gathering as time progressed.

Seventeen year old Edward Garrett stepped up close and into the face of one of the regulars and began screaming at the top of his lungs. Walton and his cohorts reached into their dark coats.

This moment had been planned, changed, re-planned and hashed out between Walton and Livingston and scrutinized by Mayweather, who examined every potential historical outcome. Every detail was considered over the six month development phase mostly taking place in Walton's luxurious, grandiose office fittingly, over dozens of bottles of Louis XIII Cognac.

The time to execute was upon them. Walton and Livingston seamlessly and synchronically removed their flintlock pistols. Livingston, the top trained military man, removed two pistols and Walton one.

All three pistols were identical with Maplewood shafts, blued, engraved steel and golden barrels. The flintlocks were swiftly raised precisely at the moment Garrett's face received the butt of the soldier's musket. Three simultaneous shots were fired, striking the three middle placed British regulars, each center mass. The sonic boom of the blasts rocked the streets. The silence that immediately followed was only highlighted by the incredibly audible thuds and cracks of the three young soldiers bodies hitting the floor.

Crispus and the others glared, shocked and panic stricken, at the trio with smoking barrels and detached expressions. "What in God's name?" Attucks said.

The mob of protestors, including Attucks, then began to run in terror in the direction from which they had entered earlier in the evening with so much confidence.

Five more British soldiers approached with their guns in firing position. Livingston, his arm board straight, fired three accurate shots in rapid succession as calmly as a mourner lighting candles in a church. The thunderous discharges from the modified flintlock reverberated off the brick buildings around, putting an exclamation point on the overwhelming silence following the last blast. Walton executed a fourth soldier and Livingston aimed and fired at the fifth, striking him dead.

Mayweather strained, vigorously wishing to object. It was the shocking viciousness and the potential worldly ruin all happening before him that left this otherwise doughty chap's mouth agape with nothing but delicate breaths escaping. He kept reminding himself of the greater good.

The last man standing had three lethal weapons fixed on him. Three weapons that were truly awesome to a man in this time. He looked to his left at the slain young men and slowly placed his musket on the ground. His eyes were full of disbelief as he eyed the men and their alien weaponry.

"Captain Thomas Prescott?" Walton asked.

"Yes," Prescott replied with his hands raised above his head.

Walton's face warmed with the intoxication of interacting with such an admirable gentleman in British history. A slight grin pulled the ends of his lips up. "We represent Crispus Attucks and the colonists. Please turn and walk away from your weapon."

Prescott turned at once.

Walton peered down at his own right arm still in firing position to make sure it hadn't disappeared as he suspected it might after this event.

Prescott slowly walked toward the station house. After five terrifying strides, he turned and the three men were gone.

6

Current Day - 2052

Streaking through the universe at 22 LYPH (light years per hour) was strangely unrestrictive to Kyle. It had a similar feel to the Brackford Dart, which Welly and Kyle rode from New York to California together in just twenty minutes. The Dart revolutionized travel around earth using a diluted version of Mauvite - that little blue gem of a rock that helps propel and protect Brackford space vessels which aids human deep space exploration.

The Dart, known for its precisely straight travel paths, seats up to three hundred and twelve passengers and can take you around the world in a couple of hours. Passengers depart from a tower twice the size of the Empire State Building in one city and arrive at a matching tower in their destined city.

Kyle remembered that trip clearly. He remembers because he hated every minute of the hyper fast vacation. It was a media spectacle. It was just a big dog and pony show - Wellington Brackford takes the historic maiden voyage on his company's earth changing super train. Wow! Is that what really matters most to humanity? It broke records for streaming coverage. More people watched that first trip than the season finale of

Head of State, the presidential reality show that takes viewers inside the White House.

All that Kyle wanted that day was to be hanging with his loner pals with not too much ambition and no care about their lacking ambition. While he made history that weekend on the Dart, he only thought of the historic events he was undoubtedly missing at Zen's or Tommy's or Ant's places.

Similar thoughts tumbled now, two years after Dart's launch, as he stared out the surfboard shaped window into the darkness. He turned his head and lazily glanced over at his intensely concentrated father. He was focused to the point of being in a trance-like state of waking sleep.

Always intensely focused on everything other than his family, Kyle thought.

Kyle let out a melancholy scoff and peered back out the window. The initial ascent was an adjustment for the body which typically made one lethargic. Kyle's calm was more than just the fatigue from the ascent. His calm was more of an internal inertia assisted by a deficit of chemical enhancements.

Everything would be different if you were still here, Ma.

The ship jolted suddenly and Welly himself jerked back into consciousness with a terrified look. Welly's expression of terror and grave concern eerily resembled his 'contemplating what sushi rolls to order' expression. He was in deep thought. New thoughts and memories emerged. He placed his hand on Kyle's shoulder to balance his mind. Kyle rolled his eyes.

No Boston Massacre - Boston Witch Hunt! British Regulars gunned down by an angry mob. Thomas Prescott accompanied by hundreds of red coats scoured Boston at dawn on March 6, 1770.

Welly could see the images of these words printed on text book paper. He could hear his teacher, the radiant Mrs. Diamond, in the front of the class announcing these facts as he scribbled notes in his marble notebook. But wait! That same teacher is teaching about the Boston Massacre. He could now visualize the image of the engraving by Paul Revere of the British Soldiers shooting down the unarmed protesters with the plumes of smoke.

Yes! Yes! This event had incensed Boston and sparked a flame which was heavily fanned by Samuel Adams and the Sons of Liberty. John Adams defended Prescott and the British Regulars and won the case before joining the side of the Patriots.

Welly was surer than sure of these events and this confidence produced a surge of giddiness in his blue eyes.

Kyle watched him incredulously and felt compelled to ask finally, "You okay, Dad?"

"Not now!" Welly fired back, desperate not to lose focus.

Kyle shook his head. He mumbled, "Whatever," and then turned to stare out the window.

Psype psype. Two different events on March 5, 1770 involving same people at same time on King Street in Boston - likely history mod - Boston Massacre very clear memory of angry mob protesting British sentry, slinging verbal assaults and throwing objects. The soldiers eventually fired into the crowd without orders, instantly killing three and two died later due to injuries sustained by the shooting. Samuel Adams, John Hancock and Sons of Liberty fueled their argument for freedom. John Adams represented British soldiers - six acquitted - two convicted of manslaughter.

Second event remembered, parallel timeframe – same location - Boston Witch Hunt - caused by British Regulars being gunned down by an angry mob. Prescott along with hundreds of redcoats scoured Boston pulling citizens suspected of involvement with the violent acts - houses torched - bedlam – twenty three jailed and tried including Crispus Attucks.

Chills rushed up Welly's arms so much so that he jiggled his arms. He was realizing the awful facts that he apparently already learned, but also knew he did not. He sat bewildered.

Embers in the hearts of Boston Patriots burned hotter than ever before....other events...think...other events remain intact. Breed's Hill? Dorchester Heights? Continentals sneakily gaining access to occupy the heights and gain high ground over Boston on March 5th, original anniversary of Boston Witch Hunt? Patriots benefitted from unseasonably mild weather and fog cover. Okay, other major events, scan. Lexington and Concord, scan.

What the?

Serious history mod possibility.

Welly gasped as if he hadn't swallowed a breath in minutes.

"Jesus," Kyle said, "are you alright?" His question was glazed in more annoyance than concern.

Kyle rolled his eyes once more.

Welly gulped a large breath of the vessel's near perfectly filtered air and removed his hand from Kyle's shoulder to wipe the single bead of sweat from his brow.

"I told you," Welly said. "Don't use the lord's name in vain."

Past is something Welly held very sacred. He often pondered the thoughts and the voices of the past; so many greats sardined in there that it overwhelmed him at times. So much so that he had written private poetry about the topic. He felt compelled to live up to or exceed those before him and when considered on a grand scale as Wellington Brackford had a tendency to do, the task was quite daunting. He felt connected to the great minds throughout history and the thought of that reliable wind at his back vanishing forever made it difficult to breathe.

Welly put his hand over his brow once again, feeling faint. He was spun around and around and still expected to hit the piñata. Only the goal here was not as minute as candy, but rather the importance was at the other end of the spectrum - reparation of world history. The incredible weight of a truck or better yet, a country, befell him as he continued to try and negotiate these new memories.

What if I'm wrong? What if this mod was really just an intense dream or a manifestation of anxiety drifting by?

He owed to himself to ask that question, but he already sub-consciously deduced the probability. It was no dream. If you know what you're doing a mod is as different from a dream as the taste of red versus white. Those men chasing and shooting were real. They were there for some reason.

But, what if it was an intense fabrication? What if the chasing men were there for another reason.

There were a million reasons actually. Welly had business in so many industries and countries. He had technology and a sharp, competitive edge that many wanted to dull or extinguish entirely. He was said to possess access to some mystical world, some enchanted vulgate or something like this that a number of people thought were bad for the world. To some less understanding people, they believed Welly to be a form of evil. There has always been fear of the unknown since the dawn of mankind and one day, Welly hoped to witness that first fear on that first dawn, first hand.

I have to call him, Welly thought. *I have to scramble the jets on this thing.*

However, he already knew layers down this could not be done. A mistake like this could be the end. If he rang the alarm on this, the government gets involved and goes and investigates and discovers it was just a dream - it could be the end of everything. The dominos he'd carefully stacked most of his adult life could degenerate, from an inspiring path for the human race to follow, into a pile of rubble. He would have to see for himself. The government was too damn clumsy. He had to see firsthand, alone.

I have to see. Have to be certain.

"Hey," Kyle said. "Are you okay? You're freaking me out."

"Someone," Welly said finally. "Is trying to change history right now!"

Kyle said nothing. Welly removed the hand covering his eyes.

"Kyle? Are you listening to me?"

"Oh, I'm sorry. Does being tuned out piss *you* off?"

"Cut the crap Kyle. This is important."

Kyle rolled his eyes. Welly continued.

"What do you remember about the American revolution? Do you remember learning about the Boston Massacre *or* the Boston Witch Hunt?"

"I don't know." Kyle shrugged and then his eyes widened to silver dollars as Saturn appeared outside his viewing window. It was thousands of miles from the vessel, but it seemed close enough to grab for the brief couple of seconds as they passed. He quickly closed his ever-so-slightly opened mouth.

Witnessing a glint of wonder in his son's eyes for a fleeting moment, Welly squinted and smirked imperceptibly.

The majestic light radiating and the divine rings of debris, and all of the cosmic chaos activity was a heartstopping spectacle to behold. From earth, Saturn looked so calm and peaceful, but up closer there was a more hectic scene with violently windblown debris that was both beautiful and unsettling. In a flash the planet was gone from sight.

"I didn't pay that much attention in class," Kyle said.

"This is an incredibly famous happening. One of the two must ring a bell."

Kyle thought. "The witch hunt sounds familiar. I never heard of the massacre."

"Son of a bitch!" Welly shouted. "That's *new* history. This is happening *now*! I mean not now. Almost three hundred years ago but as we speak. Right now. You understand?"

Kyle raised his eyebrows. He understood just fine.

"No," Welly said. "What I mean to say is." He struggled for a way to explain without sounding batty. "Did you get a woozy, chaotic feeling, an almost dream-like deja-vu type feeling within the past hour?"

"Hmm," Kyle said. "You mean when we left the facility at a hundred million miles an hour?"

The rate of speed was nearer to one hundred twenty eight million miles per hour when calculated including the rate of space being pulled into the vessel, but the point was well received nonetheless. How was Kyle to differentiate the feeling of traveling at that speed from the history mod induced delirium?

Welly was sure of the new reality barreling into his psyche as it was as "real" as the prior.

"Let me ask you this," Welly said. "What year did America declare our independence?" Welly asked knowing the date of celebration of the nation's independence no alterations had taken place.

"Really, Dad, Independence Day is like your favorite holiday. You've been droning on about America and our independence since I was like five, probably earlier if I had to guess. What the hell is going on?"

"Please....answer the question."

"Yup, never time to explain to the insignificant son. And you wonder why I am the way I am."

"Kyle, at some point you have got to take responsibility regardless if I have been father of the year or not."

Kyle rolled his eyes and looked out the window. *Father of the year-I'd settle for you being a father one day of the year.*

Welly's skin warmed and his jaw tightened as it tended to do. Never was it effortless or even simply comfortable interacting with his son since the accident. Without his wife, Kyle's mom, the equilibrium of their relationship was off. Even with all of Welly's mathematical and problem solving skills, he failed at cracking the code on a healthy father-son relationship.

Kyle's fingers were capable of pointing only in one direction and he had an allergic reaction to the mirror.

"Sevity Sev...," Kyle said, mumbling and trailing off.

"What?"

"Seventeen...seventy...six! That's the year we celebrate our independence. You're Wellington Brackford, I'm Kyle. How you doin? It's nice to not meet you."

"Okay," Welly said. "So the outcome has not changed. And we are still here. History has been altered, but the outcome is still the same - America still declares its independence in seventeen seventy six, right?"

Welly had a desperate look on his face.

"Yes, again," Kyle said slowly. "Seventeen seventy six."

Welly thought. *So some individual or more likely a group of individuals went back to March 5, 1770 and actually altered the events? Really? Actually altered history? On the ground? It's unspeakable! Un-thinkable!*

Or is it possible that I have my history mixed up? No - no - I am clear, crystal clear. How did they manage? On what vessel? All were absolutely accounted for. But why? Obviously to change the course of history and America. - a world superpower. Obviously Welly. But who? And why was history - the big picture - the outcome - unchanged?

The Boston Massacre was a spark that started the notion and the ball rolling for a revolution. Samuel Adams used this event as a rallying cry for the patriots and colonists that toyed with the concept of rebellion against King George and his men. It helped Adams and other patriot leaders win over some hearts and minds. Without that spark and that rallying cry the outcome is still unchanged. But wait! They persisted - yes, they persisted nonetheless! Hearts and Minds!

"Hearts and minds!" Welly shouted finally. "These assholes changed an event, yes, but that event did not change the hearts and minds. And *that*, Kyle, is what won the war!"

7

9 Hours from Time Nova

Welly was fixed straight ahead adjusting their route slightly. Other than the display of numbers and equations dancing overhead and in front of him, one would never know he was feverishly computing. All of this work, controlling the vessel's manifest was possible by signals direct to Welly's brain. Human operation of machines actually wasn't so much different from when Welly grew up in the world - other than the non-use of fingers. Like anything else, once it's around a bit, it's normal.

Zoning out had become normal, even noble. Many of the day's greatest minds may be found in Central Park staring at a bush all day. To see a person vacantly gazing up at the sky on a street corner was common. More than likely they were sending an important message or jotting some notes or closing a deal of some sort. Differentiating a harmless citizen from a mentally ill individual was a bit more difficult for ordinary civilians in the modern world. For police it was easier as they were recently granted permission to read the thoughts of someone suspected of being potentially dangerous. Yes, they had to follow protocol and obtain permission from a judge, but this took all of about eight seconds once the subject was either unresponsive or acting erratic.

The subjectivity of these thought reading warrants is what fueled the controversy and caused a huge stir on the Zeit. The Zeit was simply a pool of thoughts and consciousness where ideas were shared, relationships built, and arguments raged. It was the evolution of the social media platforms of yesteryear. It was the cause of sometimes starry eyed and at other times wrathful gazes from enveloped strangers. Of course, society was fully comfortable with this now. Indeed, it was also the traceable dawn of stolen ideas and corresponding lawsuits, but the part that Welly was proud of most – it was where ideas were forged and blended and extracted from the tornado of human thoughts and ultimately, the Zeit proved progressive for our humble planet.

Kyle and a large group of friends were active in Thought Circles on the Zeit, much more than Welly was aware. At times, they even protested issues by gathering in front of the Gracie Mansion with signs from sunup to sun down. He once urged his influential father to psype an articulate message over to the mayor which Welly obliged. He received a call back from the mayor almost immediately.

Welly was pleased to see Kyle engaged in something with a glint of passion. Usually, Kyle was just zoning out. But Kyle, Welly knew, zoned out for other reasons. Kyle always claimed to be writing, but Welly suspected he was still using the new age drug Frumalda, also referred to as "Frummy". It gave kids the same glazed over look as when they are psyping or deep in study when in actuality they are far from actuality.

Kyle's eyes opened slowly then catapulted open upon realizing his foreign surroundings. Thick fog floated through his mind. The feeling in his stomach was a simulacrum to a runaway elevator drop. He eyed his concentrating father as he slid his right hand into the pouch on the side of his pants. He delicately removed one of the stamp-sized translucent sheets and swiftly raised it to his mouth and coughed - concealing the transfer from his Dad.

Welly concluded his work momentarily and looked at his son.

"Well, good morning son. You were out a while. Are you okay?"

Kyle rubbed his stomach. "Not really. Kind of nauseous."

Welly perked. "Do you have a dizzy feeling? Like an out-of-place, confused type of feeling?"

"Yeah," Kyle said.

"Okay," Welly said. "Can you remember what you were just dreaming about?"

Kyle rolled his eyes.

"Important, Kyle. What were you just dreaming about?"

Kyle looked away from his dad and out into the glittered black beyond, through a viewing porthole. So stunning was it, but as was common with Kyle, enjoyment teamed with guilt. The guilt of knowing he's witnessing something great and simultaneously remembering that others will never get that opportunity again.

"Mom," he said angrily. "I was dreaming about mom."

Welly studied his own lap for a moment. He had to follow up. "Anything unusual?"

"Yeah," Kyle said. "She was alive. That's pretty unusual isn't it Dad? She was pouring syrup on my pancakes. It was so vivid I could read the label. Delhi Syrup Co with a little maple leaf logo."

Welly nodded. "Anything unusual about this one?"

Kyle sighed. "We were at the table eating. I've had a dream like this a million times. I just get this feeling. Like it's a feeling that she's been there the whole time. In the dream, the accident....it never happened. We're eating breakfast now. It's recent you know. Then I wake up and I believe it and for a second it's nice. Then it all comes back and I remember." Kyle fought off the tears and continued. "And it sucks. It just sucks. But you know all that don't you?"

"Nothing besides mom that you can remember?"

Kyle rubbed the back of his neck and shook his head. "Just the gnawing, agonizing pain day in and day out of missing my mother and the gaping, unfillable hole in my heart. Yeah that was all." Kyle let his words hang in the digitally lit captain's booth for a moment and then continued. "I just will never comprehend why someone with the means to travel in time won't go and save his wife, his son's mother, when he *can*."

"Kyle, how many times Kyle? You know my breakthroughs are critical for the advancement of-"

"Mankind," Kyle interjected and scoffed. "I know, I know. The rest of the world comes before her, before me."

"You know how this has tormented me. You know damn well. The right decision was not to change that moment and your mother would have one hundred percent agreed. I don't want to hear anymore about that."

Welly knew that Kyle still did not and may not ever know the real Welly. He never met that eight year old little boy Welly, lying on his deck in his backyard in West Babylon gazing up at the stars. This was Welly's first true love - before he met Christine and long before he met his best friend Kyle. He would gaze up at the sky for hours and knew this was his calling - the stars dotting the dark expanse beckoning him like a howling pack of wolves. He did not know how or why, but he knew it felt right.

As he progressed through his lifelong journey and accomplished his goals and suffered great loss, he only wished he was narrow-minded enough to believe that all of it was to provide a simple benefit for him and his family. He also knew that his other-worldly thoughts were precisely what allowed him to accomplish his many "impossible" endeavors. If not for these accomplishments he would not even be in a position to act on wishes, and the accomplishments are irrefutable evidence of a man's thinking above the curve high enough to never seriously cultivate such wishes, so paradoxically, it was illogical. It was a quandary that perplexed him.

Of course he wanted Christine. With his primitive heart's whole luminescence, he wanted her back. But he never forgot what he knew since he was that little boy gazing at the infinite crystal-dotted darkness; he was put here for something bigger.

After a few seconds Kyle said, "Yeah whatever. But we can break the sacred rules to go what? Save the country? Some patch of dirt on a marble. The country that doesn't even remotely resemble its intended vision? The country that acts like the Bill of Rights is made of clay rather than stone and rewards inactivity and stagnation? Isn't that what you said? In fact that's what we should call our modern nation - Stag Nation! Right?"

"I say a lot of things when I'm pissed off. I don't believe that for a second!" Welly blasted. "And frankly, I don't think you've seen enough of the world to consider that yourself."

"My *friends* get murdered at their school because of these antiquated gun laws and *nothing* is changed."

Welly said nothing for a moment. He took a breath.

"I know how hard that was," Welly said finally. "But things did change. Security measures were increased to a large extent. Change is gradual and not as immediate as we like most times. The needle moves slowly and it doesn't seem to move at all when you're watching it."

Kyle shook his head letting his Dad know that he does not get it. "Did you ever consider, *dad*, that Americans are victims of their own freedom?"

Welly felt simultaneous pride and disappointment. He was proud that his son had grown to form and express a thought such as this one, but extremely disappointed in his viewpoint. "It's this terrible freedom," Welly said, "that afforded us the opportunity to think and experiment and move the world forward for the greater good of all inhabitants of the planet. So, no, I don't think we're victims. I think we are critically important leaders."

Kyle thought and then said, "Okay, fine. But would it be so bad if we had the freedom to think and experiment without the freedom to have guns? Do we really need all these freakin guns? I mean, really? Oh yeah it's just in case we have to fight back against the big bad government. You know better than anyone that the government's military technology has advanced so much that the public's antiquated rifles and pistols would be like trying to hurt the ocean by throwing some grains of sand at it."

"I don't want you hanging out with Zen anymore. He's poisoning your mind."

"These are my thoughts. If anything, I'm influencing Zen's mind."

"Kyle, if we can fix whatever this glitch is that's happening then there will be plenty of time to debate this all. If we don't." Welly paused and looked down through the transparent section of the floor and out into the gaseous swirls of light and debris, backdropped by an endless black curtain. "Well then we may not be around to have that argument. I really need you, son."

Kyle grinded his jaw and looked out his window.

"That fine band of stars out there – that's the edge of our galaxy. That's the edge of the Milky Way. You're one of the few blessed ones that gets to see that from this distance and vantage point."

Kyle was not feeling so blessed.

Welly saw far more of the universe than any humans before him, according to his research to date, and this only strengthened his patriotism. In a place so cold and hostile as planet earth there needed to exist a dominant force of good and America was a large part of that force as misguided as it was at times. History was certainly quite ugly. Welly referred to the Dark Ages as "earth's awkward years", during which a lot of lessons were learned the hard way. But he believed the good, the bad and the ugly of history were all very important, even sacred. When destiny led him through that door to sneak a peek of the great beyond, he felt a massive responsibility. When he confirmed a lifelong suspicion that nothing disappears, but rather is eclipsed or concealed, and everything in the universe is truly connected, he felt an even greater responsibility.

His journey has uncovered that current time is comparable to a master Excel spreadsheet whereby all of the past happenings are linked spreadsheets, and the sum of all of the equations from all of the spreadsheets throughout all of time is what one sees waking up in the morning of the present day. In short, present day is the sum of all things. Make an ever so minor tweak to a spreadsheet ten billion layers deep and it might drastically skew history – potentially wipe out generations of families, give increased power to the wrong people or even obstruct advancement so much so that it renders the ability to tamper history unrealized, potentially sending the world into a tailspin, and leaving us in the stone ages.

8

Welly thought back to that fateful June day, forty years earlier, as he often did, pouring over every detail, searching for anything missed and making sure there was no additional messaging, hidden or otherwise.

Like metal being pulled to a magnet, Welly waded through the thick line of Leyland Cypress trees into the wooded lot behind his modest childhood Long Island home. After eleven additional paces, he saw in a small clearing, a triangular craft hovering just a few inches off the earth. Still he was without fear; just an ecstatic feeling washing over him telling him it was alright.

It's alright. Keep walking.

Six more steps over the soft soil of summer and Welly joined the craft in the small clearing. The craft was no more than twenty feet in diameter. It was black with a matte finish yet it shimmered and glowed like a desert mirage and lights beamed below it.

Time slowed down further. It was opposite his conceptualization of a dream in that a dream was often hazy and perception of reality during and after a dream tended to seem off-kilter, questionable. No, this was more real than reality – a sort of hyper-reality - that was etched into Welly's consciousness and more real than any food he'd tasted, drink he'd drunk or flower he'd smelled.

As he stood awestruck, taking in every detail of the craft before him, much like he did that Christmas morning with his drone, he realized there was something moving on the other side. He was unsure if he saw or sensed it first. What happened next jolted into being like lightning, like a flash-bang, grabbing hold of Welly's attention such as nothing before it or since.

Out walked a humanoid creature that stood no taller than Welly's chest. The creature now looked at Welly and again, rather than fear, Welly felt ecstasy, euphoria. He felt a specific warmth he couldn't remember feeling prior to that in his life. It was a feeling kin to the feeling a newborn must feel being held in a mother's warm embrace. That reassuring feeling that everything was going to be okay. He intuited that the presence of this humanoid caused the sensation.

As he locked eyes with the large-eyed being, the non-verbal communication commenced. It raised its hand slightly and Welly experienced a surge of information, the first part being that the message was to be clear that they are peaceful and that the galaxy was filled with peaceful beings and that sadly, the inhabitants of earth were deemed the most hostile of all the galaxy and this was a worry for other beings. But this information was not explained this way; it was explained with an energy and with fewer words if one were to explain them in earth-like terms, but they were not really words. They were communications of a different sort. The information Welly was being imparted was not told to him but rather told *into* him, inputted. He did not believe it to be true but rather *knew* it was the truth.

When the small grey being briskly walked to him, Welly still had no fear. Instead, extreme calm. The being reached its hand higher and intuitively instructed Welly to reach out and touch it. Welly pressed his palm flat against the palm of the being.

The being's smaller hand was a smooth, rubbery membrane with four appendages. At that moment, Welly experienced a surging river of enlightenment. Vast information poured into him, branding itself into his memory. He could see a birds eye view of the multiverse and could see our entire universe as it was a small marble, and a three hundred and sixty degree view showed him even more multiverses and multiverses within multiverses and on and on for infinity. This true knowledge, of our size and place here, is the ever-flowing spring from which peace is derived. He was taught in that bursting instant.

He was also given precise coordinates of the great ever-expanding time keeper, later to be nicknamed Time Nova, that existed and stored all the history of the cosmos. The time keeper being what Welly could only describe as a high traffic area used as a fountain of knowledge to drink from to learn and gain endless insight and knowledge. Further, the intergalactic visitor ensured Welly that the causality laws don't govern this great time keeper in the way time travel was historically theorized. The keeper is a universal – in the truest definition of the word - memory storage system and passing through at a precise location allows you into that time period to the second. Every single coordinate of the myriad googolplex of the coordinates available represents and holds a precise point in time. Opposite to rings on a tree, the outermost ring represents the beginning of our universe and the exact center is the precise current moment in time. The time keeper, Time Nova, grows from the center outward, expanding with each new unit of time.

Time Nova's swirling expansion continues as each nanosecond of time passes, capturing every bit of data of each planet, star, and every piece of matter and antimatter within every galaxy and all that lies beyond. A traveler entering the newest formed center of the ring would be right back into the point in time from which they just entered. Entering the outer rings, the dawn of time itself, of Time Nova was not recommended and moreover discouraged in a profoundly direct manner. It was too delicate, too fragile, the ET conveyed so definitively that Welly agreed and accepted without question.

The alterations made by a traveler will in fact be saved as all events, minor and major, are automatically saved. That change will cause other changes which will be saved as well. The way Welly would describe it during seminars in his early twenties, is that it is similar to altering an image digitally and your change auto saves, and perhaps if that image was used in other materials or is part of a larger photo then those images would be affected as well. The changes could have significant impacts to some, but some issues with photos and inconveniences to some will not affect the whole earth much at all. In the same way, issues on earth, large or small, have very little effect on the rest of the universe, but Welly knew, may have great impact on how humans explore and view the universe which to him could be catastrophic.

The universe, the creature conveyed, is composed of beings with a bottomless depth of respect for their shared space and its occurrences; so much so that a ubiquitous understanding prevented any thought of ever tampering or altering the past. It was a pool of life which all drink from and never dared contaminate. The creature added in his unique and advanced fashion that the humans were the last to know of this time keeper by design. The behavior of the human race inspired a fear in the rest of the inhabitants of the universe.

Informed was Welly that the humans only use a small percentage of their innate mind power and that some others throughout our time had also been enlightened, but silenced. Moreover, other humans manipulated such truths for selfish purposes.

Apparently, the combination of resources already existed within our own solar system and most of it, right on earth, that would allow humans to build vessels and travel much farther and that the igniting energy exists in their own bodies and minds. It implanted in Welly the exact design, schematics and materials to design the vessels they use.

It described the unlocking of the mind to communicate, just as it was doing then, and to power craft and reach much further potential, and it abruptly wished him the equivalent of good luck on his journey on this unique planet. Welly was enlightened by the ET that the reason he and all other humans cannot see the very real, existing mind 'element' (as he called it to help Welly's immature mind to grasp it) was that it exists and is continually created by, and as a result of thought. It's because it exists in a dimension incredibly close to the edge of human comprehension, but just beyond it.

This dimension is accessible, and can actually be seen by accessing a section of the brain that humans currently did not access. This element is constantly expanding and growing and causing the universe to grow as the thoughts of all inhabiting the universe continue to be exerted and exercised. And in fact, through this path and this separate area of human brain function not yet uncovered, is precisely where the ET entered to impart this other area of comprehension and knowledge into Welly - and so in addition to gifting him this incredible insight, it also unlocked this area of his brain providing Welly with an edge over the entire human race. Upon this realization, he felt it was his sole responsibility to use it to his best ability and try to further develop it in himself and others.

Operating in this new dimension, everything is particle based and one's mind and body have the ability to act as a vacuum. This is not much of a stretch as our body already has vacuum like capabilities as we suck up tiny particles in oxygen every second. But in the other dimension everything is smaller than oxygen, smaller than neutrinos, and the *entire* body gains vacuum-like capabilities that can be controlled in an incredibly large spectrum of force degrees.

Welly explained this at seminars by asking the audience to imagine a roll of toilet paper completely unrolled and only the last square of toilet paper, one hundred feet or so away from us, is uniquely covered in polka dots. If we want to get to that polka dotted square by means of any form of travel we previously had available, it would take time. We would have to travel *to* the polka dotted square in one form of transportation or another. Now picture the strongest vacuum available and set it at the beginning of the unrolled TP and you would bring the polka dotted square to you almost instantly. Now, bring forth the fastest vessel in which you can travel to the polka dotted square, and the most powerful vacuum and multiply that speed and that's how fast the polka dotted square could be delivered. Further,, if you slow the vacuuming down to super slow motion video you will see the fabric of the toilet paper bending as it is sucked into the vacuum. He liked to relieve the tensioned room by closing with, "So that's how I wipe my ass with the fabric of space."

After his encounter, he knew people had this ability yet to be unlocked, and there is another world that has always been, parallel to the world humans have long since observed. People possess the capability to build crafts with these powers, that maneuver at supersonic speeds and manipulate the fabric of space and time to travel incredible distances. Strikingly, even amongst all that had transpired, the ET added one more piece of information. Information that stood out and lit up brightly. It imparted that people can suck in particles slowly and walk through seemingly solid objects. There was a sort of rearranging and orchestration of molecules that was effortless once one accessed and operated in this other dimension.

And then something else happened.

The last bit of wisdom imparted to Welly by his ET coun-terpart, in that small clearing among the tall and full Leyland Cypresses, boiled down to a message that the impossible was anything but. It was not any of the knowledge expressed to him on that day that would keep him motivated, driving ever onward, day in and day out still to current day, as he was a rounding man nearing fifty - no, it was not what he was told, but rather what he was shown just before the ET departed. What he witnessed would stick with him above all else.

The next memory that directly followed this encounter was waking up in his bedroom in a hot sweat. He could not account for the prior afternoon or evening, but he felt different - changed, altered. The memory was that of the most realistic dream. More real even than the reality he felt as he flipped his sweat soaked brown hair out of his face and frantically searched for his notebook. All he wanted was to write down everything. Write it down in a non digital format that could not be hacked and deleted somehow.

It was a Sunday when Welly headered his page, June 3, 2012 and began writing as fast as his hand and wrist would permit.

9

Welly long since believed or *thought* strongly, that thoughts were real. Years after the ET enlightening, he read a lengthy research paper. He was as a young teenager as he read it for the first time. He'd combed over it a dozen times since. It stated definitively, based on scientific research and data, that deathly ill or seriously injured individuals with large groups of people praying for them had a much higher rate of pulling through and recovering than those without the large groups praying - thinking, focusing deeply on their wellbeing.

This fact is just one of the reasons that kept Welly going to church. He believed in the power of prayer and wanted to add his mind's and heart's muscle to the pull or the push. It could only help. That, along with the feeling he felt deep - just beyond as far as was possible - within him. The belief was so deep and profound that no earthly or outer earth experience should break it or even wobble it.

Never giving up though on the concepts and knowledge delivered by the ET, he honed his mind intensely, scrupulously, and evolved enough to observe aspects of the dimension. Later Welly discovered; when a person is thinking and you are viewing this person in another dimension, you can actually see the thoughts radiating around their head and leaving traces of light and heat waves. Light and heat waves that are beyond the light spectrum previously discovered by man. Welly, in fact, laboriously proved that the spectrum of light was no spectrum at all. Rather it was closer to a full sphere of wavelengths – colors previously unimagined, much of which was undetectable without the aid of the undiscovered mind elements.

The thought energies appear similar to the distortion of a really hot day or a mirage, but they are not that. With the aid of certain bands of the light sphere, Tysonium and Cracheria, thoughts appear to be effervescent or at times, gaseous. But they are not that.

There *is* such a thing as bad energy - it might hover in a room for a period of time, might get swept into a room sticking on an individual like dirt on a wet dog and then ruminate. It might bunch up and hang over a house or a street for some amount of hours or years. It can be seen in the other dimension. It's visible. It's real.

Welly realized why no store in a particular location could survive - seemed to be a doomed spot. The energy was bad and humans had a keen sense of the energy on a level they never even knew they were capable of accessing, like an animal senses the coming weather.

Information about thoughts being live and living and examples of people in a think-tank who simultaneously get the same thought, or people thinking above the curve and getting pelted with a brand new idea that changes everything, and the proverbial light bulb going off above their head - were all very real down to the light bulb.

Welly knew certainly how many times he had talked aloud to someone in close proximity and then thought privately to himself, and then the other person would blurt out a seemingly new thought that just entered their psyche and it was Welly's thought verbatim. Welly knew that it spilled out, oozed even, and was absorbed in by his fellow interlocutor. He knew how very real it was indeed. It was no trick, no miracle; it was mathematics.

Every being leaves behind an energy, like a mist unseen by human eyes. Some energies are stronger and can linger for years and some for only minutes. If you had a fancy, capable camera, you could conceivably stand in a room and then leave the room and snap a picture of yourself and your energy standing where you just stood prior.

Different beings from other places can access this energy, this form of themselves, and flip back and forth between densities allowing them to literally walk through what humans think of as solid, impenetrable objects. There is seemingly a whole sub "city" unseen, busier than the one seen, consisting of billions of trails and actions and life, that exists among us, everywhere.

Only through the assistance of deep meditation at age twenty eight, did Welly unpack the information regarding internal receptors he received during his ET encounter. Internal receptors (Internal Antenna as Welly would later rename them and then nickname them IAnts) were something each thought-forming being possessed. Essentially, everyone has these internal receptors, however, magnetism in some is simply stronger due to their internal make-up, the way some are blessed with perfect vocal pitch and others not.

Ideas are given off, exhaled eventually and mostly are irrational fragments. Some are new while other ideas have been whirling like colorful campfire smoke for a thousand years, meshing with lesser and greater ideas, breaking free and reforming and so on. Those blessed with strong receptors and well-working minds may receive an amalgam of ideas, quite literally out of the clear blue sky and create something never been seen or heard or smelled or *thought* of before. One of the reasons for Welly's being selected, according to the story imparted to him by the ET, was Welly's receptors were unusually strong. While they were not the most attractive on the planet, they were more than capable and ostensibly, Welly carried other qualities of interest to this being.

Welly knew instantly in the quasar of his soul, it was now his mission, his duty, his sole responsibility to use it to his best ability and try to further develop it in himself and others.

This thought 'element' as the ET described it, also solved a matter that was raging on by astrophysicists for quite some time. The previously named "dark matter" that they could not see or measure, but knew of its existence, and that was occupying much of the universe by mathematical deduction, had been renamed Wellingtonium in Welly's honor.

It wasn't easy though. It was several years of disbelief and in some cases mockery, by the top "thinkers" in the field. It was difficult for Welly to prove this to anyone as he was the only person to be able to see in this way. He had to find a way to invent something that tangibly communicated with something within the limited world that he inhabited to prove his truth. He had to tap into a frequency that didn't exist in the traditional way that anything existed. It existed the way red objects exist to a totally color blind person.

Actually, Welly often felt during those six years that he was the only person alive who saw colors and the entire world was color blind. How could he prove something is there when no one else can see it, smell it, hear it or measure it in any way? It would take Welly nearly seven years since his first seminar on the topic, to figure that out. So when he finally invented his illumination device to help the others see, it was all the more gratifying.

He also brought to light during meditation that the being inputted a reason that the dark matter and dark energy, as it was previously named, is so prevalent in far off intergalactic space is that thought is much denser and deeper than thoughts of earth. Thus, earthly thought was widely considered to be more primitive than those of goldfish in our incredibly young evolutionary journey as a species, as the ET explained. There was no judgement or shame as most beings followed a similar evolution. Some species had been honing and furthering their collective intelligent thoughts as long ago as eleven billion years.

Welly was different. He was being an intergalactic dolphin, though his delicate ego and Christine when she was with him, both suspected he gave himself entirely too much credit.

10

Boston, Massachusetts

June 15, 1775

The three present day British men turned at the etched wooden sign displaying the words *Marlbrough Street*. It was late in the morning, but many were still coming and going on and around the narrow dirt street. The trio continued to waste no time basking in the intoxication of being in another era and padded toward the guards stationed in front of the Province House estate.

Mayweather was certain this was General William Howe's headquarters this day. All of his historical data pointed towards Howe's presence at this location and he very well hoped his information was accurate. The two guards at the door and two on the perimeter were a good sign. Still, perspiration gathered atop his forehead with the prospect of the quite feasible possibility that due to poor and imprecise record keeping of the time, anything was possible. He knew the petulant Walton would care not for excuses if he was driven off course by a miscalculation. After all, Mayweather's primary value to Walton was his extraordinary knowledge of historical details.

Based chiefly upon Mayweather's information, Walton insisted this particular day makes strategic sense for the mission at hand as it is two days before the Battle of Bunker Hill. With the *proper* warning from the *proper* source, General Howe would act accordingly. He would recognize British excellence and leadership, Walton knew. It was an essence that transcends the mere boundaries of time. He would halt the revolting armed group of farmers before the ever costly, bloody British victory on the hill. He then simply leads the mighty British forces into an attack against a much weakened and demoralized enemy, culminating with their surrender. This would have to work.

This day of June 15th, 1775 had further significance as it was the day that the Second Continental Congress appointed George Washington Commander in Chief of the so-called Continental Army. Walton was enthused by this fact. It was symbolic that he ended Washington's campaign on the very day it begins.

It was an unseasonably cool morning with gusts of wind that none of the overdressed approaching visitors felt. The two statuesque British regulars, in front of the small fence surrounding the estate, donned clean, impeccably neat uniforms. The white pants & red coat seemed freshly formed; their gold buttons shimmering even with the absence of any direct sunlight.

Walton paused for a moment to take in these fine examples of British majesty and splendor.

The guards, seemingly younger than thirty, with pale faces, distinguishable only by hair color, one orange and the other blonde, raised brows as the three well-dressed visitors approached.

"Good day my lords," Walton said casually.

"What is your business?" The orange haired soldier snarled.

"We have deserted the rebel army and are in possession of extremely secretive information. It is most urgent."

The orange-haired soldier looked at his counterpart. "Regarding?" he said tiredly.

Walton stood with great posture and delivered his message. "I am in possession of information of utmost importance pertaining to a secretive mission by the rebels. The very lives of many of your brave brethren hang in the balance of my success in suitably explaining this message."

The orange haired man nodded at the other, spun and began climbing the steps of the large house. He entered through the front door.

Run along little chicky - bring me the hawk.

Walton assuredly raised his eyebrows as his plan was getting along seamlessly. He was quite proud of his invaluable weapon of oratory precision.

Moments later the door opened. The orange haired soldier returned being trailed by a three piece suited man in a white wig. The man had a stern look that brightened greatly when he spoke.

"Sirs," the man with the white wig said. "I am Ambrose Serle, secretary for his excellency, William Howe. How may I assist you?"

Walton raised his eyebrows higher still. "Tis a pleasure, My Lord," Walton said. "However this correspondence is intended to be delivered directly from my lips to his excellency's ears so as to avoid any ambiguity. Tis of the most crucial nature."

Serle raised his chin high. "I am imparting to you benevolence as I stand before you with open ears as an adequate messenger representing the nearest you may come to the great general without direct orders from his excellency himself."

Walton swallowed his pride heartily. He conceded this would be the most impactful option and more poignantly, his only option. He knew of Ambrose Serle and knew him to be a devoted loyalist and needed him to deliver the message properly. He glanced at Mayweather for confirmation of the next best move as was previously discussed and agreed to, if a scenario such as this were encountered.

Mayweather nodded.

Walton reached into his pocket and removed a perfectly folded paper with the words, *His Excellency William Howe,* inked in superb colonial penmanship.

"My good sir," Walton said as he handed the paper to Serle. "The fate of many brave British soldiers and perhaps the entire rebel cause lies in your hands and your ability to deliver *this* message."

"I offer you my assurance. Thank you," Serle said and raised his chin to the sun. He turned and walked back into the house.

"Wait!" Walton said. "My lord."

Serle spun and faced him with raised brow, demanding Walton speak right now.

Walton knew he needed to speak with humility to have a chance of being heard. Mayeather thoroughly informed him Ambrose Serle was a loyal subject of General Howe's and was outspoken in written word as later some of his diary would be published as an account of the revolution from the British viewpoint. He was detail oriented so he may likely look at the letter, but perhaps not in time. He needed to speak his piece concisely. "Late night of June sixteenth, tomorrow, rebels shall commence digging in atop Breed Hill in a cunning surprise maneuver."

Serle raised his eyebrows even higher, incredulously.

Walton continued. "In lack of such information, his excellency General Howe shall otherwise awake to this stunning feat." Walton felt the palpable indignation and knew he needed to be more convincing. He continued. "Though the rebels are untrained farmers and shopkeepers, from such a superior position atop the Hill, they indeed kill many of your fine British infantry. More than a thousand perish."

"I see," Serle said. "So the Yankees somehow, clandestinely fortify themselves atop Breed Hill in but just a single night, wherefore the majesty's troops are hence engaged in a losing battle at a cost of one thousand, did thee say? Casualties? I fear, good sir, that this correspondence may reduce his excellency to laughter if his excellency was so inclined. How *did* thee come by such knowledge?" Serle asked with a smirk.

Walton swallowed his pride along with his saliva, before saying, "My sources must remain private, however sir, this battle you will not lose. You will be triumphant, however your losses will be great."

Walton's words seem to be bouncing off of Serle's face.

Walton needed to pierce through and he felt the urgency. His time with Serle was no doubt receding rapidly. "I am not cracked my lord, but along with my first-hand information, I am a see-er. Into the immediate future I can see," Walton said.

Serle squinted as if Walton's words were brighter than the red of his coat.

Walton proclaimed, "One thousand and fifty four British dead or wounded sir. That is precise. Prevention is not costly. Simply guard the hill or take it first. If I am proven to be mad then you moved some of the King's soldiers for no reason, but nothing is lost. After all, an ounce of prevention is worth a pound of cure, hey?" Walton raised his eyebrows hopefully. Inside he was annoyed with himself for having slipped into his modern boardroom style of talk in the throes of his closing statement.

He was doubly annoyed now remembering that the tosser, Benjamin Franklin, had coined the "ounce of prevention" quote. Perhaps, he thought amusedly, some mysterious and gallant informant will get the credit for that quote in the updated future.

"One thousand fifty four," Serle repeated back. "Rising tis our toll. How unfortunate."

Walton felt like a doctor trying to convince a disobedient patient to take their medicine. "Timothy," he said to the all-knowing Mayweather. As much as he despised being so vulnerable as to ask the bloated Mayweather to throw him a flotation device, but he knew he was drowning. "Tis there anything you may share to aid him in his belief?"

There were facts past, present and future that may shock Serle, Mayweather knew, but knew equally that they would serve to solidify his likely thought that these three bizarre men were indeed, cracked. Mayweather looked at Serle while scanning his memory for this event in history – trying to uncover if they had succeeded already. He found nothing unchanged. Though generally without sleep or transcendental meditation providing a proverbial mental reboot, it was extremely difficult to be certain.

He decided his best hope was flattery. "Sir," Mayweather began. "This man before you is gifted with the ability which he claims. You are a profound writer my lord. Your consummate Christian prose and unparalleled hymns make me to believe you are a man capable of recognizing spirituality and divinity in forms we do not always understand. Tis one of those forms now present. Most sincerely."

Serle looked over the three men, investing a few seconds on each of their eyes. He fixed for an extra moment on the tall, goliath of a man, Livingston, and then spoke. "Good day, sirs," he said finally.

The three men walked over the small patch of grass and onto the road.

"Well?" Walton said to Mayweather.

Mayweather stopped walking for a moment and fell into a self-imposed hypnotic state. The two other men stopped walking and stared at him curiously.

Walton shook Mayweather back a minute and a half later. Mayweather startled and then started scanning through history. He ventured deep into his mind's eye. "Regretfully, no, nothing yet sir. I can't be certain, but it appears they don't listen."

The three men walked along dejected in silence for a few moments.

Mayweather was a boy whose baseball game was canceled, kicking up dust as he stomped. He ran his puffy pale hands down his face, mushing his skin along the way. "He looked at us like peasants," he said finally. "Arrogance! It's their bloody arrogance that leads them to peril."

Ambrose Serle crumpled up the paper delivered by the three cracked and blasphemous strangers and tossed it into the unlit fireplace on his way to see the General.

General Howe sat with impeccable posture behind his massive cherrywood desk. Legs etched top to bottom. Gold candle holders resting atop both sides. He jotted, focusing deeply, in his hefty journal.

"Three men visited. Claim to possess vital information. About the future, my lord."

Howe's quill stopped short.

"Pardon," Howe said and looked up.

"These men claim the colonists furtively scale Breed's Hill and construct fortifications in a single night. The colonists then fight the king's army, killing a thousand. One thousand fifty four killed or wounded, precisely."

Howe put down his quill and looked out the window behind him. From this vantage point he could view the top of the hill in question through the clouded window panes. He was quiet for a moment, digesting this claim.

Serle was obediently silent.

"In confirmation," Howe said finally. "The colonists, these rabble in arms, covertly climb the hill and build fortifications all in the duration of one single eve? Then dispatch over one thousand of her majesty's finest?"

Howe looked up at Serle and smirked. "All with their pitch-forks I presume?" he asked.

"Presumably," Serle said.

The two men laughed heartily.

"I'll leave you to your work, my lord."

Serle turned and left the room, closing the door behind him.

11

Charlestown, Massachusetts

June 17, 1775

The British garrison stationed on the shore in Charlestown, surveyed the land around them. Their refracting brass telescopes gleamed in the gloom of the early morning.

All in order.

The younger, and solitary blonde haired man of the group of four, scanned over Breed's Hill and continued to the heights of Bunker Hill. He shook his head and shifted back to Breed's Hill. "My God," he said to himself. "Breed's Hill. Breed's Hill," he shouted. The lenses of the garrison scanned over to view the fortifications built of earth. Protruding cannons pointed down, backed by a sizable group of Patriots.

"Get word to General Howe," the most senior soldier ordered.

Quarter of an hour later, Major General William Howe was indeed informed. He charged from his headquarters with Serle and three officers to a position to view the works. From his viewpoint he could see the astonishingly impressive works at the peak of the modest hill. Without the aid of a telescope, they appeared as ants scurrying along their new ant hill. He grimaced and muttered, "Rats."

He immediately held a brief council of war to plan an uphill attack. It was decided to advance from Charlestown and send troops from Boston over to Moulton's Hill if necessary. When the meeting was over, the room cleared - all except Howe and Serle. The two men looked at one another with apprehensive expressions before making their way toward the hill.

Howe, using the waters surrounding the hill, could have opted to circle the Patriots on the hill with his ships of war anchored nearby, but decided to march his troops uphill. There would be ships facing the hill and roughly twenty two hundred British soldiers marching up the hill. Enough so that the rabble may simply retreat under the might of her majesty's finest.

Ships opened fire first, volleying a barrage of cannon fire. Just after morning passed, British soldiers crossed the Charles River. They stormed the inclined terrain to reclaim the hills.

The Patriots waited. Their hearts thudded loudly alongside the thudding of the British army marching toward them. They waited still. Colonel William Prescott made it clear to his Patriot fighters by ordering, "Don't fire until you see the whites of their eyes!"

The British soldiers grew closer and closer. Not until the British soldiers were within less than twenty paces did the Patriots open fire. They discharged a forceful burst of shots fired. Rapid cracks boomed out from both sides. Plumes of smoke billowed out through the scattered trees on the hill. Numerous British troops were killed or wounded; the rest retreated down the hill.

Then, once again, the British troops stormed the hill in a second wave. They were beaten back by the Patriots and again, retreated after many more casualties.

The Patriots were winning the day at this point, but dangerously low on ammunition. With the third and final British charge up the hill, hand-to-hand fighting ensued. Bayonets stabbed. Fists hurled. Blood shed.

The British did eventually take possession of the hill, but at a steep price. Twenty two hundred British soldiers entered the battle, one thousand fifty four were either killed or wounded - same as it always had been.

Howe sat at the table sipping tea from the finest English teacup embroidered with the majestic crest of the Royal coat of arms of Great Britain. He took his time with his tea and traveled deep in thought. The day was unexpected and disastrous and this surprise would certainly not happen again.

Serle entered the room holding papers. "My lord. Final tallies. Colonists killed, one hundred and three. Estimated wounded, three hundred. The King's forces, eight hundred fourteen killed, two hundred forty wounded. I've tallied and tallied twice more. My lordship, tis a total of one thousand fifty four killed or wounded."

Howe placed his tea cup down hard on his saucer, clanging them. He looked up at Serle, his large, deep set dark eyes filled with fury.

"Locate him."

12

Manhattan, New York

March 20, 2045

8th Avenue in Manhattan was bustling. It was chilly, but Kyle felt warm in the clutches of his mother's firm grip. Though he and Mom, Christine, paced along quickly, he still managed to steal a few lengthy gawks at the panhandlers as they passed. These people always fascinated Kyle; the ragged clothes, unkempt hair and horrifying instability in their eyes. Even as a nine year old he knew fear should have taken the wheel and forced him to look away, but instead it pushed him to gaze a little longer.

"Don't be rude," Christine said, tugging his arm and jogging him from his fixation.

Kyle turned forward and hopped a step returning back astride with Mom. He looked up at his mother now. She wore her navy blue pea coat. Her auburn hair, shoulder length as it always was, swept back and forth along her shoulder like a gentle broom with every step. She huffed a steamy breath and Kyle spotted the concern in her pale green eyes even from his profile view. Christine had few pet-peeves, but Kyle knew well, being late was definitely one.

As they arrived at 39th Street, the red sign across said, DO NOT WALK, while the sign on 8th to Kyle's right counted down - currently at 22, 21, 20. Kyle and Christine were at the front of a pack of mostly well suited up men and women making their way to work. The combination of flowery fresh hair conditioner and after shave pungent to Kyle's young nostrils.

Kyle stared at the cross street pedestrians crossing. The people were briskly threading through one another to get from one side of 8th Avenue to the other side. He eyed their walk sign with those deliberate, determined numbers. He was old enough to know the deal. That sign would count down to zero, blink red a few times and then he and his mom would get the go ahead from their sign.

19, 18, 17.

Kyle looked at the sharp man beside him mouthing the words to the conversation he was having in neuro mode. The movement of the man's mouth was unnecessary to have a conversation in neuro mode, Kyle knew, but this technology was recently introduced and adults that grew up only speaking with their mouths were still adapting. Kyle's mind's eye giggled. The man looked like Kyle did when he ate a mega scoop of peanut butter. Kyle looked back at the adjacent walk sign counting down.

14, 13, 12.

Commuters directly across from Kyle and Christine decided to risk it and scampered over despite the other light being green. A young brunette woman, carrying a pug like a football, dashed across. A middle-aged Chinese man hustled quickly right behind her.

8, 7, 6.

That side of the street had the advantage of a clearer view of the one-way traffic. Kyle and Christine's side was lined with bumper to bumper box trucks double parked, loading and unloading – the closest of which was encroaching on the grit cov-ered white line of their crosswalk.

Impatient, deep breaths wove through the pedestrians bunched around Kyle and Christine.

5, 4, 3, 2.

The red countdown made it to 1 and the massive green light dropped down to yellow. Christine listened for a moment and then began to walk. She made it to the driver's side of the box truck on the line when Kyle heard the purr of the car speed-ing up to make the light. Kyle, being dragged behind, heard a voice shout, "Christi—" and a khaki sleeved man reached out and grabbed her shoulder.

Christine stopped just as the SUV zoomed across the cross-walk and underneath the red light. She turned around.

"Welly?"

The pack of irritated commuters shoved past this new fam-ily reunion traffic jam, shaking their heads.

"Dad!" Kyle said as a warmth exhaled throughout his skinny frame.

Christine thought and said, "What about your meeting?"

"Ahh," Welly said, shrugging. "I rescheduled," he said, being jostled by the never-ending parade of professionals. "I was thinking we can do lunch in the city."

"Yeah," Christine said. "But let's move it so we're not late to my meeting."

"Ooh, can we go to Jekyll and Hyde's?" Kyle said as they hur-ried across to the other side of the street.

Welly responded with his all knowing grin, larger than a full moon to Kyle. "Okay son, but you have to do well on your test."

Suddenly all the ambient car horns, scraping, clacking, screeching and jackhammering were inaudible. All sounds were replaced with Billy Joel's, *Keeping the Faith*. Kyle looked around and seemed to be the only one thinking this was unusual so he said nothing.

If it seems like I've been lost in let's remember,
If you think I'm feelin' older and missin' my younger daaays,
Oooh then you should've known me much better,
Cause my past is something that never,
Got in my waaay,
Oooh no,
Still I would not be here now if I never had the hunger,
And I'm not ashamed to say the wild boys were my friends,

At this verse the pedestrians suddenly started acknowledging the music and their strides became rhythmically lock-stepped with the beat. Kyle looked up at his Dad who was singing along with Billy Joel now loudly, on the bustling street.

Oooh cause I never felt the desire,
to let music set me on fire,

Now Welly was belting out the lyrics, drowning out Billy completely.

THEN I WAS SAAAAAVED, YEAH,

THAT'S WHY I'M KEEPIN THE FAAAAAAAAAITH, YEAH, YEAH, YEAH,

KEEPIN' THE FAITH

A filmy version of Welly appeared now. He was sitting next to Kyle playing the drums on his knees. The dream slipped away like water through his fingers. Beyond his father's bobbing head - the backdrop of darkness, with ever-changing numbers and mathematical symbols – fireflies, swarming around – reminded Kyle, he was on the vessel. That familiar disappointment settled in upon the realization that this was just in fact, a dream.

It was a dream that was so real it sucked him in every time. It was one that recurred for years and left him crushed, yet always thankful for those bonus moments with mom.

His father's giddiness made Kyle want to throw something at him.

Look at him. Totally entranced by his dumb music.

Kyle squeezed his eyelids shut and shook his head with vigor to send the message loud and clear that he was annoyed. Kyle knew it would cruise right over Welly's head or worse, encourage him to sing and dance even more gleefully if that was possible.

"Down three," Welly said. The volume lowered to an elevator level. "Top of the morning, laddie," Welly said in his best brogue to break the tension.

Kyle rolled his eyes. "Why not just turn it off?"

"You still don't like this, huh? I figured it would grow on you by now."

"It's grown on me like a wart."

Welly chuckled. "You know your grandpa used to love Billy Joel. That's how I got into him. I thought it might have the same effect on you. Guess not yet." Welly paused to choose his words. "More importantly, I need to ask. Did you have any really vivid dreams that were out of the ordinary?"

Kyle looked up at the ceiling of the vessel. There was plenty to view. Kaleidoscope of math equations, various maps and luminous dots, lines and text danced before his eyes. He knew his dad could and would explain every one of them if he was to concede the slightest interest. "Same dream," he said finally. "The one where you save her."

The silence strangled them both for a few long seconds.

"It's just so real," Kyle said, still staring up at the chaotic splendor above him. "I just....never want to wake up."

Welly was happy his son was putting forth a touch of emotion. He took the opportunity to put his hand on Kyle's upper back. Kyles muscles tensed.

"I'm sorry, Kyle. I really am." Welly rubbed the peak of Kyle's back. He then gave him two quick taps and brought his hand back into his own space. If Welly learned anything, it was that true and enduring progression takes time and rushing it causes delays. This was something he tried to teach his son, but so far to no success.

Kyle grinded his teeth and focused on a micro knob covered control board alongside the far wall. Welly studied his son's profile for a moment.

"You know, it's healthy to cry," Welly said. "You gotta let it out, son."

"No. I don't," Kyle said.

"It's scientifically proven that crying releases stress. It's a necessary practice if you are to remain mentally healthy. I don't think I need to remind you how important your mental health is."

"You know what? I'm tired of answers. You always have *all* the answers. For once I'd like you to say, ya know, I really don't friggin know son."

"Uh huh," Welly said. "So that's what you want me to say? I really don't friggin know son. And this would make you feel better somehow?"

Kyle shook his head disgustedly.

Welly smirked. "What can I say? I'm a pretty smart guy."

Kyle hurled two spears from his eyes into his father's.

"Look," Kyle said. "Can you please fill me in on what we're doing now. We've been traveling for a while and I'm still not totally clear on why." He just wanted the subject to change. It was too depressing anyhow. He knew his father's respect for history ran deeper than the love for his family. And he knew his mother's death was now in fact a part of history which must never be tampered with even though it's now possible with the technology that his *father* invented. The irony made Kyle nauseous.

Welly gripped the arm rest and slowly rose to his feet. His lower back felt so mechanical. It was like a rusty weather-beaten hinge. He hunched and clutched at it as he stood.

He said to Kyle, " You know, I never had back pain before it happened."

He hobbled a few steps over to the drink dispenser and stared at the machine. He issued a command inside his mind, dually processing the conversation with Kyle and the administration of his beverage. A small door opened on the adjacent counter and a mug emerged.

"I used to bend down and pick you up and whirl you around without even thinking about it. Imagine that. Without even *thinking* about it."

The mug slid along the counter on an imperceptible conveyer and slid into place under the dispenser's nozzle.

"You were a chubby baby too."

Welly laughed. The machine dispensed coffee - perfectly blended with cream and two sugars. Welly breathed in the aromatic delight.

"It wasn't until a few weeks after she was gone that the back pain came. It never left. The mind is a powerful thing. There is still so much that we don't know. For the amount that we can now control, there is still a thousand times that amount that we cannot. Stress can do a lot of damage."

Welly was not one to ingest medicine of any form unless it was absolutely necessary. He did not want to chemically tamper with his brain whatsoever. He believed, he *knew*, that everything he needed and what everyone else needed for the greater advancement of this planet was between his ears. To him, messing with his mind was like tracking down the Holy Grail and then using it to play flip cup. No thanks. He was here for a great purpose. Mild to moderate to even severe back pain was not going to derail that.

Kyle said nothing. He felt the weight of the silence that insisted upon a conciliatory response, and he refused it.

"A heck of a lot changed for me after that," Welly said, trying to offer an explanation for the last decade. "Changed *in* me."

Welly sipped his coffee and walked back to his captain's seat and gingerly sat back down.

A long silence filled the interior of the speeding vessel. No sounds other than the soft pings of the control screens and the *thwops* as they tore through folded pockets of space.

"God knows I've searched for that other me. I looked everywhere for that me from before the accident. I caught a couple of glimpses. Well, maybe shadows, or more like shimmers. But I can't get back to." He trailed off and then continued. "I've recalled countless memories. Mine and other people's. I've relived so many moments on the Zeit."

Thwop. Hushooo. Thwop.

"I don't know son. I tried."

Kyle shook his head. "Why don't you try finding *me*, Dad? I'm right here." His words rang out rapidly, like rounds spit from a Gatling gun. He immediately regretted engaging.

Welly again reached his arm across the console between them. "Hey son," he started.

Kyle shuttered and pushed his hand aside. "Can we please just drop this *right now*?"

Something about the seriousness and severity of his tone informed Welly that he needed to back off.

"Of course," Welly said. "Full steam ahead."

Thwop. Hushooo. Thwop. Thwop. Hushooo.

13

Welly thought. The vessel was scheduled to pierce Time Nova in thirty two minutes and Kyle needs to know. Explaining this to Kyle will result in endless mental daggers flipping his way - perhaps even a real one, but still Welly knew - *this was different*. Even this thought was heavy - tumbling in his mind like wet laundry.

This is more important than my *mother*, than your *wife*? Kyle would undoubtedly say. No defense is apt to satisfy his disappointment and that love and family over all else is one of the things Welly loved so much about his son - about Christine too.

Fortunately or unfortunately, Welly had cosmic perspective. He focused on the big picture and focused on advancing the human race and assisting the universe first and foremost. After all, he was tapped to do so. But he always had this cosmic perspective. Even as a little boy he spent more time looking out into the limitless black ocean above. Most nights he scarfed down his supper and skipped dessert to have a little more time star gazing before his human body failed him and needed to recharge again.

He often thought and often, he thought about his own thoughts. He wondered, with pointed curiosity, from where did these thoughts sail. Some of his favorite authors and great-est thought leaders he admired explained they drifted in from nowhere or some variation of this sentiment. This left Welly unsatisfied and he yearned to know though he never thought he may *actually* know during his life - at least on a conscious level, or at least on a serious level. But he did know. Sort of. He knew now that thoughts are matter, as real as the antique wooden desk and the various tiny dolphins littering it in his tiny home office. Thoughts sway and bend and drift and as-cend and descend and combine in as many ways as there are mathematical equations.

Wait! Welly thought. *Something is happening - happened.*

The mods were coming in fast and furious and even without his coming out of sleep as he always thought was necessary and how he trained the others. He was drifting in thought, but didn't think he was in that deep. Surely, not in a transcenden-tal state.

There would be a lot of restructuring data and new training to do at the Forward Facility after all this has been dealt with - assuming, of course, there existed a Forward Facility after this was dealt with.

April 19, 1775 700 British troops ordered by Thomas Gage - uh huh yes - march through Lexington and onto Concord? A small skirmish in Concord ends in the Patriot's arsenal of gun-powder and weapons being seized - and Samuel Adams being captured and jailed.

He scanned over that last line again.

Samuel Adams being captured and jailed? No no no!

This has major implications. Can't be true. This is throwing the timeline off. Think think.

Welly knew, yes he *knew* the accurate history to be early morning of April 19, 1775 the Minutemen - those Patriots ready to leave their families and fight with only a minute's no-tice - led by Captain John Parker, gathered on Lexington Green to make a stand against the Redcoats who outnumbered them seven hundred to seventy seven.. As the men stood lined and facing each other there was a mysterious shot fired - *the shot heard round the world*. This caused an eruption of gunfire.

And the battle caused a monumental spark that turned into a flame.

The battle went on as the British Redcoats were ambushed from the woods on their continued march over to Concord. Adams has enough time to transport the Patriot arsenal of gunpowder and he escapes. Great Britain and King George are put on notice as seventy three British are killed, one hundred and seventy four are wounded and twenty six are unaccounted for, missing. As far as the colonist Patriots - forty nine were killed, thirty nine wounded and five missing as a result of the Battles of Lexington and Concord.

The Minutemen? Where were they in Lexington? Scan! Open! Redcoats marched through Lexington as the colonists watched in disbelief.

Watched?

No!

What is it? What am I missing?

Think!

Of course. Paul Revere, William Dawes and Dr. Samuel Prescott galloping on horseback to warn the colonists that the "British are coming!"

Of course. Well, where the hell were they?

Scan Paul Revere April 19, 1775.

Paul Revere, William Dawes and Dr. Samuel Prescott were held captive in Revere's Silver Shop located at 19 North Square in Boston - the same shop that Revere made his famous engravings of the Boston....Witch Hunt.

Oh, Dear God. What the hell is going?

The men were held prisoner for forty eight hours, by three men, for reasons unknown. The three captors wore white wigs.

*They were never identified. Revere, Dawes and Prescott were fi-
nally released unharmed on the evening of April 19, 1775 with
no explanation.*

Whoa!

*So Revere never sees Dr. Joseph Warren on April 18th and
never even gets the information that the British are preparing to
march into Concord to capture the military stores. And the rest
is history. But we're still here. America still wins, right? As far as
-*

It was all coming in too fast. The usual trickles of a history
mod were twenty foot swells crashing into and then around in
Welly's head. He was whirling and getting woozy. He felt vomit
rising up and he clenched his fist.

Concentrate!

Concentrate, he did. He grabbed hold of it. He knew what
needed to be done. He focused on the calculation. It had to be
precise.

Welly and Kyle needed to pierce through Time Nova into
the morning of April 18,1775 – a day before the battle of Lexington and Concord. There. He had the calculation. Welly was
thankful for modern technology's assistance. He shuddered at
the passing thought of how long this would take with pen and
pencil and hoped one day never to find out.

Set.

The time coordinates projected out based on the moment
they would pierce through, considering both their rate of
speed and Time Nova's steady rate of expansion. Each minute
of time that Nova saved, represented just under a square mile
of penetrable space. Drilling down mathematically and then
entering physically in at a particular second, millisecond or
nanosecond, required great precision. Even with Welly's mathematical proficiency and experience, immense, complete concentration was necessary when piercing Nova.

In fact, Time Nova was not really a nova at all, scientifically speaking. It was originally presumed a supernova which is a star that suddenly and significantly increases in brightness because of a cataclysmic explosion. An exploding star, in other words. Time Nova, as it turns out, became visible to earthly telescopic instruments due to its increase in size, and not as a result of its being an exploding star.

"You see that dot, son?" Welly asked. He was out of breath despite having done zero physical activity.

Kyle nodded unenthusiastically.

"That is actually the time keeper for the multiverse. Amazing. Just amazing, huh?"

Welly commanded an image to appear between the two of them and the vessel's main windshield.

The screen displayed a live look at what appeared to Kyle as a giant, smoky, flat multi-colored lollipop without a stick. Welly tilted his head slightly and the image got larger and closer to them.

"So right here," Welly said and pointed at the very center of the lollipop. "That's current time. You go through there and you're in the same time you were before. If you venture just outside the center, starting with the closest outer ring." He tilted his head once more and zoomed into the ring next to the center. It was a pale yellow beside the white of the very center.

"There. You enter there and you will be in the past. Depending on your precise coordinates of entry. So where exactly you pierced through, will determine *exactly* what point in the past you end up. And that changes. Constantly. The Time Nova is ever increasing from the center, outward, with every moment that passes. It's recording. *Everything*. Isn't that intoxicating? Every shooting star, every piece of debris in every cyclone on Jupiter. I mean, the formation of Jupiter, every baby's breath, every snack eaten by a T-Rex and every photon that traveled to and fro, a time before time as we know it. In theory that is, of course. No one has ever actually been to the outer rings. But in theory, anywhere, or I should say any *time* since the dawn of the multiverse. You just have to know where you're going."

Welly commanded a display of a swirling grid that appeared to the right of the Time Nova screen. He looked cautiously at Kyle and saw he was actually listening for the moment.

"This is the road map we use. This, when layered over the Nova, provides us with the coordinates in time. Every ring, every subsection of each ring, every grid in every subsection, and every grid number inside each grid *and* this is expanding and recalculating every single fraction of a millisecond as Time Nova expands and grows. It's alive. It breathes. You see, son, this is why people on earth thought this was an exploding star, a supernova, because it was never visible until it reached a certain point of luminosity and as a result, the light was finally able to reach our equipment at the time, the way the light of an exploding star might. It was the expansion to a certain point, of this great timekeeper that provided enough light for us to detect it out here between galaxies, with the mere technologies at our disposal, just after the new year in twenty thirty one. The grid is spectacular and finely tuned, but I still need to double check its math with a few other programs, proprietary to *us*, at Forward."

He playfully elbowed Kyle. He knew he was pushing his luck with that.

Kyle's cynicism returned. "I know how it works. You *know* there's a whole course at my school I had to take on it. The *worst*. Everyone kept looking at me for my reaction during every friggin lesson. It was so embarrassing. I get it. We can study the past and you're the hero that discovered it. And I'm the son of the guy who discovered it. Yippee for me."

"Yeah, damn right, yippee for you. I have big plans for us. One day I'd like you to be my partner, son," Welly said as he delicately positioned the breathing grid screen over the Time Nova screen, with the precision of a surgeon guiding a laser.

"Yes, I know Pop. We could find two thousand points on that grid where you've mentioned it to me."

Welly smirked and continued working.

"I'm on my own path. I have things *I* gotta do."

Yeah, Welly thought. *Dick around on the Zeit and put energy into causes to no end. Maybe this trip would change him. Maybe he'd cut the Frummy. Maybe even like working with his dad. Doubt it. But maybe.*

"Besides, I'd want to check out the future," Kyle said.

Kids these days. Give them a time machine and they still complain. Welly thought and smirked in his mind's eye.

"The future can't be seen. So far as we know. Not from this airport. Again, so far as we know. The future has not happened. The farthest forward you can go with Nova is current time."

"So far as we know," Kyle said. "Right? Just sayin, it would be slope is all."

"Slope is cool, correct?"

Kyle said nothing and stared straight ahead.

Welly worked the numbers that both swirled around inside his mind and outside on the projected fields that poured from microscopic specks on the smooth ceiling five feet overhead. He gripped the two featureless joysticks in front of him, one with his left hand and the other his right, and concentrated deeper. His eyes were shut. He concentrated from that area of his psyche that was unlocked by the ET, and he drifted into a consciousness above his own, sipping from the great and plentiful reservoir of the universe and beyond. It was math and coordinates and all those things that frankly bugged Welly, but it directed and aimed the ship. It was energy and intuition and feeling that added the extra oomph and power and even stability to pierce the combative field of the Nova and into the precise location inputted.

Welly's breathing slowed. "Dad," Kyle said. "Pop. Are you up?"

Welly could not hear him. He was in that other place.

Kyle looked around as the brilliant light poured in from every portal of the vessel. Looking directly ahead now he saw nothing but the Nova. Only seconds earlier it was dark. Now it was there. The Nova was alive with bluest blues and the most exotic reds and oranges dancing wildly. Dashing white orbs. Glowing edges. It was chaos, but organized just so. Kyle was a deer entranced by the most dazzling headlights.

Welly focused on his thought used to steer and guide, and on his energy.

The center of Time Nova is not swirling as it appears to be but rather, expanding. The very center is black and the outer edges are constant with growth. Consistent with it's storage space, it expands generating roughly a square mile of new area per second. If you pierce through the center, the blackness, you are entering the core birthplace of storage and the current time; a time you can never go beyond so far as Welly and a million researchers believed currently. In the black center you are feeling extreme heat and pressure, pressure capable of turning a man into a diamond and a diamond into space dust if one was traveling on the exterior of the vessel.

When you enter any other part of Nova you cut through a slight membrane that instantly repairs itself upon the object's exit, but when you return through the center of darkness there is no membrane. There is extreme rumbling however, the shaking salts of time and re-creation of creation as Welly put it sometimes in lectures.

Why does it exist? How does it exist? One day perhaps a trip would be planned to the outermost tip of the outermost ring and to witness the beginning, but much more theorizing needs to be done. Besides, not sure there is much to see besides violent explosions of fusing molecules and gas.

The vessel jutted almost imperceptibly.

Then it was black again.

Welly leaned his head back and opened his eyes. His hands slid off of the joysticks and his arms slumped down like those belonging to a corpse. He took a heavy, ecstatic breath. He felt the energy was drained out of him because it was, but for good purpose and he knew it would come back two fold. It was the way one felt after getting a deep tissue massage. He wiggled his arms to shake out the numbness.

He checked the cosmic clock, translating it to the earthly and American rendition with his mind's eye to be sure they had pierced the Nova in the right location. Indeed they had. April 18, 1775 4:52 am Eastern Time. He projected it from Kyle's overhead, and it displayed right in front of him.

Kyle nodded. "Uh huh," is all he said before shaking his head.

Welly fanned his hand through the air from left to right the way a magician might fan out a deck of playing cards. A map of the cosmos appeared in holographic lights in front of him and Kyle. He fanned the hand back from right to left - this time a few inches higher than the floating map. Now a second map of the cosmos appeared.

"You see son? The top map is the precise location of every star, planet, black hole and shard of space debris on this day that we've just entered and right below is the way things stand in our day. You see that winding line? That's our route back to earth and we can make adjustments based on the lay of the land at this time. Or I should say the lay of the cosmos."

Welly grinned at his own little slice of space humor and looked over at Kyle hoping for a small smirk or an eye roll. Kyle's eyes were closed.

Welly made a slight alteration to their route based on some rogue zooming boulders - remnants of Keppler's Supernova. Then he got up and headed to the galley for a cosmic pizza.

He knew they would arrive on land by nightfall. A horse would be needed for a midnight ride to warn the Minutemen of the pending raid by the British soldiers. That wouldn't be too hard to come by. Though riding it may be the challenge. Welly rode a tame, nearly comatose horse once as a kid, but that was it. Kyle had taken lessons for a few years when he was younger.

14

8 Miles East of Lexington, Massachusetts

April 18th, 1775

The seven steps lowered onto the wet grass. The droplets hugging the tall grass glimmered in the moon's light. The tall trees surrounding the field on which the vessel landed, were monstrous silhouettes lurking. It rained as it always had during the day on this April 18, 1775 in this area of Massachusetts. Welly scanned this information on the way and he also knew it would be a clear night and then a pleasant day tomorrow - other than the bloodshed on the fields in Lexington.

As Kyle stepped down the last two steps from the side of the two hundred fifty four foot arrow head shaped vessel, he quickly realized something. The scent of the crisp air and the palpable shift of de-electrified energy made his sparse arm hairs stand on end. He was not in Brooklyn anymore. He was not in 2052 anymore either.

The wooded area that surrounded the open field on which they landed the vessel, was dense with trees. Everything was wet. The air was cool compared to the warmth of the vessel. The faint smell of campfire carried along through the dampness reminded Kyle of sleepaway camp five summers earlier.

Welly winced with every step as he exited the vessel. He grabbed at his lower back and said "Ah," and "Damn" and "Shit" upon each landing. Sitting for so long wreaked havoc on his vertebrae.

Kyle said, "I thought that was the language of the ignorant."

Welly planted both feet on the grass and took his hand off the railing. He said, "Ignorance is bliss." He thought to himself briefly and then said, "But who wants to be a blissful idiot, right son?"

Kyle shook his head and raised his eyebrows. He said, "You make *no* sense."

Welly shrugged him off and concentrated on the map and then generated it visibly. He stared intently at the map he had beaming from his fingertip. He rotated it to show Kyle.

"We are approximately eight miles due east of Lexington *here*. It's eleven o'three pm. We need to walk quickly along this path *here*. There are a few houses along the way one of which can provide us with a horse."

Kyle sprang back. "A horse?"

"Yeah, a horse. Look, son, this all probably seems insane, but I received a crystal clear mod that Paul Revere's midnight ride never takes place because Revere, Dawes and Prescott were held captive. Therefore they never warn the Minutemen and the British basically stroll right through to seize the ammo in Concord and capture Samuel Adams."

Kyle shook his head again to inform his dad that he thought he was off his rocker. "Okay."

"*Okay*?" Welly said. "This event happening this way could have, will have, would, did, whatever – have major implications. Could literally change the course of the entire world we live in."

"Right," Kyle said. "So what? We don't have that good beer anymore?"

Welly gave him that look that said, *Really? You're better than that, son.*

"I know what you're doing, Kyle. You're damn good at getting me bent out of shape, but not now. Does the name Paul Revere mean anything to you?"

Kyle inhaled deeply. "No. I don't remember that name. I'm sure I could find it on the Zeit somewhere though when I get back to my connection."

"No, no. I thought that would be the case. If I asked you about Paul Revere yesterday you would have had no problem telling me exactly who he was and significant events etcetera. Everyone in the current time will wake up just like you, not recalling what happened because it didn't happen, but it will now. Look, Paul Revere among other things, was instrumental because he along with a couple of others made a midnight horseback ride to Lexington on the heels of a raid from the British soldiers and warned the local Minutemen so they could be ready to stand their ground."

Welly inhaled deeply and continued, "It was the first major fight between the British and the Patriots and lit a fuse that helped to spark the revolutionary war. Only now he's been detained and doesn't make that ride and everything is in jeopardy."

Kyle squinted. "What are you telling me, Pop? You think *we're* capable of making that horseback ride?"

Welly looked away and then back at Kyle. "We have to be. We just have to walk through those woods and find the nearest house, borrow someone's horse without being shot and ride to the town and start hooting and hollering and telling everyone that the British are coming."

Kyle looked like he was about to speak, but no words came out.

"We can do this. You and me," Welly said.

Kyle assumed this had some deeper bond or meaning to the old man and didn't care to indulge him. "What choice do I have?"

"You have no choice, but I need you to pay close attention. Stay by me. Stay silent. You're a mute here. No interacting with anyone other than those we have to inform of the British troops. If you must speak to anyone, access the speech and vocabulary of the late seventeen hundreds. Got it?"

Kyle's eyes looked upward as he scanned his mind. "Yes," he said and widened his gaze to convince his father. "Yeah, yeah. I got it."

"This is not a game," Welly said sternly. "We are leaving the vessel here. You have the coordinates of the vessel locked in your memory. Kyle, please pay attention! Once I change the vessel's light spectrum you know it's impossible to see it with the naked eye so you have to know the coordinates in case we are separated. Change your light vision setting to L14 to see it. If we get split up - Kyle!"

Kyle was basking in the foreign wonderland in which he found himself. He was gazing across the fields of high grass lit by the moon and into the line of mossy trees. He squinted into the layer of fog emanating from the seemingly enchanted forest. *Are we really here? Seventeen seventy fi-*

"Kyle!"

"Yes," Kyle said instinctively. "Yes, I'm listening."

Welly continued. "If we get split up we meet back here. You have the coordinates now. Got it?" He stepped over to ensure his eyes stared directly into Kyle's eyes.

"Yes," Kyle said.

Welly boarded the vessel again and within seconds it disappeared from sight.

"Let's go," Welly said and began walking quickly, hunched forward forty five degrees.

After walking for twenty minutes, Kyle was still struck by just how dark it was in the thick woods. He already stubbed his toes and half tripped over fallen branches a dozen times. The other disconcerting thing was the numerous grunts and twig cracks he heard from sources beyond him and his father. Some grunts or snorts were far off and some closer. Some so close he thought he may be tackled at any moment.

Kyle scanned the index of wildlife in this region in his vast memory storage files as he was sure his father did before they even landed. He flicked away, with his mind's finger tip, the squirrels and rabbits and possums and chipmunks and even the deer. Then he landed on the moose.

A moose? A friggin moose?

If one of those things presented itself Kyle knew he's apt to turn and run directly into a tree in the darkness while the *friggin moose* does whatever the hell a *friggin moose* does. Worse even was the black bear population and still worse were the wolves. Kyle's scan led him to some articles written about the history of the area and the wolf issue.

A bounty of forty or fifty shillings was paid to a hunter for killing a wolf, around this area and time period, which served to inform Kyle that they had a *friggin wolf problem*.

A loud twig snapped like a thunderous whip crack. It was close. Kyle spun and drew in a short breath. *Screw it*, he thought and switched on his night vision.

Kyle pressed his finger on his right temple until he landed on the appropriate vision setting and released his finger. The optical enhancement package, he received on his fourteenth birthday, offered a wide array of settings. The enhancement simply altered the light which one sees and produces gas thin lenses on demand, aiding people in long distance sight or microscopic sight. Extensive optical enhancement packages, which were only ever so slightly visible to others, allowed the possessor to study the cosmos and determine with ease how many tiny craters appear on the surface of a boulder on the moon.

The black woods surrounding Kyle lit blazingly now, everything bathed in yellow. He looked around everywhere and was surprised at the density of these woods. He half expected to see a *friggin moose* standing next to him based on the volume of the last branch snap, but he saw nothing.

Wait.

Off in the distance he saw something scurry. His line of sight was disjointed by a staggered tree line. He picked up the pace and decided to walk beside his dad rather than behind him. *Better, better for both of us*, he thought.

Finally after ten more minutes of padding along the soft, mossy earth; they reached a clearing. Kyle rubbed his night vision off. It was too bright with the moonlight and left him feeling disoriented.

"Okay," Welly said. "You see that house over there?"

Kyle nodded. How could he not? There was nothing else to look at. It was a welcomed sight though – that tiny cabin and the barn next to it in the center of the oversized field. It was some form of civilization at least.

"Okay, you see that barn right there?"

"Wait. Which one are you talking about?"

"This is serious, Kyle. We can be shot for this. I'm sure there's a horse in the barn. We'll both run up. You crouch by that fence over there. You see it near the house? Crouch down over there and watch the house. I'll go into the barn, get the horse and come pick you up."

Kyle shook his head and rolled his eyes. "Maybe I should get the horse. You know your back-"

"My back is fine. Your job is to make a howling noise loud enough for me to hear if someone comes out of the house, okay?"

Welly began to creep out into the field from the woods.

"Wait," Kyle said. "No that's no good. There's a bounty for killing wolves. I'll get shot."

Welly scrolled through his mind's eye docs. "Damn your right. Impressive scanning. Good job son. Make the *hoooo hoooo* owl sound instead."

Yup. The absent minded professor sends his only son to get blasted by a colonial farmer as he howls like a moron.

"What's that sound again?"

Welly shook him off. "Get over to your position quickly," he said and began trotting toward the barn.

Kyle obeyed his father's order and sprinted toward the fence. It felt good to open up the throttle in the spacious field and he made it across the large expanse in under ten seconds. He crouched down, huffing as quietly as was possible, and fixed his eyes on the house.

He glanced over at his dad who appeared to be walking briskly in the opposite direction of the barn. Rather, he walked to Kyle's position by the fence, clutching his back.

"Okay," Welly whispered. "You were right. My back sucks. I will do the hooting and you secure the horse."

Kyle took an exaggerated breath that translated to, *I have to do everything.* He popped up from his squat and dashed toward the barn.

The barn had no door, but rather a large square opening that gave way to a hay covered floor and two stalls facing one another. Kyle's eyes were attempting to adjust to the extreme darkness, but he rubbed his temple once gently to slightly brighten the barn with the technological assistance of his implanted sight enhancers.

The large shadowy creature developed suddenly into two rubbery black pipes emitting steam. Kyle soon identified these as the horse's nostrils and saw the two gleaming golf balls glaring suspiciously at him.

"Hey, big guy," Kyle said calmly.

He reached out and rubbed the bridge of the horse's face. The horse shifted, stomping its hoof on the dirt floor. Kyle untied the lead rope from a stake nailed into the wall of the stall. Seconds later, he was leading the horse across the field he'd run across minutes earlier.

When he got within a few yards of Welly, he climbed on the horse and signaled to him.

Welly envisioned a quick one foot onto the stirrup and a swift thrust over and onto the horse and they ride off. On the first attempt, his leg did not reach high enough and he pummeled into the side of the horse with his shoulder. His second attempt, strategically, was more straight forward - leg in stirrup, use upper body strength to pull overweight torso up and then onto said horse. That did not work.

His third attempt was a combination of the first two. He gained some short momentum, lifted his foot into the stirrup and yanked, flinging himself onto the horse where he lay like a draped blanket for a few moments, catching his breath. He repositioned himself finally and grabbed hold of his son.

"You sure you can drive this thing?"

"Four years at Jamaica Bay, Pop," Kyle said and thwapped the side of the horse. They galloped off into the black night following the directions in their mind's eye compasses.

As they trotted along the dirt path, three hundred feet and closing from the battle field to be, in Lexington, the first glimpses of daylight pushed in. Welly had the presence of mind to realize he was not witnessing history, he was creating it. He was bobbing down that path, among those trees, breathing the colonial oxygen as he always vividly imagined it as a young boy during Santapogue Elementary history lessons.

He was there - here. He was *actually* here, and his back was hurting like a son of a bitch.

The next few moments would be fantastical. He would undoubtedly be injected with the all curing cortisone shot manifested by the energy of the universe and administered by historical destiny itself. He would boom out, "The British are coming! The British are coming! We're here in the name of Paul Revere and the British are coming!"

When they arrived in front of the first clapboard sided houses, Welly yelled feebly, with a cracking voice, "The British are coming!" He clutched at his lower back. "Damn it!" He yelled louder. "The British are coming!" He clutched at his back again. With every strain of his voice and pounce of the hoof it felt as though he was taking shotgun rounds directly above his buttox. "Damn it! The British are coming - the British! The British are coming! Damn it! Damn it!" Welly's face was flushing from the pain. His concentration was slipping away. "Paul Revere. Paul Reveeere! Name of. Name of Paul Revere. The British. Are. Coming!"

It was a disaster.

They trotted along and caught the attention of some men working in front of their homes.

"The British are coming!" Kyle boomed. "Gather your arms! The British are coming! In the name of Paul Revere."

Welly was impressed and a bit ashamed of himself.

Then in a voice so loud it startled Welly, "THE BRITISH ARE COOOOOMING!" Kyle bellowed.

Kyle glanced back. "Happy?"

Men, young and old began pouring out of doors bearing muskets. Welly clutched Kyle's arm. "Great work son," he said. "Head straight up through those trees and then we'll circle back around that way."

They approached a hill behind some of the small, humble homes situated directly across from the field where this first battle of the Revolutionary War was about to take place in only a matter of minutes -twenty four precisely.

Welly was relieved. "Thank God," he whispered. "There," he said as he pointed over to the rear of one of the homes. A clothes line from a small barn to the plank of wood on the side of the home. "Can you run a snag us each a shirt and pants off the clothes line?"

"What happened to not being seen?" Kyle said.

"If we are seen like this we'll be in more trouble. I don't know why the hell I didn't print some current day apparel." He looked over his son's clothes and then at his bright red and white sneakers. He rubbed his temple. *"Oh my God.* Wow. Those are the sneakers you're wearing? How could I not have noticed that?"

"Darkness," Kyle offered.

"These mods must be affecting my head. Preparing these details should have been a no brainer for me. Damn it! Well, I don't know. See if there's a pair of shoes laying around too."

"Whatever," Kyle said casually, and began walking in the direction of the backyard with the clothes line.

"Wait," said Welly. "Look around. Do you see anyone? Go quick."

Kyle shook his head at his father but then started sprinting. He hopped the three foot rock wall and then froze.

A man came bursting out of the back door of the home and Kyle dove behind a bale of hay. The man aggressively ripped a shirt off the clothes line and went back inside. Kyle booked immediately for the same clothes line the moment the man went back inside. He haphazardly snatched a whole section of clothes in a panic and ran back to Welly.

Welly and Kyle wore their new freshly borrowed colonial duds as they lay on the down slope of a small hill in some colonist's backyard. The shirts were white and the pants were the color of the tree bark of the maples behind them and were as comfortable as wearing fine sandpaper.

The vibrant red of the British soldiers were as bright as strings of lights against the wooded backdrop from which they emerged on the path. They marched synchronically into place onto the green in front of them.

"Wow," Kyle whispered to himself.

Welly adjusted his ocular lens and zoomed in so that he could see the pimples on the young Patriot faces and stubble on the faces of the elders. He gently rubbed the side of his eye and zoomed it back out a little bit. The soldiers on both sides were clearly visible in Welly's enhanced vision frame. This brought new meaning to the term theater of war.

A confluence of events and outcomes were merging and erupting inside Welly. This was causing him an uncharacteristically large amount of conscious anxiety. For a man who prided himself on being cool under most any circumstance, his heart raced now. If his mod was correct and the outcome needed to be changed then what was about to happen would determine if he and Kyle had succeeded or not. Plus, in truth, he had never been this close to a battlefield and managed to avoid any shootout type of situation his whole life with the exception of those suited men at the Forward Facility yesterday. He impressed himself with his calm then and there, and hoped to be revisited by composure.

He witnessed this very scene from thousands of miles above, on one of his vessel tours. Of course that was the original, unaltered version of events. As amazing as that was, hovering way above the actual real-time event unfolding in front of his eyes and the eyes of the ultra wealthy vessel tourists that paid a pretty penny for the excursion, it was still not like this was now. The tourists and he watched the event happen in real-time, yes, but they were so far removed from the actual danger and sounds and smells that despite the extreme close-up view their advanced lenses provided, it was not the same as feeling it. It was not the same as it was now with the damp earth beneath him as he lay on the same ground on which the soldiers stood nervously with their muskets no more than a hundred yards from him and his only son.

The colonists exchanged words with the British soldiers. They stood facing each other.

Welly's heart beat faster and faster. He zoomed out his ocular lens briefly to look at his son who lay beside him.

Is Kyle okay?

He found Kyle not paying any attention at all to the happenings on the field before him but rather fixed on the side window of the small house diagonally off to the right in which a young woman stood, staring out through the cloudy window pane, at the field.

Welly could see she was a pretty girl from here, as could Kyle he assumed, but he zoomed in on her anyhow. Her lengthy caramel colored hair was draped over her left shoulder and a look of dread occupied her pale face, enveloped her large, hazel eyes.

Welly looked again briefly at his teenage son and shook his head. He turned his focus back to the field and zoomed in just at the time he heard an intense *crack* and witnessed a British soldier falling to the ground.

He quickly shifted his focus to the woods where he saw a plume of smoke and three men running back the other way. One man with a distinct head of grey hair held his musket in his right hand as he ran beside his two white haired accomplices.

The shot heard round the world.

The vessel tour was unable to identify the shooter under the cover of so many trees and now Welly missed it from right here on the ground.

Who were these men?

Welly had to know.

He thought, *could I really find this out? Solve the mystery that would otherwise always remain unsolved? Could I do it without getting killed, or worse, altering historical events? That's the better question.*

Crack after *crack* after *crack* after *crack* rumbled out like thunder and men and boys were falling on the field. Heavy clouds of smoke lingered over the damp grass while the remaining colonists began to retreat in all directions.

Welly needed to know who were the men who fired that first shot. Was this Samuel Adams and company, as some theorized, or were these men somehow part of history alteration? Though the latter made little sense to Welly, it provided more justification for needing to positively identify them.

It was safer to go alone. There would be less chance of unknowingly stumbling into an event that could throw a proverbial wrench into the inner mechanical workings of the great time keeper. Kyle would be fine so long as he stayed right here and besides, Welly knew he'd be gone only a few quick minutes.

"Kyle," he said. "I have to try to see who those men were that fired the first shot. Please promise me you'll stay right here. *Don't* move."

"Okay," Kyle said "I'm right here."

Welly struggled to do a push-up and then got on his knees and raised his back upright, exerting an incredible amount of energy in the process. His butt was still throbbing from that miserable horseback ride. He got on his feet with a moan and then ran as fast as his body could move in the direction of the tree line in which the three men had run away from a few minutes prior.

15

After the chattering and wailing and weeping and cracks of musket fire grew steadily inconsistent and eventually subsided, and the small village became less chaotic, Kyle was making his way back to his position.

His morning did not turn out as planned. He'd been uprooted half an hour after Welly left, when two boys came bursting out the back door of the house behind which Kyle was lying. At the foot of the hill Kyle was sprawled belly down on, was, what appeared to be a rectangular bed of weeds.

The young boys, no older than twelve and ten, began grabbing the weeds and hastily tugging on them. They seemed hurried and Kyle watched them curiously. The younger boy held up his first dirt covered treasure and eyed it in the light. Kyle saw it was a small carrot. The boy threw it in his sack and continued violently pulling and collecting carrots. The other boy did the same on the opposite side.

The duo methodically harvested their way along until they were nearing the end of the rectangle, placing them twenty feet from Kyle. Out of the corner of one of their eyes, they were bound to notice a strange person lounging on their hill and likely have some questions.

Kyle decided it was better to pop up and be seen as a passer through. He rose to his feet and brushed himself off to begin his casual walk away. After brushing away a few blades of grass, he looked up and saw both boys stopped carrot picking and stared at him inquisitively.

Kyle had something already locked and loaded for these two. "How do ye?" he said boldly.

The older boy nodded while the other cocked his head in perplexed concentration.

Kyle had nothing else so he ran.

The two boys resumed carrot picking.

Kyle ran fast behind the backs of five spread out houses until finally he came across a stack of hay bales. He sat behind them catching his breath. Minutes later, Kyle heard a man and women speaking in a frantic tone to one another, their voices getting closer and closer to Kyle. Suddenly, the hay bales began disappearing behind him and it was time to run again.

Over the next few hours, Kyle ducked and dodged and hid around most of this neighborhood. Thankfully, most of the colonists were too preoccupied to pay much attention to another young man scampering about.

He was making his way back to his initial position on the hill. He arrived at the small barn in the yard with the clothes line from which he borrowed his new wardrobe earlier. He was walking past when their back door clapped open and the same man from earlier marched determinedly toward the clothes line. Kyle was in plain sight now having passed the barn. He glanced back to see the barn door partially open. He side-stepped ballerina-like into the opening and away from the sliver of light slicing into the barn.

Seconds later, the back door clapped again and Kyle crept over to the opening. He looked at the clothes line seeing that only a few items remained. He wondered if the man noticed he was down a few shirts and pants. How many clothes could he possibly have?

He looked beyond the line and saw the patch of soil where the carrot garden was previously and followed it along to the bottom of the hill and then upward toward his and his dad's initial position.

Nobody there.

Damn, he thought.

After thinking about it a bit more, he concluded his dad must be back at the vessel. He must have come back, saw he was gone, searched around and then returned to the vessel to meet.

Right? Kyle thought. *That's what he would do. Right? It's the only logical thing. The man is about his logic.*

The back door clapped again, jarring Kyle from thought. He scurried away from the opening and sat on the sparsely hay covered barn floor. The barn door started to open further. He anxiously looked around the barn like a cornered mouse, seeing if there was a place to hide. It was too late. He was stuck. He was caught.

The door opened and more daylight barged in. Kyle's mind fluttered like a cartoon flip book as he thought of what he might say. His eyes squinted and he used his forearm to shield the sunlight.

Oh shit, was all that came to mind.

In the doorway stood a statuesque figure. Light beamed around the silhouette's every curve. Kyle squinted and blinked. He saw her now. She was a girl. In fact, she was *the* girl. The girl he saw earlier standing at the window.

Her hair was pulled back now, but still covered her ears. It was tied with a pale, butter-colored ribbon. Her hair was not quite blonde hair nor brown, but it gleamed in the light more brilliantly than twenty four karat gold. She smiled when Kyle's browns met her hazels. She looked at the ground and back up at Kyle.

Oh my God, Kyle thought.

An intense heat made its way up from his chest and traversed his neck, eventually filling his cheeks and ears.

"Wow," he blurted. Something took him over, forcing the word from him like an exorcism.

The girl covered her mouth to shield her smile, but her squinting eyes betrayed her.

Kyle stood up, brushed a few hay straws from the back of his pants.

"Who are ye?" she said.

"Kyle, um," he thought about offering a fake name, but did it really matter? With hundreds of years of periodic distance there should be no harm. "Brackford, Kyle Brackford." Normally, this statement of his name was met with immense incredulity or excitement back in 2052, which Kyle enjoyed more than he cared to admit.

"Kyle Brackford," she repeated back.

"What tis your name?" Kyle asked, feeling a sudden compulsion to know all about her.

"Jennifer Crowley," she said.

"Jennifer Crowley," he repeated back.

They both smiled.

"Will your parents be angry with the, um...presence of I?" Kyle said, growing frustrated with this oldy speak.

"My father twas filled with such vexation. He took his leave hastily with other Minutemen. They are to meet in Boston and form plans. He imparted the strictest orders that I remain on these grounds awaiting his return."

"Scary times," Kyle said aloud without thinking.

Jennifer cocked her head slightly. "Tis," she said.

"And your mother?"

Jennifer looked at the hardened earth and at the scattered hay straws in front of Kyle's feet for a moment. "She passed on. Six years was I. She fell ill and passed on quickly."

Kyle felt her pain and it summoned up his own. "I'm sorry."

She looked back up at him now. "Thank you, Kyle Brackford," she said and smiled.

"I lost my mother at an early age. I know how hard it is, *tis*." He felt the need to say something else to start to backfill the deep expanse they unexpectedly opened. "For me," he said, "There is just this void. This invisible pain inside that's like mixed with regret and this feeling of dread just knowing that its, tis, unfixable."

Jennifer's eyes opened wide. She nodded her head. "Tis *my* feelings."

Kyle looked at her eyes deeply. He was struck by a profound feeling of rightness in this moment - in this place that was not his home and time that was not his own.

He said, "At times I'm stopped just completely and totally, by all the terrible things that happen to good people. All the awful things people do to one another, ya know? Other times I'm overwhelmed by the enveloping beauty that surrounds us and it's just," he took a deep breath. "Suffocating."

She tilted her head and looked in his eyes quizzically. Her large hazel eyes engulfed him.

He had it now. The fog in his mind cleared. "But right now," he continued. "Right now I can't even think of one thing that I might consider beautiful compared to you."

Her head bounced back as if spritzed with water and then she smiled.

"I'm sorry, but I'm not really sorry at all. I mean it. You are like from another planet beautiful. And your voice tis, like an angel."

She smiled and looked at the floor. She moved some dirt around with her foot.

"Actually," Kyle said. "I am sorry if I've made you feel uncomfortable. It just came over me that I had to say that to you. It was like the words were just forced out of me, ya know?"

Kyle realized his speech inadvertently reverted back and he worried about her reaction.

She squinted her eyes and said, "You speak in quite a direct and may I say, unique, manner. From where do you hail?"

"Oh," Kyle said. "I'm from a faraway land myself."

She waited, her hazels pleasantly demanding an answer.

"New York," he said finally.

Her eyes widened once again. She glanced down at his sneakers. "Tis where such interesting shoes are created?"

Kyle looked down at his red sneakers. "Uh," he said. "Tis."

She drew in a large breath and said, "Dreamt have I of taking leave for New York," She looked up at the barn's rafters, seeming to recall her dreams. "Kyle Brackford from New York," she said finally. "May I bid? What is thy purpose in mine barn?"

Kyle thought for a moment. *Fair question.*

He said, "Just resting. I ran all," he thought and scanned for morning. "Morrow," he said.

"Yes," she said. "I saw thou running and removing apparel from our line."

Shit, Kyle thought.

"Sorry. Mine apparel were soiled. Why didn't thou stop me?"

"Well," she said. "I too witnessed you riding in to warn of the British arrival." She smiled brightly. "Kyle Brackford bravely warns Lexington of impending doom. Most heroic," she said and gazed deep into Kyle's eyes.

He was lost momentarily, but quickly found himself and panicked. The potential historical significance registered. Those endless lessons and speeches from his dad must have seeped into him somehow, despite his best efforts to shoo them away.

Oh no! he thought.

Impulse mixed with pure fear and purer desire overtook him. He leaned in and kissed her. It was, once again, a force that he felt no control nor will to fight against. To Kyle, she was beyond stunning and her lips were juicier than ripe plums and a kiss just felt more right than anything he'd felt in a long time and he went for it.

They kissed.

When their lips unlocked, they remained face to face.

"Paul Revere," he said with their noses touching. "To Paul Revere goes the credit."

Her hazels were wide as they had been thus far.

God, he thought.

They kissed again. This time more ravenously.

Kyle felt like swallowing her mouth whole, but he contained himself and channeled his feelings and navigated to impassioned, sensual kissing.

Their lips separated.

"Paul Revere," she said and smiled.

Kyle nodded.

They kissed again.

After a minute or three hours – Kyle wouldn't be sure – they came up for air.

"Kyle Brackford," she said and smiled again.

"Jennifer Crowley," he said back. He was overcome with the need to apologize again. "I'm sorry. I just have this feeling for you. It's like overtaking me. I know it is, tis, strange for me, I, to say to you, thee, thou."

Jennifer smiled. "Thou are blunt. Imagine a man stating to a woman precisely his feelings toward her immediately upon making her acquaintance? And the woman returning in kind? How wonderful a world."

Kyle laughed. Her enthusiasm was infectious.

"So play pretend will I that in such a world I now reside. Smitten am I with thee. Overtaken, yes, perhaps this is the phrase of the day."

A silence fell between them.

She said, "Shall you stay for lunch, Kyle Brackford?"

Kyle thought for a moment. He could picture his dad waiting for him at the vessel, pacing back and forth. Kyle had a sinking feeling in his gut. The right thing to do was clear, but he knew he could not leave yet.

He raised his eyebrows and nodded instinctively.

She smiled and held out her pale hand daintily. "Come," she said.

He grabbed her hand gently. It was soft and warm and everything the hand of a beautiful girl should be. He followed her out of the barn.

16

Welly waited in front of the invisibility camouflaged vessel, pacing back and forth. He contemplated walking the eight miles back to Lexington and then knocking on every door in the village by the green. Stopping him was the probability that the two would pass each other by a wide margin in the woods and Kyle would be back at the vessel while he raised concerns from the colonial townsfolk.

He was already mad at himself from going rogue on a wild goose chase. The long, lonely walk back to the vessel provided him time to think about the level of stupidity he displayed. Even if he caught up to the shooter of the shot heard round the world and identified that person, how would that help this mission? The only justification was that the person might be connected to the history mods somehow, but that was weak and not likely true, Welly admitted to himself.

Worst of all, the woods proved to be incredibly dangerous as musket fire erupted all around him and he nearly got himself killed. He sought cover and laid face down on the dirt behind a moss covered log for almost an hour. So, unless the shooter was in the dirt behind that log, he was not going to make a positive ID. At his rate of speed these days, even in nearly perfect conditions, he would not have caught up to them. He also had to admit *that* to himself.

Out of habit, he kept shifting mentally to ping Kyle on his slab to psype him a message, remembering again each time that without the Zeit to carry those messages, that form of communication was not possible here. It crossed his mind that if he were still waiting by the vessel here in two hundred seventy years or so, technology would catch up and this kind of mental communication with his son would be back on track. So, he had that going for him. Knowing Kyle, he knew that waiting that long for him was not out of the realm of possibility.

Welly just hoped he wasn't on that damn Frumalda, Frummy garbage. Welly knew he was not the only parent dealing with this issue. It's becoming something of an epidemic with youth, he read on the Zeit. Kyle showed signs. He was withdrawn and constantly spacing out, lost in the ether. Welly did his best to confront him in an open way letting him know he was young once and he could talk to him about anything and no judgements. "I'm writing!" Kyle's response had continually been. But Welly was indeed young once and learned a thing or two and he was pretty damn sure he knew the difference between drugging and writing.

Damn it! Welly thought. He couldn't shake the feeling that Kyle was deliberately breaking the rules to hit him where it hurt most - right in the sacral plexus of temporal paradox.

17

Kyle finished slurping down his potato soup and popped his final scrap of bread into his mouth, letting it soften and combine with the broth. The tastes of basil and salt and fatty oil were somehow unfamiliar and new and exceedingly fresh and delicious.

Jennifer sat in the chair to the right at the humble, unevenly squared wooden table. She watched Kyle with great curiosity and Kyle enjoyed that more than the soup.

"Delicious," Kyle said.

Jennifer smiled. "My father canst cook well. Clean, he canst not."

Canst? Kyle thought and then landed on it. *Ahh, can.*

Kyle smiled and began to rise and lift his bowl off the table. Jennifer snatched the bowl from his hand and smirked. "Sit, unbend. More?" she asked.

Those hazels. They made it hard to breathe. Kyle felt something below his chin, like his throat closing. He shook his head. "Full," he said.

She smirked again, peeling off another layer of the protective foil around his heart – probably the last one. She walked a few feet over to the container of cloudy water on the counter top and dipped the bowl beneath the water. As she sloshed the rag over the bowl, Kyle eyed her frame wiggling. It was barely perceptible beneath the puffy fabric of the dress, but it was perceptible enough to drive Kyle wild. Once again he was over-taken. He envisioned himself making his way over to her and kissing the nape of her neck.

He thought about his dad waiting for him and the supposed gravity of their mission here. His mind flashed back to just af-ter his mom died when he got to go to his dad's work with him. It was something he looked forward to then - a bright blip on an otherwise dark period of time. But shortly after their arrival, his dad was whisked away to an allegedly quick meeting. Kyle still remembered that small playroom, and being surrounded by all the latest toy gadgets and gizmos and just staring at the door for hours.

Without realizing, he was on his feet now in Jennifer's kitchen. He seemed to float to her, carried by unseen forces. He brushed her hair aside, putting it over her right shoulder and began kissing the back of her neck. She dropped the bowl and the rag into the water and leaned her head back indicating to Kyle that she liked this affection.

He ran his hands up her tight frame and caressed her chest and kissed her neck more passionately. She spun around and began to kiss him now. Then she broke away from him and grabbed his hand. Smirking once more and leveling him with those eyes, she yanked on his hand and dragged him down the short corridor in the direction of the bedrooms.

18

In five minutes it would be three o'clock and still no sign of Kyle. Welly had been alone with his thoughts for hours. One thought occurred to him in between the frantic dread about Kyle being out *there* – was when the last time he was granted such a stretch of uninterrupted think time. It was probably two days after Christine's burial; after most of the people were gone and food had been eaten and the cards had been read and the flowers discarded, Christine's old high school friend Lindsey and her daughter spent the day with Kyle. Yes, that was it.

Typically, Welly did his thinking in smaller, intense bursts. There was little choice as his office doors, those cold metallic ones Welly loathed, at the Forward Facility, were constantly slid open with the next guest being ushered in by Cecil, his longtime assistant.

When there were no guests, Cecil was psyping him notes about someone trying to set something up or asking if an employee can grab his ear for five minutes. He made it a point to make time for his staff for two reasons – one was that he knew the importance of being heard and this little yet enormous perk may make the difference in someone feeling good about their work and their importance and their contributing and their wanting to contribute more and so on – and secondly, Welly was blessed with some great minds at his dispose and you just don't know where the next stroke of brilliance that changes the course of mankind forever, may come from.

Otherwise, he was doing what he was always doing which was moving the ball forward and innovating. Along the way he knew it would be critical to have as many people engaged and honing their mental skills which is why so much of his time was spent teaching Data Stay as well as other workshops. He wondered if any of his best students were catching these many mods. He hoped, but doubted. The training was still in early stages, relatively. He would find out soon enough.

If kyle would just get the hell back here.

He found anger more comforting than the real emotion he was filled with which was fear. He skirted around the thoughts of Kyle being seriously injured or worse and tried to focus on being pissed off at Kyle. That was better right now.

Welly looked around again at the tree line. Birds fluttered from tree to tree – flapping blots overlaid on the still blueish backdrop, the green leaves rustling as they took off from one branch and landed on another. Welly inhaled a deep breath, savoring the clean, pure 1775 air.

Yeah, this was abnormal on so many levels. His time though, was so fragmented and ever interrupted, that Welly knew he was growing frugal with his shrinking bandwidth the older he got. This was likely a bone of contention with Kyle if he was being honest and now was as good a time as any to finally be honest. His coveted bandwidth reserved in large part for the world's future – his divine purpose.

He had been so thrifty with his precious bandwidth in the name of dedication to his purpose. As much as he believed, he doubted at times. Even with the belief of what he needed to do for everyone's greater good, he supposed he could budget his time better – make time for his son as much – no more – than he made for others.

There it was.

It was something resting and probably even festering just beneath the surface for some time now that he just did not want to look at directly. It was too painful. In fact, when he thought of how much love he had for that kid and how he considered him - always since he met him - to be his best friend in the whole world, he felt akin to a monster for how he pushed him aside so much to focus on his work.

No more. Once I, we, get this mess taken care of things are gonna change. Yes sir. Yes indeedy.

He was here now, alone, and nowhere else to be except right here. He was forced to be alone with his thoughts. It was not easy as it turned out, though, not having enough time to simply clear his mind, alone, was a harbored complaint of Welly's. It was a complaint which often tumbled around in his head clumsily like baby Kyle tottering around the living room.

Yes, so here he was. Out here among the thickets of grass and trees and birds and bees. A gentle breeze blew delivering with it the scent of blooming tulips and Welly was reminded that there are no coincidences.

So here he was.

And there she was, as she always was – right there in the front of his mind blocked by the wall of wet tissue paper of everyday life.

"I miss you Christine. Everyday. I miss you," he said out loud and was surprised at his horse voice.

He shook his head hoping to shake the pain away. It was the little moments he missed so damn much. Those moments that fill in the gaps between monumental landmarks in one's life – they were most precious – they *were* the monumental moments.

Welly remembered a day when he ran out of boxer shorts and he needed to get to work. The Forward Facility construction was still not finished and the company had nice enough digs right down the road at Flatbush and Utica. Welly checked his underwear drawer and then the dryer and then the laundry baskets.

"What the hell?" he said, surprised. "I have no clean underwear. What is going on with Fabienne?" he asked Christine in their bedroom.

"Unemployment I guess. I fired her," Christine said, raising her eyebrows as if to say oops – did I forget to mention that.

Welly stopped in his tracks – his towel gripping his hairy stomach and pushing out the chub like a tourniquet. "What? Why?"

"Well. You remember I told you on Monday that she had a dizzy spell and I got home and she was on the floor?"

"Yeah, but she got checked out and was fine, right?"

"Yeah, but I didn't tell you that when the ambulance guys were carrying her out on the stretcher I looked at her clothes and her jewelry she was wearing and it was all my stuff. The final straw was as they fumbled around with her at the door I saw she had my Boppy Bear socks on."

"Oooh," Welly said and winced. "Not your Boppy Bear socks. So you actually fired her?"

"I did," Christine said. "I called her up and told her not to come back. I didn't want to tell you cause you have so much going on. I'll find a new one eventually. In the meantime I'll handle the cleaning."

Welly walked over to the overflowing dirty clothes hamper and found a pair of dirty boxer shorts. He pulled them out and smelled them deeply. "That sounds great honey."

"You're an asshole," she said and smiled.

Jackpot. That smirk was the equivalent of a belly laugh for Christine and Welly knew it.

"They're clean enough. I've got big things today. Underwear doesn't matter today. You know I'd walk right down Flatbush Avenue with no underwear at all if it would advance our people."

Christine rolled her eyes. "It would probably cure world hunger at least. Everyone would lose their appetite."

"Oh I thought you were gonna say everyone would be too turned on to eat anything."

"Oh sure," Christine said.

Welly had his khakis and button down on a few seconds later and said, "Wish me luck."

"Good luck," Christine said.

He reached out and hugged her tightly, feeling her cotton t-shirt, pressing against his dress shirt. He could still smell her extra whitening super duper peppermint toothpaste.

He wept in the field next to the vessel.

Oh God.

Then there was the other thing. The thing Welly slid an even thicker, steel wall in front of, and then an even thicker wall on the pathway that delivered him to the steel wall. An immovable wall. His mind's eye darted and bounced off it like a ricocheting bullet if ever it approached.

No.

The other thing was too much. Much too much.

Oh God. No!

Why should he venture to that wall this day he thought. It had been so long since he was so much as a thousand miles from it - let alone close enough to see it.

What's the correlation? What's the significance of this place? Or is it this day, this April 19, 1775?

Huh.

I'm always searching for the friggin answers. Kyle's right. It's the way I'm wired. Faulty wiring job. Ha.

Don't think about it. Don't. Just too much open space for deep thought here is all. That's all. Now leave it alone!

He shivered at the harshness of his inner voice and then was consumed with guilt. Sometimes he felt like wiping out all the painful memories - just deleting them from his mental hard drive. He knew he never could do it though. Those memories meant too much to his life. They *were* much of his life.

Memories were not just memories for Welly, or for those of his disciples who worked at honing the art of Data Stay or the Mind Trip. Mind Trip was not virtual reality – it *was* reality. Those, like Welly, who honed their minds to be able to journey into a hypnotic recall so deep and so intense that they *were* experiencing it, generally did so often. These people had little use for devices and instead might sit on their front porch or in a crowded subway car in a deep trance on the exterior, but on the inside – deep on the inside – they are floating down a serene river, perhaps catching their first fish, or on a ride-on mower with sunny skies and a gentle breeze, mowing endless rolling hills with a never-empty fuel tank. It may have been your own experience or a manufactured one. In fact, a whole industry cropped up around creating experiences such as these and predictably enough, much more perverted ones as well.

One accesses them through visualization and navigation with their mind's eye to the title of the channel or memory they wish to experience and entering in, by thought command, any information needed including payment if necessary. Payment may be applied by deep connecting within your journey in your mind's eye to an encrypted portal where it is safe to enter by use of thought, your ID and password information.

If it's a trip you want to re-experience, you may not need to rely on the Mind Trip manufacturer or creator and their server a second time, you could use your Data Stay abilities and save it to re-access over and over and likely over again - if you've sharpened your skills.

If it is a paid trip, the creator will get paid on the experience itself one time only by the Mind Tripper, and then make most of their money through product placement within the experience. That billboard way off in the distance of that rolling hill you're mowing is a soft drink you could really use after sweating in the sunlight for three hours now. That beat up old sticker right by the gear shifter on that ride-on mower is a reminder of who has the cheapest insurance and best service.

Welly knew all of this quite well as one of his companies, Brackford Enterprises, was the leader in the Mind Trip industry. It was exciting stuff and Welly was astonished and, well, a wee bit horrified to see the sweeping, controlling effect by which it grabbed hold of first, America, and then the rest of the world. The number of mind honing studios outnumbered coffee shops already.

People were clearly addicted to diving within themselves, but that was part of the way, Welly thought. It was part of the jagged road on the journey toward the destination. Welly believed the answers to propel humans forward lay within an expansion of use of one's brain and an expansion of one's psyche. Since people already possessed the capability of such an expansion upon coming into this world, this mental exercise must be a good thing – right?

Welly had to admit it did not always feel like such a good thing. The recall was so real. He was there with Christine and that was amazing. Then he was back and it was like he was mourning all over again. His chest tightened and more tears poured out of him as he awaited Kyle's return.

19

The ground that Welly lay on was still a bit damp, like a wrung out sponge, but it didn't stop him from dozing off. The long trip and the abundance of mental angst swept his legs out from under him.

The retiring sun beam streaks scattered over the trees in the distance, giving the clouds above an orange underglow. The birds played their out of sync melody of innate flutes in short bursts.

Kyle ever so carefully padded his filthy sneakers up right beside Welly's sleeping body.

"The British are coming! The British are coming!" Kyle whaled.

Welly abruptly raised halfway up in shock and Kyle howled with laughter. Welly winced and squinted as if he had just taken a swig of lemon juice. He slurped a great gust of air through an invisible straw and Kyle's smile vanished.

"My back," Welly said. "My damn back."

He laid back down and stared straight up at Kyle's nostrils floating roughly five and a half feet above him.

"Hey Pop," Kyle said. "I didn't mean to--"

"Oh it's bad. Damn it's bad," Welly said.

He wiggled slightly on the moist ground and hooted in agony. He forced himself onto his side and then blew multiple gusts of air as if blowing out birthday candles. He then flopped over onto his stomach and stared down at Kyle's once white and red, now grey, dry-mud covered sneakers.

God damnit! he thought. *Sorry, God,* he then thought and then yet another thought came to his mind as he stared at his maturing son's large feet. His mind briefly flashed back to what felt like ten minutes ago when Kyle was just a little tyke.

Little Kyle was tooling around the coffee table in the living room appearing to have more volts of electricity running through him than Frankenstein as his body jolted this way and that. He was in a red and green and blue striped collared shirt and miniature khaki pants with no socks or shoes, exposing his truly awesome little guy feet.

What a great wardrobe designer Christine had been. There is no doubt the clothing selection suffered for Kyle once she was gone, and before Kyle could pick out his own clothes. There was the brief and everlasting awkward time period when Welly got more strange looks than he cared to remember. But he did remember his best friend, AKA baby Frankenstein, falling onto the Persian rug and lying there much like Welly lay at Kyle's feet now.

Christine was still there then, so Welly's back pain had not yet begun. He quickly whisked the little guy off the floor and picked him up over his head so he could make motorcycle sounds on his belly. It was simple then. That's all he had to do to make his best buddy laugh and that's all Welly needed to feel full.

Welly shifted back onto his side making him appear like the magician's assistant who was about to be sawed in half. "Kyle," he said. "Can you help me move my legs?"

Kyle sighed with purposeful audibility.

It didn't exactly match the whisking that Welly had done for him fourteen or so years ago but that's okay. All would be forgiven my child.

Kyle found his way over to his dad's feet and slowly moved them upward. He knew the drill. Next he would have to help him get on his knees and a push-up position with his arms and from there help him stand up, which is exactly what he did.

Welly stood hunching and holding the side of the camouflaged vessel. It was so well blended into its scenic background that a passerby would have seen a man leaning on air and defying gravity.

"Thank you son," Welly said

Kyle shrugged and raised his brows as if he had better things to do. And he did. He missed her already - an incredible amount.

"Can we just get the hell out of here?" Kyle said.

"Well, are you okay? Are you going to tell me what the hell happened to you?"

Kyle looked at his dad's eyes and then down at his feet.

"I was scared," he said. "Someone spotted me and I ran around the village hiding until someone took me in and let me sit in their house."

Welly looked up at the sky and shook his head.

Kyle said, "It was fine. I was just scared to leave until now. I'm fine. Can we just go?"

"Yes, we have to," Welly said. "We'll talk on the way."

Welly's dirt speckled loafer finally made it onto the metallic floor of the vessel. Welly let out a huff which was interrupted by a tightening sensation in his right calf. The surprised feeling sent a jolt through him and he fell over.

Kyle saw now there was a man behind him wielding a musket.

The man bellowed, "Halt." He then stumbled up the stairs, tripping on the last step and nearly crashing into Kyle.

Kyle instinctively reached out, grabbed the slight man's shoulders and shoved him to the ground. The musket fired upon hitting the floor and a ball whizzed right by Kyle's left ear and shattered a digital device on the upper wall. The sound in the small space was akin to a stick of dynamite exploding. It was deafening. Kyle's ears rang with bells of pain so much so that he thought they would bleed.

After the brief shock-spell broke, he jumped on top of the skeletal man and laid his weight down on him.

Welly stood with the aid of a railing on the side wall and said, "What is your name, sir?"

The man said nothing.

Welly took in a breath and said slowly, "We do not mean to harm you. What is your name?"

The man said, "Ebenezer. Ebenezer Cartwright."

Welly looked up and focused deeply. He entered the name into his extensive memory record's databases, family tree files, criminal records and found a hit. He let go of the rail and walked over to Kyle. He held up his pointer finger to Kyle, showing him the glowing tip of it.

He whispered in Kyle's ear, "I am going to immobilize this man but he may wake up and tell people about what he saw. They may very well think he's a loon and therefore change the course of his life and possibly the lives of his descendants."

"Okay," Kyle whispered back. "Great. Just do it already. He's squirmy."

Welly thought and then continued whispering, "Most of his descendants have no known notoriety except for one. His seventh great grandson is a prominent lawyer."

"Pop," Kyle said. "We'll be okay."

Welly huffed. "This is bad."

Welly held up his pointer finger cautiously. The tiny light radiating from the tip of the finger brightened. He pressed the finger into the side of Ebenezer's neck and he became entranced immediately. His neck relaxed and his eyes fixed on a sight in the endless distance only he could see.

Kyle felt the man's body go slack and said, "I have to get me one of those."

Welly glared at him.

"Self defense," Kyle said and held up his pointer finger. "This thing is just a crappy flashlight."

Welly shook his head and said, "Flashlight can be quite helpful. And don't get any ideas. You've got years to go before you can even apply for a permit for an update like that."

Kyle shook his head.

Welly said, "Kyle, can you manage to drag this man onto the grass without hurting him?"

"This guy weighs like sixty pounds Pop. I got him."

Kyle grabbed Ebenzer's sweat-soaked armpits and raised him up slightly. "Gross," he said and dragged him out the open door and down the steps onto the grass.

Welly rubbed his forehead. He felt a headache coming. Glancing up he observed that the electronic device the man, Ebenezer, shot was one of the debris avoidance navigation tools.

Ugh. Great.

Welly quickly reconciled this loss with the reminder that with the incredible tools at his disposal aboard the vessel, there was redundancy upon redundancy so in theory that device was not mission critical. Things could have certainly gone worse. All considered, they were pretty lucky.

Kyle re-entered the vessel shaking his head. "Can we just get the hell out of here already?"

"Sit," Welly said. "Strap in."

The vessel hovered above a large swath of grass and Ebenezer's body. His body lay awkwardly like that of a crime scene body.

The vessel spun forty degrees counterclockwise and jutted into the sky, quickly out of the vision of anyone inhabiting earth.

After the trip back to Nova was safely on its course, and after an exhaustive amount of bickering and Welly getting no clear answer as to where the hell Kyle had been and why, Welly retired to his suite to get the other half of that sleep. This time he was in a dry, warm bed.

He hit the pillow which molded around the shape of his head like soft molding clay and fell asleep almost instantly with the savory knowledge that the vessel was heading precisely where it needed to be heading - back to Time Nova.

Once through, his first order of business would be to reach out to his old pal Denny. Welly would ask for a MOM - a meeting of the minds, whereby both would speak by way of thoughts conveyed by an optimum likeness each generated, and housed only in the mind's eye. Welly would request such a meeting and the meeting would be granted.

But for now, sleep.

20

Cambridge, Massachusetts

October 5, 1775

General of the Continental Army, George Washington, from his Cambridge headquarters just finished penning a letter. The correspondence was to be delivered to John Hancock and the Continental Congress headquartered in Philadelphia. It informed Hancock of the interception and deciphering of a treasonous letter from Dr. Benjamin Church, Director General of the Hospital for the Patriots, to the British General Thomas Gage.

Church would be arrested soon after, stand trial for treason and be convicted of communicating with the enemy, and be imprisoned until 1777. After falling ill in prison, Congress would have him exiled by way of a schooner, bound for the West Indies that is ultimately lost at sea.

In his letter to Hancock, Washington also describes some letters from the Colonel Benedict Arnold regarding his expedition in Quebec, before signing off as follows:

I am with the greatest Respect & Regard, Sir, Your most Obed. & very Hbble Servt

Go: Washington

George's large body was filled with stress. It entrapped and surrounded him on so many fronts. He sealed the envelope and instructed his personal servant, William "Billy" Lee, to expedite his correspondence.

Washington stood alone, with superb posture, surveying the nature from the large, fine English made window of the Longfellow House which served as his Cambridge headquarters. He inhaled deeply. The autumn colors had a calming effect. From this window he saw a staggered line of trees. They were uneven blotches of red and yellow and orange - blotches from a drying paint brush dabbed along the blue canvass. He took in another breath before remembering - winter would be arriving soon.

15 Miles East - Concord, Massachusetts

Walton, Livingston and Mayweather stayed at the inn for the second consecutive night.

Walton shifted around in the wooden seat at the empty wooden table of the restaurant at this Massachusetts's lodge. He relished the thought of arriving victoriously back to modern day with his beloved modern furnishings and modern cuisine. Living in colonial 1775 was the antithesis of comfort and made his soft, normally well lotioned skin, crawl with annoyance.

The inn was a large colonial house situated on a dirt road surrounded by a scattering of various trees – pine, oak and a few red maples. There was a barn and two other small supply buildings dotting the property as well. A carved wooden sign hung on a stake on the front lawn that featured three letters – Inn.

The ever punctual John Livingston glanced suspiciously at the proprietor as he entered the dining area.

Walton had no choice but to grin.

Livingston looked like a grown-up in a child's playhouse in this room – in fact, he looked that way in most of the establishments the trio visited. The people of this time were just a bit smaller physically, and Livingston's size was much more differentiating and at times, shocking to the colonists. At six foot five he towered over everyone, but his well-developed build, his gargantuan biceps and forearms were nothing short of freakish to these folks.

"There he is," Walton said. "Welcome back to another fine meal at the Concord Inn," Walton said.

"I enjoy the food," Livingston said in his usual stone manner as he sat down.

"You simply enjoy food," Walton said. "Deep fried shoe leather would do just the same for a brawny bloke with your appetite, no?"

Livingston half nodded. This was the nearest to a hearty chuckle as could be garnered from him.

Walton leaned forward and spoke quietly, "Only chap who likes food more is that podger who'll be stomping in any moment, cracking up the bloody planks beneath his bloated feet hey?

Livingston half nodded again. This time raising his eyebrows slightly.

"I can't endure much more of that one," Walton added.

"His mind-" Livingston offered and was interrupted.

"I know, I know," Walton said. "I will say though, my mods are arriving now with greater clarity as I hone. Between the two of us operating the vessel."

Mayweather entered the room. He spotted Walton and Livingston – the only diners in the small room – and trudged over to the table. "John," he said and then looked at Walton as he pulled out his wooden Windsor chair.

The shiny waxed chair, simple in its build, featured evenly spaced hand carved wood rods for a backrest that would make an inmate feel at home should one be kneeling behind the chair peering through. Mayweather, the historian, knew this chair was undoubtedly an antique in current day, capable of fetching a pretty penny or pound. He could indeed even predict within a few pounds for how much the item may be sold.

"My Lord," he said to Walton as he sat down.

The chair creaked loudly.

Walton glanced over at Livingston.

The middle aged man with thinning, unkempt hair brought over three rolled cloth napkins and unrolled them on the table in front of each man. His hands trembled and the silverware clanged upon each napkin's unveiling.

Walton sighed and shook his head.

"Thomas, tis Thomas, yes? May you simply bring us three of your finest pheasants? Whatever tis thou killed today. Please? Gramercy."

Thomas nodded politely. "Beverages?"

Walton rolled his eyes toward the wood beams on the ceiling. "Water. Your cleanest."

Livingston said, "Beer."

"I think I fancy my first flip," Mayweather said cheerily. "Please. Many thanks."

Flip was a combination of beer, rum and molasses.

Thomas turned and walked away.

Walton scowled at Thomas's back and then said, "Gentleman, we are evidently being trailed – just behind us in time things are being undone which we all agree, has to be why we have not yet succeeded. We need a decisive blow. I'm thinking Trenton may indeed be the turning point of all importance."

Mayweather raised a finger to interject, but Walton steamrolled onward.

"We know Washington crosses the Delaware on Christmas and most cowardly sneak attacks the British and Hessian forces before scurrying back across the Delaware. I propose he does not cross the Delaware and instead his flat boats are sunk and our countrymen are properly informed of the position of the rabble in arms."

Walton took a triumphant breath.

Livingston nodded.

Mayweather shook his head. "Sir, respectfully, I've been giving much thought to this and concluded, ironically, my lord. I *think* now this is a war of thought. The seed of passionate thought and spirit planted and watered to grow into roots so indomitable they enwrapped the mightiest military force in its time and pressed it into submission."

Walton was disgusted, being reminded of this truth. "What are you proposing?" he said.

"Up until now, the time we are in currently, the thought of separation from King George by most colonists is still *not* most prevalent. The thought of these colonists is an undirected passion for preservation and freedoms, but still a loyalty to the crown despite all that has happened. One man gave shape and structure and a path through prose and stoked the embers in the hearts and minds of these colonists. An Englishman of course, my lord. Thomas Paine."

Livingston grunted.

Walton thrummed his fingers on the wooden table top and thought. It sounded like galloping horses. He stopped mid-gallop and said, "You're proposing if that raggedy pamphlet Common Sense is not published then these hearts and minds are not given the clarity of direction and what? Do they just flounder and float on?"

"Perhaps," Mayweather said. "The pamphlet was published at the same point in time that the transcript of King George's speech to parliament arrived in Philadelphia. He declares the colonies were in open rebellion against the crown, but the people here are given clarity to their anger and this fuels a longing for separation, rather than striking the fear and pause it might have otherwise."

Walton thought. He nodded. "You have thought about this a great deal, have you?"

As much as Walton hated Mayweather's bloated body in which he clunked around, and the many infuriating sounds and smells produced by this body, he had a profound respect for his mind and abilities as a strategist. His mind being filled with history and extraordinary mod recognition capability is what landed him a seat at this table. He was also the only one that Walton knew to be able to operate and navigate the space vessel to the Time Nova.

Mayweather nodded.

"We take out Mr. Paine," Walton said. He slapped the table and added, "Where in hell is Thomas? I'm parched."

21

Welly's mental alarm sounded and the walls in his room let off a surrounding, dreadful *eh eh eh eh*, letting him know there was fifteen minutes to Nova. There could be no chance of him not waking up.

He said, "Stop," both orally and within his mind.

He slung his feet over the bed and stood up. He clutched the lower section of his back. "Damn it! Damn it, damn it, damn it. I'm sick of-"

A violent wave of chaotic thoughts bludgeoned him. He forgot about his back and now had an instant migraine. Sharp, shooting pain. He sat on the bed and clutched both hands on his head and then slid them down to cover his eyes. The pain subsided and burst out, subsided and burst, and again, just like a throbbing toothache in his eyeballs. He squeezed the closed lids of his eyes and thought of Thomas Paine.

Thomas Paine? Okay okay. Thomas Paine, writer. Common Sense. Right. Okay. Common Sense. Okay okay. Strong argument for independence, challenged authority of the crown, stoked the flames of the colonists.

The 16 pamphlets of course - American Crisis published later in 1776. It was read aloud to the patriots a few days before Washington's Army's Christmas sneak attack on Trenton to serve as a morale booster.

Yes, of course. 'Tyranny, like hell, is not easily conquered; yet we have this consolation with us, that the harder the conflict, the more glorious the triumph.'

"What?" he asked finally, out loud, as if someone else were making him think these thoughts. "What the hell is it?'

Suddenly a competing thought walloped in and the migraine intensified.

He didn't.

Parts of this history were fuzzy, evasive, as if trying to conceal themselves.

Thomas Paine missing, vanished. Vanished?

Thomas Paine, editor of the Pennsylvania magazine, vanished on New Year's Eve 1775. Some of his untitled thoughts and writings found and published in his honor following his disappearance. Other unfinished works published years later. Year, year? 1888? Considered well-crafted and on display.

Well-written period piece examples. Next chapter.

Next chapter.

He could hear this echoing through his skull. It was the voice of his fourth grade teacher Mr. Staeger.

Next chapter. Next chapter. Next chapter.

Another thought crashed into his psyche. *Hearts and minds.*

Shit!

Hearts and minds!

Welly vomited. He hadn't much on his stomach before and even less now.

He stared at the chunks on the cold metallic floor beside his bed with his pulsing, bulging eyes. He said, "Spill," and the metallic rectangular tube floor moulding unhinged itself first from the lower part of the wall, and then unhinged in various jointed sections once the floor was scanned and the spill size and location identified. The newly formed semicircle of rectangular tubing glided over to the rotten pinkish yellow mess.

Once in position around the spill, mist was sprayed from the imperceptible holes on the tubing.

Welly smelled the lemony cleaning agent and it took him back to someplace nostalgic, though he could not pinpoint exactly where. He stared at the technology working. The mist was breaking down the slop, doing its job.

"Ten minutes to Nova," a computerized voice blared out, jolting him.

He wiped his mouth with the back of his hand and staggered over to the door. This was bad and extremely urgent, but even worse, he couldn't think about it right now. The trip through Nova must be precise.

Welly hollered, projected his voice down every corridor at Kyle, "Wake up! We're going through Nova. You need to be strapped in." He felt the acidic burn in his throat and rubbed the outside of his neck and it did nothing to soothe it.

Kyle was sitting in the co-pilot seat front and center of the vessel just as he had been the first time through Nova. He gave Welly a crafty smirk and an eyebrow salute to tell him, *I'm already here so hah.*

Welly lacked the strength to return fire - between his slamming head and lower back pain. He sat and the straps wrapped around his body snugly. Inside his head was too hectic. It went from an open highway to a traffic jam to an eighteen car pile up. Time was of the essence and though he had psyped a few key notes in his memory regarding Thomas Paine and his writings and impact, he had to focus on getting through Nova precisely now.

He brought the commands outside of his mind's eye and on display for Kyle and he to observe. He crunched numbers and double checked the entry location of the Nova grid. Dead center like a bullseye was always the necessary target upon re-entry into current time.

Time Nova increases its size, saving all things in its memory, from the center outward with every passing nanosecond due to it constantly birthing new history storage causing it's expansion. The outermost edges are the oldest points. Presumably, the outermost tip at the end of the outermost ring being the earliest point in the great time keeper's recorded history, the dawn of time itself.

The knowledge of precise and mechanical workings of Nova was essentially stumbled into by trial and error like so many great discoveries. It was on that fateful first trip through Nova with Welly at the helm alongside the late great Martin Brown. It wasn't until their third trip through and the third time they almost accidentally changed the course of history, bumbling around like two kids playing with matches on top of a nuclear reactor.

He knew well now, seventeen years after that maiden voyage, down to a pinhead, where the vessel needed to go.

The light intensified greatly - a spectacular sight for those not suffering from a migraine. Welly's mind and energy was necessary here - no question - and he knew it. The vessel dipped as he withdrew his focus.

Up up. Got it. Stay the course.

The vessel started to shake. The bumping temporarily broke the spell cast on Kyle by Nova's splendor and he looked gravely concerned.

"Pop," he said.

"Got it. Got it," Welly said full of vibration. "Stea- Steady-"

Kuaaaah!

Welly vomited all over himself leaving ooze and splotches of pulp covering the center of his harness.

They were through.

"Sorry son. Sorry. I'm sorry," Welly repeated for a third time. He had the look of the last man out of the bar at the end of the night.

"Jesus, are you okay?"

"Lord's name son."

"Holy shit. Is that better? Are you okay? Do you need me to do something?"

"Check the all time sync clock." Welly lifted his arm as if it were under water, and pointed. "There."

Kyle looked over and squinted. He said, "July twenty second, twenty fifty two, five o' four PM."

Welly checked it against his devices. "Good," he said finally.

He unlatched himself vacantly. He removed the entire harness and entered it into the wall chute for discarding.

Kyle watched him like a science experiment gone wrong. He moved about like a man with no soul, a man dead from the inside out. He was used to seeing his dad off in that other place. He'd seen that most of his life, but this was different. This was eerie.

"Hey, are you sure you're okay?"

Welly looked at Kyle as if seeing him for the first time. "Yes," he said. "I'm just. I'm not sure really." He grabbed his head with one hand. He was both trying to subside the pain and get his bearings. "Received a mod. Sizeable. Maybe greater than any before. I can't tell if maybe we are too late. This is major, son."

Welly's consolatory tone raised the flesh on Kyle's arms.

"I have to work longhand for a bit."

Kyle looked at him with complete incomprehension.

"I need to actually write down words. On *paper*," Welly said and acted it out, wiggling his hand in the air like a crazy person until he finally waved it forward to say *just forget it*. His migraine was beginning to dissipate.

"I have to get some important info down on paper and we have to hide it somewhere safe so that if I forget everything completely, I can be reminded by something physical that might not cease to exist based on alternate series of events. So long as it was placed there after such events and it will be. My mind is trained and I am working through all this, but I'm not so sure this is sustainable."

Kyle considered this idea.

"Okay," Kyle said. "But if you forget everything won't you forget where these hidden papers are too?"

Welly started to correct him when he realized he was right. Kyle was absolutely right.

"I'll think of something. I have to get writing now. The world needs me. I have to do it now. Right after I pee. We're on full, uh, autopilot. That's it. Autopilot. So we're good. Oh, I'll be in the office quarters. And afterward I'm reaching out to Denny, Dennis, Neuhas."

This all sounded bonkers to Kyle. He looked at his dad who seemed to be coming around, but he wasn't quite sure. He stared at the wet splats of vomit on his pants. "Are you sure you're up for a chat with the President of the United States, Pop?"

"That doesn't matter right now. I have to write now and then I'll explain."

22

Welly returned to the front of the vessel ninety minutes later with a stack of two hundred fifty typed, single spaced, glistening pieces of paper. Each page printed and coated with Live Sea Scroll preservative - *'guaranteed to last for more than a thousand years'* as their ad claimed. Welly always wondered who might challenge this claim except for possibly a descendent of someone who coated a will in the preservative, way down the timeline stream and likely long after Live Sea Scroll Co was happily out of business. But, the stuff seemed to work.

Welly accessed some files that he suspected he would need. They were safely stored in his mind, but for how long? He transcribed them by way of psyping the information. It was pertinent information about the American Revolution, events before, during and after, a summarization of modern history, key information gleaned from his ET encounter, information about his life and roadmap to build a vessel and precisely how to get to Time Nova.

The upper part of his forehead, the part that used to be thickly covered with hair, shined with perspiration. "Two hundred and fifty pages right on the nose and fully preser-"

He stopped mid-sentence realizing Kyle was not in the seat anymore. He glanced around. He was alone. He stomped over to the Captain's chair, sat down and pulled a metallic drawer out from the small control station in front of him. He placed his writings inside the drawer and closed it back up.

Welly traveled in his mind through a vaulted door and encrypted space and fenced off areas to arrive in a secure enough compartment to place his call.

Call Dennis Neuhas 87379447%$()@*^ Brackford, Wellington. Jefferson Lincoln 687-FTD-906-1600-IUUY-9

He continued prompting for another minute or so until he was connected - deep connected. Almost immediately, he was right there in the mental space with the president - the POTUS. For Welly, the meeting took place on a Victorian porch that looked out onto a tremendously large and lush green lawn backing up to a lake far off in the distance. For President Neuhas, Welly always assumed he set him and Welly inside a scene with an abundance of mahogany and wainscot and tall ceilings.

"Denny. How the hell are you?" Welly said with a purposeful overly casual tone as if he was calling him to confirm their tee time for golf.

"Been better," Denny said.

Dennis Neuhas was in the oval office sitting behind his desk with both hands on his ears pressing his skull into a deep concentration. He was getting good at this form of communication but he was still no expert and he had to work at it a bit more and the average Jane or Joe. He was seventy three years old, but his hair was still golden brown with the assistance of modern day technology.

"I just finished reviewing the report," Dennis said. "I just can't fathom it. I'm at a loss. I really don't know what to say here."

"So you are aware of the mods - the historic modifications?" Welly said, feeling a sort of distribution of weight at least knowing that the government, who had been remarkably slow on the uptake with their development in the Data Stay work-shops, had been able to pick up on the mods.

That told him his work was *working*. Indeed, there was a path clearing to this being something more than just his own special ability. It would all be worth it if he could successfully pass the torch on to his fellow man to carry on. But, if he could not right these manufactured wrongs, the special visits, all his years of work, and personal sacrifice would turn to steam and then vanish. He felt a wave of panic layer over the lightened load and it heavied again.

Denny cleared his virtual throat. "You know," he said. "We are not as backwards as you and the others at the Forward Facility might like to believe. That said, just what in God's name are you trying to do? You have some sort of allegiance to England? You want to change the outcome of the American revolution? Level with me, Welly. What is this about? Your ancestors?"

These questions delivered Welly to the immediate comprehension there was zero doubt in his quote-unquote pal's mind, that *he* was responsible.

What the hell is he talking about with ancestors? Welly thought.

He scanned his memories quickly for prior conversations with Denny and keywords such as *England, English, British, and ancestors.* He came upon their golf outing a year-and-a-half ago. What a beautiful and utterly miserable day, Welly recalled. The Florida weather couldn't have been more perfect, but Welly's back pain was at an eight most of the day and shot up to an eleven with every feeble drive.

He had it locked in now. On the sixth hole, Welly mentioned that his family had come over from England after the war. He waxed poetic for two minutes about how much they struggled and how hard of times it must have been. He meant it purely as paying tribute to his ancestors and professing his gratitude for how easy Americans have it today, relatively speaking.

He scanned for a few seconds more and uncovered nothing else. That must be the clarifying connection there. Unreal. There was no great passion or debate in that conversation. Dennis had shared his family's lineage on the golf cart ride and Welly acted in kind.

There was no damn loyalty anymore. People just turned on you like a dime - it conjured up memories of that racial accusation incident. When you're accused of something, you find out who your friends are and Welly had found out, he didn't have many. The list was shrinking yet again.

"Denny," Welly said calmly, knowing there were potentially three dozen or so others listening to the conversation and would likely analyze every syllable of it. "Really? You know me. You know how patriotic I am. You also know although I don't love the idea of countries in general, I believe America to be the gold standard and the leader that shall pave the way for others. You know I believe that in my heart and you know I always have, don't you?"

There was a few seconds of silence.

"I thought I knew that. And I wish I could still believe that. The sure fact is that there are only four others registered and capable of getting a vessel to the Nova and back. They've all been detained and are under our careful watch. The only vessel in use right now is Christine Two. What other conclusion can I come to, Well?"

Fair enough, Welly thought.

The *who* was the part of this puzzle that he just could not figure out. He did know it was conceivable that someone unknown developed and mastered their technology. Welly toured the world and gave as much knowledge and training as he was able to in lectures, but the vessel operated, in some part, on a deep psychotic, almost hypnotic concentration few others succeeded in attaining as of yet. Those that did, needed to work directly with Welly for a minimum of fifteen months. Welly was advanced, perhaps decades ahead, he knew, as a result of his knowledge implantation from his extraterrestrial encounter.

"I don't have a good explanation or alibi for you," Welly said. He conceited this as he was determined to sound as genuine as was possible because he *was* being genuine. "There must be someone more advanced than we've been awa-"

Dennis cut him off. "You have to come in. There's no way around it."

"No," Welly said. "I have to come in."

"That's what I just said," Dennis said.

"*I* have to come in because *we* need to work *together*. I need your support and we have to right this and I can't do it by myself. I have no choice. I *must* convince you, Denny. There are other forces at work here and I'm going to need your and the government's support. Please Denny."

There was a long pause. "I'll keep an open mind for you Welly. How soon can you be here?"

"Tomorrow morning."

23

Kyle lay in the plush bed in his quarters on the vessel, staring blankly at the reflective ceiling. He was happy to be through Time Nova and operating in current time. He was navigating in the Zeit through his mind's eye, researching.

Jennifer Crowley, daughter of Joseph and Anne, parents who considerately filled out a census that stood the test of time. Kyle viewed the one-dimensional image of the filled out card. The writing was oldy cursive and Kyle could barely make out the words. He surmised it was from 1762 and Anne and Joseph Crowley had one daughter - Jennifer.

Jennifer's age on the card was not present. She said her mom passed away when she was six so she would have been about three or four in 1762. Her mother was still alive then.

Kyle thought of their life. Little Jennifer tootling around. Father Joseph is hard at work and mother Anne tending the home. Beautiful countryside. No war.

He wondered what more became of her father's life. How long was Jennifer alone before her dad returned?

He scanned on, searching for Joseph Crowley Massachusetts throughout the 1770s.

Military Records. Battle of Bunker Hill. June 17, 1775. Men listed below alphabetically - casualties and losses. Casualties?

He scanned down more hastily hoping he would not see the name, knowing he would.

Crowley, Joseph was listed in bold print.

Kyle paused his search for a moment and thought.

He never made it back. Jennifer was left alone.

A heavy stone sunk from his throat to his gut.

Alone, he thought again, the word echoing inside his mind.

He wished he could visit there and see her through virtual mapping, but VM only helped you visit just about any place on earth *post* VM memory links being invented and perfected by, of course, Brackford. This technology creates an amalgam of publicly shared memories, photos, videos and text to video imagery to take you virtually to a time and place to experience virtual history. One can see and sometimes even feel the grass, peer up at the blue skies, feel the warmth on their face. From a living room or crowded subway car or toilet, one can leave on a journey to Paris to visit the Louvre and see the Mona Lisa up close and personal or zip over to Japan to stand at the base of Mount Fuji or better yet, on the peak. As long as a few humans had been there and shared some of their experience, there was usually enough to meld together a lifelike experience.

Kyle continued up the census stream and located a Jennifer Crowley dated 1782. He scanned over squiggly lines intended to be written words - *city of New York, county of New York, state of New York?*

Huh, Kyle thought and ran his hand up his forehead then cut through his hair. *She made it.*

He scanned on. *Permanent Residence - Bowery, House Number - 18, Name - Crowley Jennifer, Age - 23. Must be her. Relation - Mother. Mother?*

Kyle's mind's eye scanned faster now past nativity, citizenship, occupation and then pounced down to the next line. Under the space that the last name Crowley was written above, was a single quotes sign and next to that was the name Kyle.

Kyle's heart jostled and he was jarred out of the trance-like state he'd been in conducting his research. His eyes blinked and saw the cold metallic room once again.

He drew in a heavy breath and then focused back into his mind's eye and his research, finding the census card again. He hovered over first and then locked on to that squiggly K, y, l, e. Panning over to the right, under Relation - *Son, Age - 6.*

His heart seemed to stop and then restart. Immediately he began doing math and piecing together the timeline. It did not fit for him to be the father, did it?

If it were mine the child would be seven at least. Right?

He scanned down and over. No father was listed. Could there have been another man swooping in just as he had? Could it not have been as special and as deep between them as he knew it to be? The other guy could have died in the war. Maybe that was *her* true love. But maybe-

A brilliant and reassuring thought rolled in knocking all others aside like a strike bound bowling ball.

She named her child Kyle. She named her child Kyle, after me.

He continued scanning through census records, but found nothing more. After something like the twentieth dead end, he took a break and swiped clear all the clutter in his head.

In his mind's eye he smiled and in the exterior world he smiled as well, unknowingly. Euphoria and exhaustion culminated, the final seasonings added to his waking stew. He didn't drift to sleep; he sank, like a rock in a river, to sleep.

Kyle and his mom arrived at 39th Street. The sign with the digital red letters across the street said, DO NOT WALK while the sign with the red numerals across to the right offered the countdown currently at 22, 21, 20. Kyle and Christine were at the front of a pack of mostly well suited up men and women making their way to work. The scents of flowery fresh hair conditioner and after shave merged and wafted over to Kyle.

19, 18, 17.

He felt a lock of his dirty blonde hair feather his forehead.

He looked at the sharp man beside him mouthing the words to the conversation he was having in neuro mode. The man looked like Kyle when he ate a mega scoop of peanut butter. Kyle's mind's eye giggled.

14, 13, 12.

Commuters directly across decided to risk it and ran across.

The young brunette woman, carrying a pug like a football, dashed across to Kyle and Christine's corner.

The middle-aged Chinese man hustled quickly right behind her.

8, 7, 6.

That side of the street had a clear view of the one-way traffic. Kyle and Christine's side was lined with box trucks double parked, loading and unloading – the closest truck encroaching on the grit covered white line of their crosswalk.

Impatient huffs wove through the pedestrians bunched around Kyle and Christine.

5, 4, 3, 2.

The red countdown made it to 1 and the massive green light in the sky dropped down to yellow. Time seemingly slowed. Kyle felt submerged in water momentarily. The traffic light's color change exclaimed with the heavy thump of a sledgehammer pounding frozen ground.

Christine listened for a moment and then began to walk. She made it to the driver's side of the box truck on the line when Kyle heard the purr of the truck speeding up to make the light. Kyle, being dragged behind, heard a voice shout, "Christi—" and a khaki sleeved man's hand reached out and grabbed her shoulder.

Christine stopped just as the SUV zoomed across the crosswalk and underneath the red light. She turned around.

"Welly?"

The pack of irritated commuters shoved past this new traffic jam shaking their heads.

"Dad!" Kyle said as a warmth exhaled throughout his skinny frame.

Christine thought and said, "What about your meeting?"

"Ahh," Welly said, shrugging. "I rescheduled," he said, being jostled to and fro by the never-ending parade of professionals. "I was thinking we can do lunch in the city."

"Yeah," Christine said. "But let's move it so we're not late to *our* meeting."

"Ooh, can we go to Jekyll and Hyde's?" Kyle said as they hurried across to the other side of the street.

Welly responded with his all knowing grin, larger than a full moon to Kyle. "Okay, son, but you *have to* do well on your test."

"I've been studying for *three* days," Kyle said.

Welly smiled. "How did I get such a great kid?"

Kyle shrugged. "You're a lucky guy I guess."

Welly laughed. "Lucky, blessed, charmed, fortunate-"

"Great. All those things and more," Christine said. "But we really have to get moving to this meeting or it won't matter how good Kyle does on that test. C'mon."

Christine walked in front of the cars and trucks lined up at the red light. Kyle and Welly walked behind. Welly raised his eyebrows and bulged his blue eyes out sarcastically to Kyle. Kyle giggled.

"First Mom's meeting. Then Jekyll & Hyde's," Welly said.

Kyle sat in a small waiting room that housed a wooden chair and a small wooden table with some children's learning magazines. One of the magazines was digitally enhanced and a video on a loop played on the cover, previewing the contents inside. Side by side were two similar cartoon farm pictures and a blue circle was drawn around details on the photo on the right - a find the differences game, Kyle recognized.

The heavy wooden door swung open and Welly exited the room with Christine and gave Kyle a subtle thumbs up.

Behind Christine was a man with salt streaked black hair sporting a burgundy turtleneck. He looked at Kyle with curiosity. "Kyle Brackford," he said. "We look forward to your attendance here in September. We are encouraged by your test results and we hope you will exceed our expectations."

Kyle stood and willed himself across the room to shake the man's large hand. He did his best to look the man in the eye as his father had always insisted. "Thank you. I will do my best," he said, the words emanating from some unknown vocal cord suppressed somewhere beneath his stomach.

"Very well," the man said. "Good day." He nodded at Welly and Christine and re-entered the room, closing the door behind him.

"Let's eat," Welly said.

Kyle, Welly and Christine were in the back of a taxi. Kyle was the last one in and tasked with closing the heavy door. He arched his back as straight as he could so he could see out. A heavyset man and a young brunette woman in a rich black skirt suit and a merlot scarf, kissed goodbye. Her lips grabbed hold of the man's bottom lip and she pulled it back at the end of the kiss, making the man appear as a hooked fish. The couple looked passionately into one another's eyes for a long moment.

Kyle smiled. So much going on. So much to see. The action was endless outside of a Manhattan window.

"Seventh Ave and Christopher Street," Welly said to the driver.

"No it's Seventh and Grove Street," Christine said.

"No, pretty sure it's Christopher," Welly said.

The driver started driving.

"You have no sense of direction."

Welly shook his head in protest. "Seventh Ave and Grove Street sir."

"Can I get chocolate milk?" Kyle said.

"Kyle! Hello! Kyle, damn it."

Kyle snapped to and realized by his dad's tone that he must have been calling his name for some time.

"Yes. What?"

"What's the matter with you? I've been calling your name for five minutes."

"I was focused. I was writing."

"Writing?"

Kyle shrugged and looked at his father reinforcing this, unconvincingly. He was too groggy to be convincing and he was still reeling from that dream.

"You know I'm smart, son? And I know *you* better than anyone. If there is anyone you can talk to. If you're taking that Frummy stuff, you know-"

"I'm not!" He debated if he should tell his dad about the dream. "I was *writing.*"

Welly shook his head. "Okay, right. Come out to the helm in a minute. *Please.*"

The door was closed and Welly was gone before Kyle had a chance to speak again.

Kyle's ecstatic jubilation was replaced with aching loneliness. Being accused by a disbelieving parent is a very lonely business. Whether they're right or not didn't matter much. It mattered that there may only be one or two people in the whole world that were there to believe in you and when that was gone and that crust of ground beneath you broke away, you were slipping through the depths of space, alone.

His mind flashed back to the dream from which he was just shoved. It was vivid. More than vivid. It felt so damn *real.*

He ran through command prompts in his head, accessing footage saved from that day in Manhattan. He went straight to the exact time and location of when it happened knowing his impatient father awaited. He could see from any available view saved. There were only a few from that date and time as the technology was not fully there. He had the view from the person at the crosswalk directly across from him and his mom. There was the view from the person's memory in the building across the street and two different views from 8th Avenue's cross-street pedestrians. Kyle usually utilized one of these views when reliving this moment.

He re-experienced it dozens of times from all available angles and it had never changed the outcome, only hardened the cement. But today was different. Something now felt different. Something had changed.

He studied the large group of eager pedestrians and saw his mom at the head of the pack. He looked to the edge of the visible area behind the pack. The footage was jerky and wobbled around as it always had with this and most other memory accesses, but Kyle stayed focused on the outer edge of the pack of pedestrians. There was this innate sense telling him his father would appear any second in the khaki shirt.

Christine began to wrench her head around and started to walk into the street.

Now! Kyle thought. *Right here.*

Christine rushed out and reached behind her for her son's hand and was battered by the speeding truck. Her body was punched out onto 8th Avenue where it lay strangely on the pavement, un-alive.

The driver of the truck jumped out with the same horrified expression she always had before. The same people walked on, and the same people gathered to try to help. The same boy yelled "Mommy," from the depths of his soul and ran over to be with her, hoping she would be okay.

Kyle exited the footage and wiped his hand down his face, his loneliness and despair and anger renewed.

Hope could be a wicked jester.

24

Welly concentrated on the control station. His focus was intense, frantic. His eyes bounced around epeleptically.

"I'm here," Kyle said.

Welly snapped out of it.

"What do you want?"

"You know, son," Welly started. "It's all about tone. Communicating in the right tone can take you anywhere you want to go and the wrong tone will send the wrong signal and leave you high and dry."

"Yeah I know," Kyle said. "Like your stupid dolphins, right?"

He could see the hurt take hold on Welly's face now.

"Come on son. Why are you always so angry with me?"

Kyle thought, *Because you weren't there. You weren't there that day. You weren't there any day after. You left me for the world in your mind and I hate you for that.*

"You wouldn't get it. You're the elite. You're the problem. You don't understand the struggles and the inequality because you don't live it."

Kyle felt the words oozing out and taking a form he had not intended.

"Kyle, really? You can't really feel that way. I know you hang with people on the Zeit that are still going on about these social issues and racism, but that war has long since been fought and won."

"Oh, I know. You won't even acknowledge it. Of course. Your big vow. You should see what people say about you and your vow on the Zeit. You're not as beloved in the whole world as your lackeys might lead you to believe."

"Kyle, what is this about? Why are you attacking me? I wrote that letter to stand up for human rights to try to put an end to the hazardous sights set on good people by reckless idiots who want to continue to drag people into this mire of dedicating boundless energy into someone's appearance, something that they cannot control. Those sights were set on me and I was attacked for judging employees strictly on aptitude and competency and results. When I didn't comply with *their* idea of fair and balanced by way of hiring less qualified people simply to level the color or creed scales in my company, they came at me with pitchforks."

Kyle stared straight ahead.

Welly continued, "So, yes, I thought long and hard before I wrote that letter. I could comply and take the easy route and watch more good people like myself fall to their knees due to the pressure or I could take a stance. I took a stance because this identity shit has to end! If you gather up all of the collective energy that is poured into acknowledgement of anyone by their ethnicity whether for good or bad, and the unquantifiable adverse effects that ripple from each, you can make the argument that humans can set themselves back for hundreds, possibly even thousands of years by not nipping this in the bud. I'm just doing my part."

"Yeah," Kyle scoffed. You're doing your part alright. You want to save a country that thought it was a good idea to keep slaves for hundreds of years."

"There is no perfection, Kyle. That was absolutely terrible. It will forever be a stain on those generations, but no man has ever been without major flaws. You show me whoever you believe is the most righteous, picture perfect person on the Zeit and I'll show you a flawed man. All these holier than thou people are full of it because *no one* is perfect. So I say, why waste so much time on maddening flaws? Why not be productive despite them?"

"Whatev," Kyle said. "Just saying. You're trying to save a failed experiment. Maybe it would have been better if the British won."

"No!" Welly shouted louder than he anticipated. "You're not listening damnit!"

Kyle recoiled.

Welly took in a deep breath and said, "*We* are trying to save a country founded on beautiful, amazing ideals, a country that so many good and decent, imperfect brave men and women fought for. *I* believe in those ideals and *I* believe in those decent people and their sacrifice. You better get your mind right."

"Whatev," Kyle said and looked out the window into the darkness.

"I don't want to argue," Welly said. "Can you help me, son? I need you to copy my commands here. This part is easier with two."

Kyle drew in a sharp breath and nodded.

25

Philadelphia, Pennsylvania
December 31, 1775

The air was bitter cold yet the Philadelphia street was warmed with the sounds of clangs and bangs of silverware on pots and pans as the new year was rolling in.

The man with the thick mane of wavy hair locking up the heavy wooden door of the Pennsylvania Magazine office wore his heaviest and finest English coat.

About six hundred miles to the north, the Battle of Quebec was just ending. It marked the first major defeat of this war on the American side. In a month more, the Pennsylvania Magazine would publish its report of Benedict Arnold's bravery for the Patriot side in the unsuccessful attack of the British in Canada. It would feature the story of treason by the Patriot's chief medical officer, Dr. Benjamin Church, but before those stories hit the masses, a much greater piece was to be published - *Common Sense*. This piece would light a path of fiery torches by way of the written word; bringing clarity and posing an unflappable argument for liberty and a damning argument against monarchy.

The thick haired man checked the latch and listened to the sounds of his countrymen ringing in the new year before breathing in a healthy serving of the frosty air. As he turned and started clicking along the cobblestone street, he popped his collar up to block the icy breeze.

The small group of men a few paces ahead did not seem to mind the deep chill as they tipped and gulped from their mugs. Indeed they were fine gentlemen - Queen Anne Britannia silver mugs for these chaps who now raised them up and clanged. They paused and looked over as the man approached.

"By God, you are Thomas Paine. The writer," Walton said as he spun with a carnivorous grin before taking a swig from his silver mug.

The man, Thomas Paine, looked over the three men briefly. If his intuition delivered a warning, he concealed it well. He raised his thick eyebrows.

"To whom do I owe the pleasure?"

"The pleasure tis mine. I admire your work. May I shake the hand that produces such fine editorial delights?" Walton said and handed his mug to Mayweather. "Please."

As Paine expressed a momentary look of befuddlement, Walton protruded the crystalline fragment from his finger tip and activated it. It glowed with a mostly imperceptible blue light.

Paine extended his hand and said "Tis my-"

Walton shook his hand, extending his pointer finger to Paine's wrist to his spirit gate pressure point. Walton's laser-lit finger gently brushed the pressure point and Paine dropped like clothing stuffed with straw.

"Big fan. Big, big fan," Walton said hovering over Paine's limp body. "I'll tell you gents - if someone is seeking a challenge, this is the bloody wrong century. Too easy." He smiled at Mayweather and Livingston. His smile morphed to an icy grimace and he said, "Alright, then. Let us not faff around."

"Well, let's hurry on," Mayweather said and placed the two mugs on the ground.

He grabbed Paine's arm and propped him up. Livingston followed suit and picked up the other arm. As they heaved up the dead weight, Walton merrily sauntered over to the two mugs and gracefully picked them up - his long jacket flapping in the wind. "Don't mind if I do. This way blokes. Our friend has a boat to catch."

The two men trailed behind Walton like the circus act behind the ringmaster, dragging Paine down the narrow street. Three men and a teenage boy passed them, giving them a groggy stare.

Walton said, "Rather bit much rum for my friend here," and pointed back at Paine whose head was staring straight down at the cobblestones.

"Tis a happy new year," the eldest man said.

"Indeed!" Walton said. "Happy new year!" he shouted.

The band of men and the teenager laughed and walked on.

The trio and Paine reached the docks. Mayweather huffed and huffed, trying to catch his breath, and dropped Paine's arm. Livingston held onto Paine's other arm and stared at Mayweather bemusedly.

A ratty bearded man stood cross-armed in front of a large ship. Walton said, "This is the package you are to deliver back to England with your freight in the morn."

"Payment," the surly man grunted and stroked his beard.

Walton looked at Livingston. Livingston held Paine's hand over his shoulder with one hand and reached into his inner coat pocket with the other. He pulled out a sac and handed it to the captain. The captain grabbed it. His hand yanked downward and then back up. He looked at the men with widespread blue eyes before opening the sac. His eyes grew even wider as he eyed the gold.

Walton smiled. "For your children's children, mate," he said.

"Orlop," the man said.

Mayweather and Livingston looked at Walton for instruction.

Walton looked back and nodded. "Go on. Deliver him down to the belly of the beast as the chatty fellow suggested."

Mayweather and Livingston dragged Paine over the planks and boarded the boat and bickered in the dark, feeling their way around.

Walton and the captain stood on the dock and stared directly at one another in silence.

Some crates toppled over further down the dock and both men looked.

Walton looked at the captain suspiciously.

"Rats," the captain said. "Big as rabbits."

"Perhaps they are rabbits," Walton said.

The captain grunted.

"Lovely," Walton said. "Plans for the evening?"

"Tavern," the captain said.

"Ahh," Walton said.

Livingston and Mayweather returned from the boat, crossing again over the weather-beaten planks. Mayweather huffed and grabbed at his chest to assist his inhalations. Livingston nodded at Walton, confirming the task was complete.

"Happy New Year," Walton said curtly to the captain and paced away. His men followed. The captain grunted.

5 Minutes Earlier

Kyle and Welly peeked out over the stacked crates at the men who abducted Thomas Paine. Welly was trying to get a scan of the man's face that had dropped Paine with a handshake a few minutes prior. He had not been able to get a frontal look at the man. With a good scan of the man's face he could sift through all memory records, all information he had stored, and see who he was dealing with.

Welly saw only the top half of his eyes as he peered out over the barnacle encrusted wooden crate. He blocked out the pungent odor of drying fish guts and focused.

He rapped on the crate, but the men did not look over or flinch.

"What are you doing?" Kyle whispered.

"Attempting to procure a facial scan," Welly snapped.

"Attempting to get us killed," Kyle said aloud to himself.

Welly rapped on the crate again - this time harder. The unbalanced stack of crates tumbled down. The men on the dock looked. There was no time for Welly to move out of the way to not be seen, but a divine crate tumbled down, obstructing him from sight.

"Shhh! Shhh!" He told Kyle. "I got it. I'm scanning. Scanning. Ho-lee. Are they coming?"

Kyle moved slowly and looked out through a sliver of slotted crate. "No. They're talking again."

"Francis Walton," Welly said.

"Francis Walton. Francis Walton," Kyle repeated trying to locate the clarifying connection. "Prime Minister of England Francis Walton?"

"Yes. He's trying to change the outcome of the American Revolution. He's trying to change history. Francis friggin Walton!"

"Wow, Pop. Look at you."

"Yeah yeah. Brooklyn oozes out of me sometimes when I get frazzled. Not much I can do about that."

"The other guys are coming out. No Thomas Paine."

Welly peered through the slots. "Okay, got them. Wow. John Livingston, soldier of fortune. British SAS. Special Air Force. This guy is like Rambo."

"Who?"

"The other is Timothy Mayweather. Historian, professor, Pulitzer Prize winning author. He's got brains and brawn with him."

Kyle watched as the three men walked away in one direction. The fourth and only bearded man trudged down the docks separately.

"We have to get on that boat and get Paine off there," Welly said.

"And then what?"

"I don't know. Take him to a quiet place with a stack of parchment and plenty of ink."

"Great plan," Kyle said and rolled his eyes.

"Let's go," Welly said and meant to spring up like a Jack-in-the-box, but only bobbed and then crouched immediately in pain. "Ah."

Kyle shook his head and grabbed his father's elbow and helped raise him to his feet.

"Stride casually," Welly said and began striding casually, attempting to straighten his hunched back repeatedly.

"Is that your casual stride?"

"You don't see anyone right?"

They both looked one hundred and eighty degrees around and then continued over to the planked bridge to the boat. The creaky wood seemed to be amplified and echoed out through the empty streets. They searched the dark boat for a door and found one fit for a toddler. Kyle pulled it open.

There was no light inside the space. They stepped down the three stairs, feeling with their feet and grasping at the walls with their hands.

They were in a small room clutching around blindly. Suddenly a light came on and lit up a planked wall and illuminated a smaller door. The light beamed from Kyle's fingertip.

"Shut that off!" Welly said. He pushed open the swinging door, ducked in and took the next three wobbly steps.

"You're welcome," Kyle said and followed.

In a claustrophobic space lay the man - Thomas Paine. After being zapped by Walton, he would have slept there for between forty eight and seventy two hours was Welly's prediction. Long enough to be out at sea and possibly never to return to this mainland again.

"I'll grab his feet," Welly said. "Kill that damn light. We can do this by memory now. Grab him up by his armpits."

Kyle turned off the light and listened to his father's instruction. "Damn," he said. "This guy is pretty heavy."

"Dead weight," Welly said.

They muscled up the first set of stairs and then dropped him in the midway room. Both of them huffed for a moment and then resumed their work without speaking. They muscled up the next three steps and were out onto the deck of the boat, Paine's head bobbing like a buoy by Kyle's knees.

Welly put Paine's feet down gently. Kyle dropped the rest of him, thumping his head on the oak.

"Careful Kyle," Welly said. "Those brains are a critical part of the outcome of the world."

Kyle respected that as an aspiring writer himself, but his arms were feeling rubbery with fatigue.

Welly's lower back pulsed with hot, slicing pain as he scanned the dock and the dimly lit buildings and everything else in his field of vision. He locked in on the most beautiful sight to behold at that moment. Two small legs, a squared, sturdy storage area and a single, beat up wooden wheel - a wheelbarrow.

"Kyle. Look. There. Right over there. The wheelbarrow. Go get it, son."

They had to safely stow Paine and get back to the vessel, and back to current time.

26

Current Day

Welly tried hard to focus on his thoughts as his Jeep sped along the highway track at two hundred and three miles per hour. This stretch of highway, three stories elevated over the original, bustling I-95, known as the Trackway, was pretty desolate.

The concept for the Trackway was outstanding and there were really no tracks at all - at least in the traditional sense. The raised highway harnessed bands of existing energy and expressed them inward from inside the barrier walls alongside the three lanes and upward from the slits in the lines separating each lane. This energy controlled your speed, propelling your vehicle and decelerating if needed and made sure you were in the proper lane at all times. The only issue was that the cost of the enhanced vehicles needed for travel on the Trackway was still too high for most travelers.

Welly's company was in the midst of working out a plan to help subsidize the cost of the vehicles, with the federal government, when the shit hit the fan. Actually, despite Nova's mostly circular shape, it was not a fan.

Welly smirked.

His mind was free for thought as he needed not concentrate on his driving while on the Trackway. Yet his thoughts came hard. Usually they were free flowing and easy like a leaf in the summer wind. He was stressed knowing how important it was to think now, more than ever.

Concentrate. Focus.

Oh, how he wished the ET would visit him again right now. Yes, now that he utilized their ideas and information and clues to build new worlds and technologies and upgrade the human race, helping it to go from crawling to jogging only to realize some rogue joggers are sprinting towards doing evil.

But the ET was not there. Welly started to doubt they would ever be back. He spent countless nights investigating the skies with his instruments or just looking up in anticipation while he walked his pug Jerry around the neighborhood. So many feelings, so many hair raising feelings, but they never came.

Some nights he stood on his roof and focused deeply on the stars and the planets and beyond, in search of a signal, but nothing. Nothing except for the dream. Yes, the dream. The night of the shooting star. The dream that was so vivid that he strongly suspected it was not a dream at all.

At times he would even focus his field of thought and vision so hard he wobbled on the border of the fourth dimension. That bustling unseen layer was always a great deal more active at night than his neighborhood, but no energy transmitted directly to Welly from his all-knowing friend.

The only closest thing was the dream. That tangible dream on the night of the shooting star. Yes, Christine was pregnant with Kyle. Of course, but there was no information there. Was there?

His destination was only two hundred thirty miles away when he started. He was thirty minutes into this mini road trip, but he would have been there with time to spare if he jumped on the Dart. The Dart would have shot him there in five and half minutes, but he needed this time to think - alone. Some of his best thinking was done on the road and besides, he wanted to be with his custom Jeep because you never know.

What had Kyle been railing about on the trip back after hiding Mr. Paine?

It worried Welly more than he cared to admit to himself.

He accessed the memory of Kyle speaking and replayed it:

"This freedom has run its course. Now the free are too free. Free enough to explore their uglier sides, their weaknesses, laziness and the great vision has imploded with zero morality and borderline lawlessness. It's all due to strong laws handcuffing the government and anyone who ever sided on the good."

Welly had let him rant on and listened closely to try to discern if it was Kyle's own thoughts or perhaps something he picked up on the Zeit somewhere. He couldn't tell.

Welly weighed the validity of such a seemingly crazy idea.

Was society perfect? No. But there is no utopia. Not yet anyhow.

Welly continued to access the trip back. He walked away from Kyle at some point. He was angry. He walked to the shimmery kitchen, as he called it. Everything in there was self cleaning and always shining and sanitized. He fixed himself a sandwich with Juksy, the special spread similar tasting to a mixture of marshmallow, peanut butter and banana, but there was a crunchy texture throughout with the infusion of vitamins and minerals. He accessed the memory *of* his memory as he gobbled that down - wishing he could bottle up Kyle's baby cuteness and save it. He did have it saved with Zeit memory, but that *feeling* was not reproduced. That feeling in the moment - that true love - that was not savable in the Zeit. *That* was utopia.

I have to figure this out. Time is ticking. Or it has ticked already. Think damn it! Focus!

Where is he going next?

A turning point?

The beginning?

The Liberty Tree - that beautiful elm in Boston Common where the colonists staged their first act of defiance against the British in 1765. Of course the Loyal Nine, who eventually become part of the larger group The Sons of Liberty; and their clandestine meetings to plan a number of protests to rebel against the Stamp Act. August 14, 1765 the crowd gathers and a straw figure is hung from the tree with the initials AO for Andrew Oliver, colonist appointed by King George III to impose the Stamp Act.

This gathering and hanging and the straw figure itself Welly had the privilege of actually seeing with his own eyes along with twenty seven space tourists that paid the obnoxious sum for the experience. They hovered that day about twenty thousand feet up and watched the events live with ultra magnification lenses. It was a thrilling trip and exhilarating to witness what was marked as the first act of defiance by the colonists against the crown.

Does stopping this flare up, stop the revolution? If the Brits don't tar and feather Thomas Ditson and make him march in front of the tree, does that quell the angst? Siege of Boston, Lexington and Concord April 1775, Battle of Bunker Hill 1775, Liberty Tree cut down by Loyalist Job Williams and friends August 30, 1775. Significant enough. Bunker Hill. Bunker Hill.

Think.

McDonald's iced lattes on sale.

This proximity advertisement flashed across his thoughts which meant he did not activate his blocker. A digital display materialized seemingly in the sky up the road ahead. The overhead display was a three dimensional video projection of a middle aged man who looked a lot like Welly, happily munching an Egg McMuffin.

That's it! Welly thought. *I'm famished.*

He swiped the *Bring Me There* icon with his mind's eye and his car made it over to the exit ramp, down the first, second and third exit slopes and into the McDonald's parking lot. He could practically taste the caramel.

His front thought remained on Bunker Hill while his side thought weaved through the open McDonald's gateway to the bright ordering screen waiting in the otherwise pitch dark room in a thought cavern housed in his mind. Welly's avatar stood and looked at the door sized screen.

Welly shifted his perspective now from full view to POV and swiped around on the screen while his flesh body sat still in his Jeep. He found the Egg McMuffin and swiped two into his screen's sack. And then added a large caramel iced latte. Oh, and a hash brown. He pushed the pay now button and the transaction was completed with cryptocash.

Welly immediately exited his car. The food should be waiting on table fourteen as the screen informed him.

He entered the gleaming seating area. Only one other table was occupied by two men. Welly sat down at the table with the number 14 digitally hovering in the air above it. He tore open the wrapping and grabbed hold of the first McMuffin.

Ahh, he thought and salivated. He was hungrier than he realized.

He started happily munching much like that man in the image projected above the Trackway.

Gotta love marketing, he thought.

As he chewed, he tried to access the history again, but his brain was getting hazy. He hadn't realized how hungry he was until he was devouring his fast food favorite.

Welly could access just about anything he might need. Of course, everything that any human did is recorded by the Nova. Most individuals are also recording their own lives on auto record and it is saved and accessible to them at any time. Every conversation. Every recital. Every sunset. Every end of the night show at the amusement park. Most can jump back into any memory and revisit and re-experience. They can also visit and experience the experiences of others on the Zeit if one has added their experiences for public consumption. If one wants to experience the life of a celebrity that can be done and usually for a fee and of course, product placement neatly positioned inside those experiences as well. The majority of people are always on auto record. If one is not, others might worry about their motives.

Many experiences today are more boring than Welly remembered as a child. Less and less people were talking out loud. For some, like Welly, engaging in oratory conversation was becoming more and more melodious. Such a high number of people living out most of their life on the Zeit. Relationships, work, fun, sex. It's evolution, Welly knew, and he was the biggest fan of evolution, but ironically, he may be among the biggest fans of nostalgia as well.

The unstable guy sitting at the table next to him was loudly sharing his well thought out views about "hot shit". The man was eating a breakfast burrito and telling his friend, "No hot shit. I don't want *no* hot shit on food. No thanks. No hot shit for me." Welly looked straight ahead, chomping his food, and smiled wide with his mind's eye.

He threw away his wrappers, napkins and cup and went into the bathroom to pee for the umpteenth time of the day. Ever since he hit his forties, being a quadragenarian as it were, he was peeing more than breathing it seemed. He went into the stall as he always did when presented with the option. He pulled up his shirt and pulled down his pants, sucked in his gut and surveyed the land as he deposited his liquid refuse into the bowl. Yes, everything was there - the writing on the wall so to speak. All in order.

When he got back into the Jeep he repeated aloud "*No* hot shit. I don't want no hot shit. Hot shit hot shit hot shit. I think we're all in some hot shit right now," he said and laughed as pulled back on to the highway.

His mind flashed to the conversation, or more accurately – heated exchange, between him and Kyle on the way back to current time.

What had made Kyle so damn anti-American? Had it been his pal Bobby getting shot and that he felt so little had been done about it? Or is he just trying to push my big red button?

Welly drove back on the road still thinking about the trip back. After the vomiting, after his writing. After the call with Denny. He and Kyle argued about issues and about Welly's being vacant so often throughout Kyle's childhood.

He had no choice. He had a mission. What he *saw* that day. What he saw that day he met the ET, always told him there were more worlds to explore and he may possibly be the only to know they were even there for the exploration and perhaps the only one to blaze the trail.

Yes, he recalled it vividly. It was right after the ET told him anything was possible and he gave Welly a half wave with his four fingered hand. It looked so much like young Welly's own hand, only with a slight bit of webbing in between each finger.

Welly remembered clearly sensing the ET was pleased - pleased that Welly received the message, pleased that Welly was *able* to receive the message. Then the ET performed the act that would replay for Welly often in the years to follow; would pick him up by the nape of his neck when he felt like slowing down or giving up.

The ET walked toward his vessel and then into it. There was no door, no hatch, just smooth, rivet-less, flat black material. The being simply slipped through it, like vapor. Seconds later, the vessel went straight up and out of sight as if God hit the high striker with the hammer at the Cosmos Carnival and the vessel was gone.

Welly merged his Jeep onto MD-295 S which rapidly turned into DC-295 S as he crossed into Washington D.C. He was obeying commands of the global positioning system while exploring inward more intently. He laid out a timeline in his mind's eye and surveyed it.

The elm tree, the Intolerable Acts, Lexington and Concord - been there and done that - quite literally. Bunker Hill was major yet memories seem to be syncing and never felt a mod surrounding this event - odd. Thomas Paine, yes, hearts and minds.

He shuffled around to the so many significant battles, searching.

Manhattan, Brooklyn, Long Island.

There were so many monumental moments.

The writing of The Declaration of Independence?

Blow up Thomas Jefferson, Benjamin Franklin, John Adams, Roger Sherman and Robert R. Livingston and what do you have? Does that change the world? Yes. Does that cause Britain to win the war?

Huh.

I don't know for certain.

It's so hard to say with history as any one event changed may set in motion a trajectory of new events whereby minor and major events alike take place that would have otherwise not taken place and where that trajectory ultimately ends might be exponentially enormous and game changing - world changing.

Welly merged onto I-695 N and it became I-395 S shortly thereafter.

He racked his brain. Thoughts jumped from event to event. Suddenly, a single thought bullied its way through all the others, piercing like an airplane through puffy clouds. All other thoughts, previously climbing over one another, scattered like grenade shrapnel and there was one word.

Trenton.

Of course. Trenton.

Washington's Continental Army was on the run. Supplies de-pleted. Most of the enlisted commitments are set to expire. They are hanging on by a thread and they take Trenton by surprise on Christmas.

Welly took the Maine Ave exit and merged onto 12th Street towards Downtown.

"Trenton!" he said out loud. "Of course. That is the turning point. That is the hot shit," he said and laughed at himself. He felt relief as he felt a shred of control. It wasn't much, but it was enough to remind him that he hadn't felt that way in a little while now.

"Trenton," he said again to confirm with himself and then swiped aside the timeline in his mind and activated the song list. Scanning through his titles he finally said, "Yes!"

Joy to the World by Three Dog Night started blaring out of his speakers.

JEREMIAH WAS A BULLFROG

Welly and the lead singer belted it out in harmony.

WAS A GOOD FRIEND OF MINE

I NEVER UNDERSTOOD A SINGLE WORD HE SAID

He turned right onto Pennsylvania Avenue.

BUT I HELPED-

The music continued to thump and scream, but Welly stopped singing suddenly. He was struck by a leg buckling ex-haustion. He had been working in overdrive and was mentally spent, sure, but this fatigue was more extreme, crippling, dis-ease-like.

He tried to blink it out and the world around became wa-tery. The Jeep swerved. He pulled over, parked and fell asleep as if someone just yanked out his power cord - his forehead resting on the gray steering wheel.

27

Wap! Wap! Wap!

Welly jolted awake, his eyes squinting out the daylight. A giant furry creature was whacking the hood of the Jeep. Welly blinked quickly and saw only the man's tall hat was black, massive and furry. He wore a blazing red uniform, looking just like one of the Queen's Guards of Buckingham Palace.

My God, I've slept all the way around to Halloween.

"Move along. Off you go now. Move along."

Wap! Wap!

"Okay, okay," Welly said and drove on down Pennsylvania Avenue.

I need to pee again. How long was I out?

Still hazy, but waking, he tried to focus on his driving. Something was different. He couldn't quite put his finger on it.

The words spiritual leader flashed across his mind and the memory of a junior high school field trip to this area. But had he been on a field trip to this area? He was pretty sure he had not been, but then again certain that he had been. Yes, his teacher was crying at the tall gates when the Spiritual Leader's motor pool drove past.

Wait. Spiritual Leader? Who the f-

Welly's brain skipped a beat as he met with a road block flanked by more sentries directing him to turn down the side street. It wasn't the sight of these guards that shook him, but the site looming large over their shoulder strips with those gleaming gold buttons.

It was not the White House. No. Of course, it was not. Another broken dam of memories poured in and he knew certainly it was the Walton Palace.

Dazedly, he turned down the side street and parked the Jeep in an open parking spot. He was seized with the desire to walk around in this place, to find something concrete; something that might confirm the facts he knew as facts already.

Whirling and blinking lights caught his eye. It was a gift shop. Perfect. He padded quickly over to the corner store and then realized what had been different. The street signs. That was it. They were not the standard green with white lettering he remembered in this area. They were the antique white, etched in gold lettering of an old fashion style that he.....also remembered in this area? He felt a headache coming on as the automatic doors opened and he entered the gift shop.

The repeating face of every size and style ran over Welly like a bulldozer. There were mugs and t-shirts and keychains and collectible plates and posters. Whether the face was in color, black & white, pencil sketch or made up of a thousand carefully placed words on some items, Welly had no doubts who the man was and in fact, knew that he *knew* already. The man he'd been following a step behind through time. Francis Walton.

He stumbled into a rack of hoodies and attracted the stares of a few browsers. They quickly returned to their browsing. Welly stepped over to the display of books. *The Chosen One*, one title read. Welly picked it up and flipped it over to read the blurb on the back. It was sensational deja vu as he turned it over - the clashing feeling of holding a brand new book for the first time combined with the clear knowledge that he already read this book multiple times. The feeling was strong, palpable.

He dropped the book and the stares returned momentarily and were gone again.

Indeed, Welly knew the story. The divine visitors came on their chariot of the universe and prophesied that this boy, Francis Walton, would be born on that day and that time and that he was the Chosen One - selected by God, to lead the people into the promised land.

"Dad," a voice yelled. "Dad, dad!"

Welly placed the book neatly back on the stack and thought why can't people pay attention to their kids.

"Dad, dad, dad!" the voice called again.

Welly looked around for this kid trying to get hold of his father. The annoyance felt nice - took his mind off the collapsed world around him for a second. He saw no person speaking, but the voice came back again.

"Pop, can you hear me?"

A dart of information flew through and Welly reached out his arm to the high stacked hardcovers for balance.

I know that voice. It's my son.

For a second he forgot all of that, but it was back, for now. "Kyle," he responded through the Zeit channel. "Are you okay?"

He touched his lips, astonished. He just spoke without moving his mouth. He looked around the room at the shoppers for a reaction to his loud speech with himself, but not one appeared interested.

"Yeah. I think I am," Kyle said. "I woke up at the house and there was a group of foreigners taking pictures of me laying in bed."

"What?"

What house? Welly thought. *What is going on?*

A swell of frustration splashed over him like cold water.

"Yeah. Only it wasn't my bed. It was some old fashioned weirdo bed. I yelled at them, but they didn't speak English and so I barged through the group and there were people, like, everywhere just wandering around the house. So I just ran out and down the block and I'm just standing here on Flatbush Avenue and my head is pounding. And everything looks so....different."

The panic crept into Kyle's voice. The contrast was stark compared to his usual composure and it worried Welly.

"It's okay. Listen, Kyle, stay right there. I'm going hyper speed back to get you. Give me just a little bit. Okay?"

"I'm sitting down here, Pop. My head is pounding."

"Oh, and can you send me the address of the house?"

"Address? Are you okay, Pop?"

"I think so."

"Four fifty two Flatbush Avenue in Brooklyn. Just tell the car to take you home."

"Four fifty two Flatbush. I'm on my way."

"Oh and Dad?"

"Yes."

There was a long, lingering silence. Then Kyle said, "I think Bobby's alive. I have all these new, old, but new memories. I can't explain it. I'm going to walk down the street and see."

Welly tried blinking the orientation back into his brain.

"This all. Nevermind. Four fifty two Flatbush. I'm on my way."

Welly disconnected and exited the store.

28

As soon as the friendly female voice from the GPS, talking inside his brain, helped him get back on the highway, his thoughts were so voluminous and erratic he felt like a crazy person of the worst kind - the kind that knew they were crazy.

He was losing control.

He tried to focus and suddenly a memory rose to the surface like a lazy bubble. It was the night of the waking dream and the shooting star. Welly felt relief as it felt he may be able to grab hold of this one thought, this one memory and hold onto it, gripping it like a man grips a lone vine as he sinks into the quicksand.

Why?

Perhaps since he revisited the night so many times, it was branded there somehow. Perhaps it was something of great significance. Perhaps it was just the next short order served up by the universe. Perhaps all those things.

He was walking Jerry, he and Christine's Pug. Yes, Jerry was still alive and they walked on Flatbush Avenue just in front of the house.

Yes, of course, the house. There it is.

How could he forget? He loved the house. It had been the Lefferts Historic House and Welly had purchased it from New York City when it fell into disrepair after having low volumes

of visitors for a number of years. The city was considering sell-
ing it to a real estate developer to build condos, but Welly
couldn't bear to see more history end up at the landfill, forgotten. He paid an obscene amount of money for it and then it
was home.

He focused and remembered that night. Jerry was busy taking care of his life's work - peeing on everything. The target
this time was the tall black antique lamp post directly in front
of the house that loomed overhead obediently holding a light
out for the duo. Once Jerry released a sufficient squirt on the
base of the lamp, the two walked on the street a bit.

That night Welly felt small. He felt dwarfed by the seemingly immense size of the street and the large lamp and the
trees to his right and he just felt small. There were some nights
he felt ten feet tall strutting down that same street, but not
that night. He felt the world pushing him down. Down into the
ground. It pushed.

He stopped. Looked up. He always looked up.

The night sky was so close. There was no black that night,
but patches of deep smeared blues in the parts where there
were no clouds. The clouds were low and moving, pacing along
and opening a view of the stars like the curtains on Broadway.
The clouds were like campfire smoke that night the way they
moved and that night sky behind them, so vivid and full of life.

He felt all that weight heavy on his shoulders, he remembered. Less than six months before he had proved his thought
abilities and the existence of the other dimension and in-
vestors fell over one another to make offers and up theirs to
best the other, and so on. With the deal done for the land
down on Flatbush on the water just north of the Belt Parkway,
and with the plans finalized, and the Forward Facility construction set to break ground just about the time the baby was
to be shooting through into the world, the weight was heavy.

What if something is wrong? What if something is seriously wrong with the baby?

He clearly recalled those thoughts among the scattered worries that night. Such a beautiful night, so many worries.

Welly could have gazed up there all night basking in the sweet sky and apprehension, but Jerry was yanking him. He looked down at the anxious dog and started walking again, back toward the house.

He looked up as he walked, stealing one last glance and that's when he saw the shooting star. It was so fast and so lasting, blazing from one cloud cover to another. Welly was thankful.

Yes, and it was later that night when it happened - the waking dream.

29

He had to urinate like Jerry now. It was so bad it felt like he was carrying a bowling ball in his pelvis. He'd have to get off on the next exit.

Welly drove, deep in thought. The roads were different. There were more trees, but Welly drove on obeying the car's instructions mindlessly. He felt like he had just awakened from a black-out migraine and although his head didn't hurt, his brain was mush.

He felt a tightening in his crotch that reminded him again. He had to pee badly. He pulled the Jeep over to the shoulder and just beyond onto a patch of hardened earth, sending pebbles ricocheting off the wheel well. He zombie walked up to the first tree in the line and began soaking the bark.

He looked down out of habit to focus on his manhood as he was finishing his business and something caught his eye.

What the hell is that? Is it a bug?

He jumped back and brushed at the area right above his pubic hair. His heart rate began to slow as he realized it was just a tattoo.

He looked around behind him and was thankful no one was standing there watching. He must have looked like a nut. He certainly felt like one.

He cocked his head and stared transfixed at the ink south of his belly button. The ink marks were numbers.

Numbers?

They appeared to be relatively fresh as the digits had a dark, almost wet appearance. Even more odd to Welly - the numbers were upside down. Upside down that is to someone admiring his bizarre tatt in a more bizarre location. But to him, standing and staring down as he was currently, the numbers were perfectly readable.

40.66425,-73.9639186

Lifting his head, he pondered.

What the? Coordinates? Has to be coordinates.

He scanned his upper thighs for something more. Combed his pubic hair to search for any other covered characters but there was nothing. Shaking his head in disbelief must have shook loose some intuition. He raised his shirt and stared down again frantically. Just below his belly button beneath the shade of black hairs pointing in every direction was one word. And apparently, so there was no confusing the letters accidently for an acronym, there was a clear exclamation point beside the three letters.

DIG!

Raising his shirt higher, he scanned his stomach and chest. That was it. He buckled his pants finally and walked briskly to the Jeep. Things were starting to swirl into focus a bit as he stomped the pedal sending more pebbles into orbit.

30

Welly drove on Flatbush Avenue. He was a few houses away from his house when he saw Kyle and Bobby standing on the sidewalk laughing hysterically. He almost didn't recognize his son because he hadn't seen him smile so wide in so long. He pulled over and enjoyed what he was viewing for a moment longer before beeping his horn. Bobby and Kyle looked around and finally their four eyes landed on Welly's vehicle.

They walked over and both entered the truck. Kyle in the front and Bobby in the back.

"Oh, hey there Bobby. Good to see you," Welly said.

Kyle raised his eyebrows excitedly at Welly.

"Howdy Mister B," Bobby said.

Welly looked at Kyle. He said, "Kyle, I believe we have to take care of that matter."

"I know, I know," Kyle said. "But can't Bobby hang with us for a little?"

The answer was undoubtedly a big fat no, but Welly was witnessing a light in his son's eyes that had been so dim for so long. Even still - this was too important. Welly began to shake his head and heard Kyle's voice in his mind's ear.

"Pop, please. I don't ask you for much. You know that nothing good ever sticks for me. Can't he just hang with us for a little? Please."

Welly's mind flashed back to when Kyle was four, just beyond the baby Frankenstein years, Kyle latching onto his pant leg as he tried to leave for work. "Please can I go to work, Daddy! Please, please, pretty please." Pretty please must be genetic hardwiring, he once thought, as it seemed to come standard with every child. It broke Welly's heart to have to leave to the sound of muffled wailing when the door would shut behind him. But he couldn't bring Kyle to his work then and he couldn't bring Bobby along now. Or could he?

He sighed.

Against his better judgement, he glanced in the back seat at Bobby and he said, "Bobby, we have to take care of some secret type of business. Government-related type of stuff. I trust that you can keep this top secret?"

"Mum's the word, Mister B."

"We actually have to go to that house right there," Welly said, pointing to his former residence.

"The historic house?" Bobby said.

"Yes," Welly said. "Kyle and I have to go around back if you could wait in the front and just run around back and get us if anyone suspicious pulls up or if you see anyone dangerous or anything unusual."

One thing Welly's business experience had taught him was that tone and cadence really went a long way. Body language is important, but a lot of other people's reaction is based on your mannerisms and your tone and by keeping extremely calm and casual, so keeps the mission at hand.

The tour guide stood in front of the large window that looked out onto the backyard of the historic house. He faced the group of tourists and explained, "Indeed, this house is constantly maintained so that not a fiber is destroyed and with your help we will preserve its historic beauty for the next three hundred years."

The tourists became excited and began speaking hurriedly in Cantonese to one another, as they witnessed Kyle and Welly both shoveling up the historic ground outside the window behind the tour guide.

They began to snap pictures rapidly as the loads of earth flew into the air. The tour guide remained facing the tourists and began making gestures as if he was showing a prize on a game show while they snapped picture after picture.

He said, "Why yes, this is a very exciting landmark in New York City and we thank you for visiting us."

Welly and Kyle were then seen in the yard behind the guide opening up a metallic box. Welly opened the box, grabbed the papers, viewed them, then returned them to the box and shut it.

The tourists' cameras snapped frantically once again and the tour guide put his hands together above one shoulder and then above the other and then took a bow.

Kyle and Welly walked briskly out of sight of the window.

31

The papers proved helpful. Welly was grateful for his past self's thoughtfulness in crafting such a well-rounded history, highlighting things he knew that he needed to know. It served as the electrified paddles to his brain, awakening the detailed memories tucked away in a lower level storage room in his mind. He had this nagging feeling, bubbling just under the surface that he was missing something. Then again, there were so many nagging bubbly feelings over the last ten hours that it was getting hard to tell them apart.

Welly's notes were concise and led him and Kyle to the vessel, Christine II, which was stashed in the marsh near Marine Park Nature Center off Avenue U. Invisibility camouflage was activated so no one would see it, and it was in a location that no one would bump into it by accident.

The papers also provided him with the needed refresher of the precise methods to fully recall and to re-implement Data Stay. It informed him that if the notes were being read, and therefore must have needed to be read, then essentially that meant they were on their own and no help from the government was to be expected - if there even remained a government as they, and they alone, once knew it. They were likely the only ones now who might even recollect any part of the true past as it was before the mods.

The papers finally instructed them to navigate the vessel back to Time Nova and attempt to restore the world. Getting back to Nova and beginning the mission was of paramount importance and they wasted little time.

The vessel was quiet as it swung by invisible magnetic fields through the darkness, slowing to just north of ten light years per hour. The glow from the floor lights beneath the console set a calming mood. The lighting reminded Welly of the white lights on his Christmas tree when they were the only radiant thing in the room.

He was at peace momentarily. The outer world rushed past him and washed over him. He felt at one out here. He was one. He knew that this is where he came from. This was home. We were all born out of stars and the stars all out of nebula.

Birth of a star occurs when atoms of light elements are squeezed under enough pressure for their nuclei to undergo fusion. Welly couldn't help but think of his loyal and nervous accountant Whitaker. Surely there were stars being formed in his stomach every time he presented the quarterly reports.

Yes, a star is from where he may have originated. He stuck on that thought for a moment and then remembered he stuck on that very same thought seventeen years ago when he and Martin Brown stumbled into a new world, or an old one as it were. This seemed to compute to Welly. It should make sense that for many years that dim speckle outside of our galaxy was thought to be a supernova, but in actuality was the great timekeeper of the universe.

What was it all for? What did it all mean? God and science were to be separated always - according to some of his colleagues. Yes, but if all serves God then so did the timekeeper, right? Why? Perhaps one day he would know. Welly's best guess was knowledge. Perhaps knowledge was not something as useless as power, perhaps it was everything.

One constant, he felt as he traveled on this journey called life through this strange world in which the lucky ones spend a hundred years, was fulfillment came from learning and growth. That must be at least part of the reason for Time Nova. It can offer answers and a myriad of lessons undoubtedly. Though there were some topics, locations, destinations, some axes of time, still off limits - well, according to the government that used to be.

No journey was scheduled for when any prominent religious figure lived or any extremely controversial historic event. However, an approval to schedule a trip to witness the construction of the pyramids was getting closer and closer. This seemed so important a few short weeks ago. It was important, exhilarating, thought provoking - all that. Welly had been high on caffeine and research and it had seemed so close, but now everything seemed so far.

The grand illusion, he thought, as he sipped his black tea. Ahh yes, the grand illusion.

Welly often marveled at how purposeful he was and the other humans with whom he inhabited earth all the while knowing that we are being pulled out with the tide and there is nothing we can do about it. We eat right, we exercise, we plan, we plot, we execute, we frantically gather money and belongings and we all try to outrun the clock and we all know it's impossible.

He shook his head and took another sip of his steaming metallic cup.

Tea?

He had another thought now. He shouldn't be drinking this beloved British beverage on principal. He laughed at himself and took a small sip. In the calm of the lights and the silence of the vessel, he reflected.

He thought about how stars are the result of a balance of forces. It was the force of gravity compressing those atoms in interstellar gas and eventually there is a fusion reaction. He thought of Christine. Never had there been such an obvious balance of forces in his life. He and her came together and made their own star. Their star who was currently not shining so bright. His inner light was dimmed again yet there were blue flames where his eyes once were, since they had to leave Bobby behind.

There was no choice in the matter. This was bigger than Bobby, bigger than Welly and bigger than everyone. His son was so furious he wouldn't talk to him.

If he only knew how much I love him, he thought.

It was almost impossible to convey this message in earthly words or with his damn limiting body language and nervous system. Christine was gone and he was failing. When he needed real advice, he would always go to her. He didn't have the proper tools to fix his relationship with his son. Did he ever? Would he ever? The forever optimist barely alive inside him, covered under several tons of life's rubble and debris, said yes. It was a faint gasping yes, but it was there. It was there, however unconvincing.

None of it would matter if he and Kyle failed to restore history to its proper order. He concentrated deeply, urging the misty distortion to dissipate to the best of his ability. Everything in his mind was still swathed in a heavy humidity. The emphatic thought, based on his memory, was the disappearance of Thomas Paine. Or had it been based on the correspondence from his past self? It made perfect sense that these history modifiers altered the hearts and minds of the Patriots by silencing Thomas Paine, and that sent them on a new trajectory whereby Britain quells the unrest and restores loyalty to the crown. Welly knew better than most, the power of thought.

Still the nagging sensation continued. It was a watered down deja vu. It was there. It was gone. Something was ever so slightly off-kilter. It was somewhere lurking beneath logical thought. It was further down in the bowels of intuition. If it was real, it was slippery. Too slippery to grab hold.

Brushing it aside and focusing on the facts and what *was* known, was the sensible thing to do. Something clearly went awry with the rescue and restoration of Mr. Paine. It needed to be fixed. He swigged the last spot of tea and accessed the controls in his mind's eyes. A little over three hours until they were piercing the coordinates in Time Nova.

32

Concord, Massachusetts

April 4, 1776

Walton and his associates were once again lodging at the dreadful inn. Although Walton claimed he would rather be sleeping on the infamous rat-infested British prison ship HMS Jersey, nicknamed Hell, citing he was less likely to contract dysentery there, the inn was the only decent place for many more miles around. Another appealing feature was the location of the inn being less than fifteen miles from Washington's supposed Longfellow House headquarters in Cambridge.

The information Mayweather provided about that white haired rabble-rouser was faulty at best. They had been unable to stop the Siege of Boston, and the alleged liberation of that city by the Patriots. Then, one certain historical fact after another certain historical fact regarding George Washington's whereabouts, led to dead ends. General Pitchfork, as Walton referred to him at times, was more elusive than Walton would have ever suspected.

It almost seemed he was falsifying dates and locations in some of his letters to throw intercepting spies off his track. Perhaps the letters he sent were embedded with specific codes

which were never properly documented and therefore indeci-
pherable. Either way, Washington was, by now, off with his
army heading to New York and Walton was vacationing in
lovely Concord with two prats.

Walton fidgeted in the wooden seat at the empty wooden
table of the inn's restaurant, waiting. This time there was to be
no debate. He knew what needed to be done.

John Livingston ducked under the thick wood beam and entered the dining area.

Walton nodded at him.

Livingston sat directly across the table and nodded at Walton.

The two sat in silence for a minute. Walton's apoplectic energy enveloped the room, seeming even to force the flame atop
the melting nub of the candle on the table to dance wildly.

Mayweather jollily entered the room. His hair wet and
combed back. He spotted Walton and Livingston and marched
over to the table. He sat between the two men.

The chair creaked.

Mayweather placed his thick hands together, rested them
atop the table, looked first at Walton and then at Livingston.

The waitress brought over three rolled cloth napkins and
unrolled them on the table in front of each man. She wore a
humble dress, puffier on the lower half and tighter on the upper. The top of her full breasts were apparent to all with the
dress's low cut.

Walton eyed her cleavage as she stood beside him unrolling
his silverware. He glanced down at the unevenly crafted silverware and then back to her cleavage.

"I have not seen you before, my lady," he said, his eyes still
fixed on her cleavage.

He licked his lips as she spoke.

"Thomas tis my Uncle," she said.

Walton looked her down and then slowly up, lingering his gaze on her chest before finally meeting her eyes. "Yes, I'm rather sure I would have remembered you. Much nicer to gaze upon than Thomas."

She smiled courteously. "May I bring you some drinks? Beer, flip, whiskey, grog or water perhaps?"

Walton said, "You certainly are efficient. It feels like a whiskey night my dear."

Livingston said, "Beer."

"I'm rather enjoying the flip," Mayweather said cheerily. "Please. Many thanks."

Walton was not surprised by how much Mayweather was "rather enjoying" it, but he *was* irked by that fact.

The waitress walked away briskly.

Walton eyed every step of her exit with a carnivorous stare. "I will have her tonight," he said.

Mayweather chuckled. "But will she have you?"

Walton turned his gape to Mayweather. "I can do anything I want here as everyone here has long since perished. We walk among ghosts here do we not? Hmm? I will pillage anything I please. The ghosts will long for nothing. Besides these people are aiding the patriots. One of those dreadful little shacks on this property is storing arms and provisions for those rats as we dine."

Mayweather no longer smiled. He looked like a boy with a popped balloon. He said, "Sir, you can't be—"

"Back to the business at hand," Walton said. "We've tried it your way. Several ways. Now it is time to try it the right way."

"My lord," Mayweather interjected quickly. "The next major event is the completion and the execution of the Declaration of Independence, but as we--"

"Yes," Walton said. "I agree it is symbolic, yes? It is an incredibly important foundational document, yes? But it is *not* the turning point. It has been and always will be, Trenton. Trenton is indeed the turning point of all importance."

Mayweather said, "My lord," and Walton raised his hand.

Walton continued, "As I've been saying for some time now. We know Washington crosses the Delaware on Christmas, attacks the British and Hessian forces before scampering in a most cowardly fashion, back across the Delaware. But he shall not cross the Delaware and instead his flat boats shall be sunk as our countrymen will be forewarned and this time, I guarantee, they heed our advice."

Walton took a triumphant breath and glared at Mayweather.

Livingston nodded.

The waitress delivered three silver cups and set them down. She said, "Wouldst thou like food?"

Walton sipped his whiskey and winced. He turned his head, looked directly at the waitress's cleavage and grinned. He said, "I have a most ravenous appetite tonight."

33

Mayweather sat upright in bed. He wore his standard blue striped pajama pants and shirt, but tonight he did not read as was his nightly tradition. The ghastly sounds emanating from the room next door prevented him studying or sleeping.

The walls at the inn were thin, but perhaps cast iron walls may have made little difference battling the ferocity of these noises. He heard Walton's rabid grunts and demeaning shouts as the pounding continued like a drum from the depths of hell. The girl whimpered and offered only the word "please" in her defense.

Mayweather's powers of visualization, from years of honing practice and repetition, haunted him now. He pictured Walton's face now down to the bulging veins in his reddened forehand. The anger. The spittle on the side of his lip. He was a monster.

Shame and rage filled Mayweather as he sat in his small bed and listened to the pounding and the whimpering. He knew if he interjected Walton may kill him or possibly he would order the sadistic Livingston to do it. If he interjected and somehow lived – the all-important mission in which they were engaged – would die.

Mayweather thought a real man, a noble man, would not let this deter him from putting an end to such vile behavior – or at least trying. So what was he?

The pounding grew louder and faster. Mayweather clearly heard an audible smack and shook his head hastily. With that he shimmied his bulbous body to the edge of the bed and threw his legs over the side.

"This must stop," he said to himself aloud.

Just as he slid on his second slipper - it did stop. The pounding ended and he heard scurrying footsteps, crying, and a door opening and shutting.

Mayweather dropped his head down and placed both hands on his hair. He grabbed two fistfuls of his hair aggressively and squeezed them like a sponge with no water left to give. He tried to crush the regret from his soul through those clumps of hair. He shook his head, attempting to undo these moments from his memory.

34

The next morning was cold and misty. Mayweather was bundled like a mini hot dog appetizer as he walked past the waitress from the night before. She was sweeping hastily. She stopped. Mayweather stopped. She looked at him over the handle of the broom. Mayweather saw her yellowing eye socket and sorrow in her eyes.

He shot his gaze away in shame and walked through the heavy door of the inn. Walton and Livingston were outside already.

"Finally, Sleeping Beauty," Walton said. He smiled. "You look like shite."

Mayweather nodded and raised his eyebrows.

Walton said, "Let us carry on then. We have some traveling to do."

He waved his hand, summoning, like Mr. Rogers. His giddiness and glee sickened Mayweather.

Livingston and Walton began walking briskly and Mayweather lagged behind.

Mayweather was unable to hear the exact words Walton was spewing, but it didn't matter. The tone sufficed. Walton was acting as a tour guide who derived great pleasure from his work, or the manager of a car dealer hyping a new feature on the new line.

Mayweather shuddered.

Livingston broke away from Walton and crossed the dirt road to prepare the horses and carriage waiting there. There were two horses; one a glossy black beauty renamed Destiny and the other, a bulging Palomino renamed Fate. Fate's gold coat shimmered like a polished penny even under this overcast sky, his white mane shone like a string of lights. Fate jostled with excitement as Livingston approached.

Walton spun to mock Mayweather, his clear blue eyes more gleeful than his wide grin. "Come on," he said. "You're slow even for you today." Walton eyed him up and down and shook his head disapprovingly. "Perhaps a bit too much of the old flip, hey?"

Mayweather simmered. It was becoming hard for him to breathe or speak. He huffed and kept walking toward the waiting Walton.

When he arrived within arm's reach, Walton somehow grinned even wider. Mayweather heard a loud crack like that of a starter pistol shooting a blank to begin a race. His mind emptied. He lunged at Walton, grabbing him by the neck with both hands. The force of his lunge and his weight caused Walton to fall back onto the tall grass.

Mayweather's grip tightened. His weary, bloodshot eyes were bright red footballs emerging from his eye sockets.

Walton's eyes were no longer gleeful which gave Mayweather a dark, but fleeting sense of satisfaction. The primitive terror in Walton's eyes at his own hands was sickening.

Walton raised his hands weakly gesturing his surrender.

Mayweather thought of loosening his grip, but his rage persisted. He squeezed harder, knowing Walton's windpipe would collapse and it would be over.

Mayweather's mouth gaped open like he just remembered a critical forgotten detail. A darkness swept over the red skin of his face making it gray now.

Walton turned off the laser from the crystalline implant in his pointer finger and dropped his fatigued arms to the ground. He knew Mayweather was gone. He just received three quarters of the concentration of energy and electromotive force produced by a bolt of lightning, directly into his tree trunk neck.

Livingston appeared overhead.

"Get him off me," Walton said.

Livingston rolled Mayweather over onto his back beside Walton. He lifted Walton to his feet with one tug.

Walton hunched over and grabbed at his neck. He paced in circles and coughed weakly, trying to regain his composure.

A nicely dressed woman wearing a bonnet approached. "Pray," she said looking down at Mayweather. "Art thou injured?"

Livingston placed a blocking hand in front of her and said, "Smallpox."

The woman jerked upright and stepped back. "I bid thee well," she said and walked back in the direction from which she originated. When she was down the hardened dirt road and safely beyond the inn, Livingston rolled Mayweather over once and then over again until he was fully surrounded by thickets.

Walton and Livingston crossed the road and boarded the carriage. Livingston cracked the whip and the wooden wheels rolled away leaving Mayweather's charred body to absorb the fading clicks of Destiny and Fate.

35

Welly was hungry for real food. The supplement strips he consumed earlier only held him for so long. He craved salt and carbohydrates and could think of nothing else to satisfy his hunger better than one of those pre-prepared spaetzle and brown gravy meals in the automat.

He set all controls to full auto and heaved himself out of his captain's chair. He un-hunched and stretched his back slowly until he struck too painful a point. He lowered and raised himself a couple more times and then trekked with purpose across the metallic floor toward the galley.

On his way, he accessed the automat with his mind's eye and made his selection. The cooked and frozen noodle meal would be moved by micro conveyors, from its room with a window view, into a small heating tunnel and exit onto the counter fragrantly steaming and ready to enjoy.

Welly's salivary glands went into hyper drive as he pictured himself shoveling in that first helping of gravy smothered noodles.

A smile was beginning to form in his mind's eye when he was thrown forward with great force. His head slammed into the beveled edge of the galley's counter. He bounced off, his body spun, sending him to the floor flat on his back, unconscious.

3 Minutes Later

"Pop," Kyle was saying repeatedly. "Pop, what the hell happened?"

The lights on the ceiling above him waved and sparkled and were distracting to Welly. Kyle then moved in closer to his face, blocking much of the light. That was better.

Welly blinked and squinted. He said, "What happened?"

Kyle said, "That's what I was asking you. It felt like something nailed the side of the vessel. Flung me out of bed."

The dam of pain broke and Welly's forehead throbbed. He grabbed at it.

"I hit my head. On the counter. Damn it. I remember now." He winced. "Damn it. Must be a result of the debris avoid-," he said, trailing off.

Kyle watched as his dad's wince turned to stupefaction and then almost instantly to astonishment.

"Damn it," he said. "I *remember* now!"

Kyle stared at him blankly.

Welly grabbed hold of the thought tightly now, with a vice grip. The word arrived in a divine flash, gift-wrapped with a plan to match. Plot points were forming in his mind all by themselves with no concerted effort. A path was clearing. It was a long path and required playing the long game, but it reconciled. Indeed, it reconciled. It all clicked into place like a correct lock combination.

He said, "Trenton!"

36

Manhattan, New York

July 9, 1776

Welly's ivory hemp shirt was hot lead sprawled over his sullied, sweaty body. The sun hung low on that hot, thick morning. It was hot and the labor was hard, but he was getting adjusted to all that came with being encamped in Kips Bay in the last couple of days.

Trench digging in the July heat is a far cry from Forward Facility rooms that adjust to your exact ideal temperature and most comfortable humidity level. Welly preferred the crisp and cool at fifty degrees over forty percent, which he chalked up to his being born in early November.

He was peeved at himself, or at his pampered life, this morning. He thought of his gelatinous and grab-able midsection and scoffed in his mind.

Have another caramel latte, extra caramel. Just take another gym drop.

Of course, there were drops for every ailment in current day 2052, every self betterment issue, every feeling essentially.

Good old manufactured emotional improvement ooze. Welly thought to himself.

Damn society grew lazier and more reliant on processed goods. Nevertheless, he convinced himself to use the gym drops. He told himself that his time was better spent developing ideas and processes that will improve the world as opposed to spending time grunting at the gym with the few people that still exercised traditionally. He was smart enough to know that many others undoubtedly shared similar convicted justifications for their using drops for this or that, but Welly knew his convictions to be justified more justifiably.

He was less than half a football field away from the small waves breaking on the beach. Being a New Yorker he knew he was close to the future site of the Water Club restaurant to his left, which he had dined at several times in the future. He knew he was standing on, or right about on, the future location of Waterside Plaza.

He liked being here. He had his bearings. He was close to home somehow despite being so far away in time. A feeling similar to vertigo did overtake him from time to time when he looked to his right down the East River and saw no tall buildings, no Freedom Tower, no Williamsburg Bridge. From Welly's position, all that was visible were patches of green and beige scenery and a smattering of small smudges of buildings.

Welly used his forearm to wipe the sweat from his forehead. He glanced down at the hair on his arm. It was greased and flattened and shimmered as if generously smeared with hair gel. He rested on the wooden shovel handle for a moment and looked up at the open sky for assistance. Today was an important one indeed.

Welly had been hard at work and keeping a low profile with a resolute focus on his objective. In a few more hours he would make his way downtown to witness history. At six o'clock he was to report to the parade grounds on New York Commons as the General himself, George Washington, was going to read aloud for the first time his freshly received copy of the Declaration of Independence sent to him by John Hancock.

Washington had arrived in New York to prepare for a battle with the British having just landed another ten thousand soldiers across the water on Staten Island. Welly was about to witness history and intended to start the process of tampering with it, or un-tampering.

There were other times throughout history that Welly could have chosen to gain easier access to Washington. He considered them all. The issues with a great many of those times was recordkeeping in these days was not always abundant or concise. He sensed the grander clock ticking and felt he could not risk any wild goose chases. This particular moment in time was well documented by multiple sources. Unless something changed that Welly was unaware of, he was going to be able to get relatively close to the Patriot General.

Aside from the confidence in knowing Washington would actually be at this place and time, Welly also wanted the information to be fresh in the General's mind. It was critically important. With so many mods having occurred, even minor ones, imminent timelines were detaching in crucial sections. The precise times of actions in the upcoming August Battle of Long Island, Brooklyn Heights, may have changed ever so slightly, seeming to alter which night Washington chooses for his midnight retreat. His weakened army becomes even weaker leading up to events that follow, including Trenton.

Everything was becoming increasingly scattered and disorganized in Welly's memory. He did his best to neatly organize and compartmentalize all the key data and then the next tornado would rip through and so the sifting and rebuilding would commence yet again.

Today he felt confident though. He could help in the cleanup and restoration of this toppled piece of important history. He was still clear on Washington's upcoming whereabouts, and the Battle of Long Island was little more than a month out.

Two birds, one stone.

Welly kept digging. He had his pick and his shovel and his job was straightforward - build fortifications with earth. He and the other soldiers worked from just after coffee and buttered bread all the way until beef and beans at the end of the day, or, every seventh day, Welly was informed, there was an approved ration of salt fish. Welly didn't plan to be around for the salt fish.

The work was back breaking labor, but Welly's back hurt him less. Yes, his back ached. It ached just like the rest of the bones in his middle aged body. His whole body felt heavy at the end of the work day, but somehow better than it had in years. He felt weak, but stronger than ever and fulfilled by the labor, rejuvenated by its purpose - by *his* purpose here. Muscles awakened that were dormant for decades. Though there was no scale to verify, Welly bet he lost five pounds during the few days here with the infantry.

Truth be told, he spent most of the hours in the day happily lost in the work - lost in this other world where he was known only as Will, William Stevenson, as his printed papers confirmed. No Mr. Brackford or sir or, Mr. Brackford sir, or anything like this. He was another ordinary soldier doing an ordinary job for an extraordinary cause. The cause was bigger than all of them and they all perceived that on some level.

Yes, he was covered in dirt and yes, his gamy scent was so sharp he smelled his own odor, but it felt good. And that chunk of wood-fired, spice-less, grizzle-covered beef at the end of the day never tasted so damn delicious.

He wiped his brow again and looked over the scattered dirt piles and then back at his shovel handle. Yes, sir. This is as real as it gets - a man and dirt. Welly thought about dirt quite a bit of late being that it was his only companion for long stretches these days. He was connected to it. One with it. This stuff we walk on every single day and ignore. This brown life-giving soil which without we could not exist. This muck from which grows everything that sustains us while we try to keep it out of sight and mind and especially off of our clothing. We are one with the dirt as we are with all things of the universe as we all come from the same star dust and, we are somehow *more* one with dirt. Dirt is where we all end up. It's where our vessels spend all time after their brief blip in the living world. Dirt is the greatest recycler on the planet. It can also save a soldier from an incoming musket ball knocking their block off.

Welly reached for his wooden canteen. It reminded him of a small wooden musical drum with a straw hole in the side. He drank a healthy gulp from the small hole.

Ahh that's good. But damn, what I wouldn't do for an iced caramel latte right now, he thought and chuckled to himself.

He looked off into the distant clear sky high above him and all the men laboring out here.

Kyle, he thought. *I hope Kyle is okay. He's just a kid. Please God, look over him.*

On the vessel, after humoring Welly by listening to the details of his inspired plan, Kyle had sunk back into his state of loathing. He blamed Welly and America for the accidental shooting death of his friend Bobby and he blamed Welly for the death of his mom. Welly thought he articulated his points quite well, and even thought some little progress was being made. When the vessel landed, Kyle threw a few items in his knapsack, including Welly's slab and ran off into the woods.

Welly chased after him, shouting his name, but it was clear almost immediately that he could not catch up. Kyle would have to come to his senses and come back on his own.

He knows the plan, Welly thought. *He'll come back.*

37

The man himself. Alive. In the flesh. The General walked towards the makeshift stage before the large crowd, in full regalia, complete with bright blue sash; it was perfectly surreal.

He was tall. Taller than the others. And once upon the top of the three-step landing, he was a hundred feet as he stood with great posture and presence surveying the mass before him.

The crowd of troops gathered on the common in downtown New York City was completely transfixed on their fearless leader in front of them, general George Washington.

Welly's plan was set and it was simple. His plan required a piece of paper, a rock, some tree sap to stick the rock to the paper for a little weight, and some minor strain to his elbow and shoulder. He stood in the crowd and held a piece of paper, folded in thirds the long way, just up at about the height of his ear. It was high enough to be noticed but low enough, so he hoped, not to be a distraction to the several gentlemen huddled in behind him.

The fresh cool breeze pouring in from the water was rank, as it brought with it the medley of body odors of the hard-working troops who'd been at it all day.

Welly himself was among the smelly. His clothes had been sweated through and dried and sweated through and dried yet again.

Quilled in dark ink, at the top of the folded paper he held, was a symbol. It was a compass on top and an interlocking square below with a capital G in the center. It was the Masonic symbol.

The applause came to a halt as the general cleared his pipes to read the Declaration of Independence aloud for the first time. Welly held his own paper steady, making sure it cleared the broad shoulders of the man in front of him so it could be viewed unobstructed by his excellency.

General Washington boomed with Shakespearean might, "The unanimous declaration of the thirteen united States of America.

When in the course of human events, it becomes necessary for one people to dissolve the political bands which have connected them with another, and to assume among the powers of the earth, the separate and equal station to which the laws of nature and of nature's God entitle them, a decent respect to the opinions of mankind requires that they should declare the causes which *impel* them to the separation.

We hold these truths to be self-evident, that all men are created equal, that they are endowed by their creator with certain unalienable rights, that among these are life, liberty and the pursuit of happiness."

The general paused briefly and looked up with his all-seeing gray eyes. He seemed to look directly at Welly, but quickly glanced back down to read the next line, not acknowledging Welly's attempt to get his attention.

Welly raised his elbow up with the smoothness of an elevator. The paper was slightly above Welly's flapping hair when the general bellowed his next passage. The whole of Washington's face quaked with fervor, perspiration gathering atop his forehead just beneath his powdered white hair.

He said, "The history of the present king of Great Britain is a history of repeated injuries and usurpations, all having in direct object the establishment of an absolute tyranny over these states."

Washington took in a breath and looked up from his papers which, Welly knew, in current-day, would undoubtedly be secured under thousand pound glass. He locked on to Welly's raised paper with the masonic symbol drawn on boldly with black ink. Washington squinted. His eyes seemed to slither through the crowd and make their way over to within inches of Welly's eyes. Welly's heart stopped and he feared it may not restart again.

Washington looked at him for what felt like ten long minutes, but more closely to three seconds. Then his eyes were back down to the next line, his voice booming louder, further strengthening with conviction.

From everything Welly knew about Washington, he was a man who paid great attention to detail so he was confident he would not forget this one.

Washington read aloud vigorously. Passion exhaled from the depths of his soul and seemed to permeate the crowd, including Welly. Every soldier, young and old, was motionless, spellbound as he rolled on. Welly no longer heard the words, but felt them. They were real. They were crafted with great care and precision born out of raw and unflinching skillfully channeled emotion.

Washington said, "And for the support of this declaration, with a firm reliance on the protection of divine providence, we mutually pledge to each other our lives, our fortunes and our sacred honor."

As Washington's face rose to view the crowd, the troops erupted in applause and shouts of independence and grunts and hoots and hollers.

The enlivened group began dispersing and would be heading to their march down Broadway to Bowling Green. If history remained true, and Welly recalled that this part of it did, then at Bowling Green the reinvigorated troops would topple the statue of King George III sitting atop a horse. The statue's lead would eventually make its way to Connecticut where it would be melted down and formed into musket balls.

Welly knocked and banged his way through the crowd moving in the opposite direction, all the while holding his piece of paper at the same height above his head. He walked in the same direction as Washington exiting the stage right. As he drew closer, he witnessed Washington witnessing him, yet again, and as he made his way to the front of the crowd he crumpled the paper until it formed around the rock. With both hands raised above his head now, he tossed the weighted paper on the ground about ten feet from Washington and Nathaniel Greene.

Washington observed the paper casually as he patted Greene on the back and gave him some sort of praise.

That was it.

That was as far as Welly would push it without risking a spectacle and a paradoxical cataclysm. He hoped the hook was sunk, but shuttered with anxiety based on the potential outcomes one way or another.

Welly walked briskly away and headed in the direction of his vessel which was parked a few miles away, uptown, where the east side of Central Park would be in modern-day.

38

Much of his walk he thought about Kyle. He had to trust the instinct buried way down. The instinct that convinced him everything would be okay. It was a feeling. But it was more. It was an assurance that he feared was denial. But this feeling was based on more than intuition. It was the waking dream experience the night of the shooting star that provided a basis of reality for this feeling.

Welly thought, *But was it just a fallacy based on some contrivance from an overworked mind?*

He thought about that night. That night he knew he would never forget and the occurrence that he would always, deep down, believe was real.

Other than the moonlight pressing on the closed wooden blinds of the large window on the side wall of Welly and Christine's modest bedroom that night, the room was dark. Something woke him. Maybe it was just the presence.

He had remembered laying down after walking the dog and giving him his nightly treats. Anxiety levels raised. There was a lot going on at that time with his professional life but when his head hit the pillow at night he would think about his coming child. His mind would race to all the possible worst-case scenarios that might arise with baby or mother or both. God forbid.

Welly's eyes opened slowly on the glowing red 2:16 displayed on the nightstand alarm clock. The memory from there on was so clear and so vivid. So *damn* vivid. Unlike any other before with one possible exception. It was unforgettable, etched deeply and completely.

Turning his head to the right toward the side of the bed that Christine always laid, he somehow perceived or perhaps, intuited, what he was going to observe before he observed it. It started as a combination of deja vu and a dream-like feeling he would, years later, become expert in deciphering. This was different though. It evolved almost immediately into ultra reality, a feeling more real than not only any other dream, but any other experience in his waking life.

He was looking at a cloaked figure sitting on their bed. It appeared to be sitting either on Christine's legs or just beside them.

The being in the black cloak was leaning over Christine's enlarged belly as she lay asleep on her back. The cloaked figure concerned itself with Christine's belly. It focused intently and rubbed the surface of the belly as it focused.

It paused, sensing Welly was awake, and ever slowly tilted its face in Welly's direction. With the hood of the cloak too large and the face of the being either darkened or covered, Welly couldn't make out much more than a dimly lighted area around the eyes. The figure showed no sign of worry that Welly was watching - he seemed to just study him for a moment in the darkness.

Welly could not move his body, but he was not concerned. He remembered clearly feeling no concern at all in the presence of the being. Rather than being filled with extreme fear and panic, Welly was filled with a euphoric feeling. As the figure shifted its attention back to its seemingly important work on Christine's belly, Welly was intoxicated by an exceedingly strong sense that everything was going to be okay.

For the first time since Christine had told him that she was pregnant right there in that very bed, he felt a blast of relief.

He did not *think* everything would be okay at that moment. He *knew* everything would be okay.

Welly circled back on this night so many times over the years. The exact reason the cloaked figure visited Welly and Christine he was not aware of, but he was never scared after that night.

He finally reached the vessel in the small clearing of the wooded area. It was quiet. All the sounds of clangs and jeers had faded out and dissolved into the summer evening ten minutes ago. Welly hadn't noticed. He'd been so deep in thought.

As he finally acknowledged his throbbing, sweaty feet, he actively recalled how that night in the bedroom ended, for good measure.

He had turned his head away from the cloaked figure and shut his eyes and fell back to sleep.

He never told anyone. Not even Christine.

The vessel was doing its job. It had absorbed the details of its surroundings, displayed them on every square inch of its exterior, and instantly updated as they changed. It was essentially an engineered technologically advanced metallic chameleon - or a techameleon as Welly referred to it.

He arrived at where he knew the vessel's steps were and stopped. He sensed something was behind him. He turned and looked.

There was a maple tree with a massive trunk and large limbs that twisted and spun off in every direction, appearing to be violently emerging and breaking free from their base in an attempt to grab hold of something in the night sky. Something emerged from beside the tree's giant trunk.

It was Kyle.

Welly sighed and smiled in his mind's eye. There were many things he thought he could say to him when he saw him again.

He came up with multiple pearls that may start the process of mending their relationship and clearing up the unclear. The look on Kyle's face told him now was not the time. Kyle's head was tilted down and his eyebrows raised.

Welly stowed his pearls and said, "Hey, son."

Kyle raised his eyebrows slightly and walked toward his dad.

39

Fort Lee, New Jersey

November 20, 1776

Welly was doing his best to catch up with the colonial army using the technology of the day - a gray horse he called Smokey for obvious reasons. Smokey was fast when Welly whacked his neck and although Welly needed speed, he winced with every step over the frozen countryside. His lower back pain had returned with renewed indignation.

He tried to focus on the scenery, the plan or anything beside his lower back, but found it damn near impossible. It was jaw-grinding, eye-narrowing agony and for what? He was probably too late as it was. His digitally printed musket was strapped to his back and bounced up and down, patting his lower back with every stride by Smokey.

He was trying to reach Washington's army before they abandoned Fort Lee and began their retreat towards Trenton. There had been no mod that told him anything had changed with this bit of history and if that was true then not too far behind Welly was five thousand British and Hessian troops led by Cornwallis, heading to take the Fort.

Of course, Welly knew, the colonial army had learned of the attack and made a hasty escape. They left in a hurry. They abandoned many heavy artillery, tents, entrenching tools, food and Welly hoped to discover if they left behind anything else of great importance.

Cornwallis's army left from Lower Closter Landing, which meant they were no more than a few miles to the rear of Welly as dawn was arriving. Welly planned to be with the colonial troops well before the abandonment of the Fort. This should have been no great feat for a guy with the equivalent to a time machine, Welly thought, but no such luck.

Welly's original landing place was a meadow surrounded by woods in what was known as Englewood Cliffs, New Jersey in present day. There were no houses anywhere near the area and no visible inhabitants. The timeline would have worked fine as he had more than twenty four hours to reach the fort and that was well before the troops retreated.

The landing was scheduled for the middle of night and was smooth. He was in New Jersey right on the Hudson River just across from Inwood in upper Manhattan.

As he exited the vessel to check on his selected landing location, he experienced an intense feeling that he was being watched. He could see nothing after staring into the bright lights of his instruments and mapping screens and the visibility outside was near zero. Maybe that heightened his other senses, giving him the ability to sense eyes on him, and perhaps his hearing sharpened as well. He heard a small twig snap nearby in the frigid inky blackness, due northwest from where he stood.

He froze on the last step of the vessel.

A huff of air was exhaled straight ahead - something was alive in the darkness. He found the courage to move his left foot back up a step in his own retreat, back to the vessel.

He was overcome with instinctive and primitive fear.

He heard something stretching like a rope being pulled tight. His eyes began to adjust, and he could see crouched shadowy figures approaching.

As another twig snapped he began to make out blurred shapes, and then he saw what looked like people cloaked in animal hides creeping hunched, in unison. Sounds of more ropes stretched. Without thought he climbed the remaining steps backwards, opened the door and fell inside, closing it with his foot as he lay on the floor.

He heard a hostile rapid pinging repeated on the metallic door. He rolled onto his stomach and did a push-up. He slowly rose and hunched over to the vessel's viewing portal and took witness to something truly amazing, terrifying and regretful.

Dozens of Native Americans surrounded the vessel and fired their handmade arrowheads at his arrowhead shaped vessel. The arrows dinged the sides of the vessel and fell softly onto the frost covered grass to be reused later.

Welly had to launch the vessel and exit the area, but did not want to harm these people. Thinking quickly he activated the exterior lights with a mental command prompt and the equivalent of twenty thousand candle lights assaulted the eyes of his attackers. They backed up and shielded the younger warriors. Welly could see there were hundreds of them stitched into the wooded area across from his landing location - the light stealing through the trees like greedy fingers, illuminating the original owners of this land.

The vessel rose up and out of sight within seconds.

The Native Americans stood disbelievingly and stared at one another.

Kyle slept through all of it.

Welly quickly researched and relocated. They were another ten miles upriver, along what would be the Palisades River somewhere around modern day Tenafly. Between hovering to finalize his research with all of the information he could sum-

mon to ensure not making that mistake again, and being farther from Fort Lee, they were way behind schedule.

He hoped his visit and interaction with the native people
would not have any rippling, history changing effects, but
there was no time to change that now.

On that trip to the next safer landing location, he reflected
on how many spaceship-like objects were etched and drawn
and painted into momentous events depicted in art. Those
that were blatantly obvious were cast as coincidences or
deemed fodder for conspiracy theorists, but Welly wondered
how much was actually conspiracy considering he, himself,
was real. He wondered how many of those painted spaceships
were historic tourists and if any were history modifiers.

He couldn't wait to tell Kyle about what had happened even
though he feared Kyle may just call him some cool new age
word for moron.

He never got the chance though. When the vessel landed
for the second time, Kyle burst out the door and ran off into
the dark night, bag in tow.

Smokey galloped up the road approaching the Fort. Welly
had no time to behold its historical splendor which he desperately wanted to do. If those five thousand determined troops
were not bearing down on him, he surely would have taken his
sweet time.

He stopped Smokey by the log fence that surrounded the
entire perimeter of the fort and slid off like a jellyfish, wishing
he *was* one, so long as it would make the evil throbbing vanish.
He thrust his aching body over the fence and padded, bent forward as if studying the ground, toward the main building.

He looked at the wood planked building and observed the
door was swung open. Items were scattered on the floor outside the entrance - two shovels, unfolded cloth of some sort
and two toppled over wooden barrels. Welly could hear a deep

bellowing sound as he approached and as he got closer, he could hear it was singing.

"Yo ho ho. Ho ho yoooooool"

Welly removed his musket from his back and cautiously crossed the wooden saddle threshold into the fort. He saw a man asleep on the floor and another man standing, happily drinking from a metal cup next to a barrel labeled - *RUM*.

The gulping man was thin, gaunt to be more accurate. His wiry frame moved about with a skittish giddiness. He was older. Welly assumed he had twenty years on him. He stumbled and looked at Welly stupidly and vigilantly for a moment. His bloodshot eyes brightened once he took Welly in.

"Yo ho laddy. Fancy some remm? Plenty er it laddy," he said and pointed at the barrel. He laughed conspiratorially.

Welly slipped his musket back into his holster. He said, "There are five thousand British and Hessian troops marching to this fort. Right now."

The man recoiled slowly at the seriousness of Welly's voice. "Ahh. Well I can't say there nuff remm for that a many," he said and laughed heartily.

""I'm leaving," Welly said and stepped forward toward the man. "Please come along."

The man shrugged and squinted at Welly as if trying to focus on him. He stared into his cup weighing his options. He gulped the last of its contents and threw the cup aside. It toppled and clanged next to the snoring man on the floor who did not flinch.

The man stumbled into a large support beam and bounced off like a buoy.

"There are no finer men," he said as he stumbled toward Welly. "No finer, finer men in this b'ness of retreat than our lads. Hey? Lemus is my name. Miller. Milleh. Leems." he said and grabbed his arm around Welly's shoulder for support.

Welly was sure Lemus would be on the floor, down for the count if he had not latched onto Welly at that precise moment.

"Brack. Uh, Will Brack," Welly said, "Will Stevenson, but friends call me Brack."

Welly fought through the added pain of Lemus's hundred pounds hanging on his frame. He willed the skinny man out to the wooden fence outlining the perimeter and let the man go. He stood and looked at Welly and wobbled. He was standing as if being held up by marionette strings.

He said, "Finer men at this b'ness of retreat I say. Never."

Welly could hear the rumbling of the British and Hessian forces approaching. He could feel it in the ground and feel the dread in his core the way an animal feels a storm approaching.

"Come over Lemus," he said.

Lemus nodded and then flung himself over the fence. He lay there, face down like a prize fighter who was just delivered a heavy uppercut to the chin.

The rumbling grew louder.

Welly looked out into the distance, but saw no red yet. He grabbed Lemus and thankfully, Lemus sprang to life. Welly helped him onto the back of the horse. Lemus sprawled over Smokey's rump like a saddle. Welly winced and boarded and took off.

The thunderous rumble sounded as if the whole British army was marching right behind them. Welly didn't look back, just whacked Smokey hard and prayed Lemus wouldn't flop off.

40

November 28, 1776

Washington and his army that now included Welly and Lemus, were on the run. The army was dangerously depleted having very little entrenching tools and food. None of the men slept much during the week and half since Welly and Lemus caught up and joined with them.

Lemus expressed to Welly as often as possible, that he was enjoying himself much more in the warmth of the fort with a whole barrel of rum to himself. It became a running joke between the two that unknowingly was keeping their spirits lifted during these trying days and brutally cold nights.

November 30, 1776

British General Howe wrote a letter. He offered a sixty day window to the Patriots to end their effort with favorable terms for all those who came forth and pledged their allegiance to the king.

Patriot support in New Jersey and across the board for the colonial cause, was waning.

The letter proclaimed all who would come forward in obedience and pledge their allegiance to the king, would receive a free and general pardon and reap the good of their majesty's paternal goodness in preserving rights of their property, restoration of their commerce and securities of their basic liberties.

Thousands from New Jersey arrived at British camps to pledge their allegiance to the king.

41

Trenton, New Jersey

December 2, 1776

Washington's army arrived in Trenton. Onlookers of the army referred to them as a pitiable excuse for an army and the most ragged, wretched group of individuals they have seen. One of the onlookers, the artist, Charles Wilson Peele, peered at the paint-like vibrant red trail following behind the arriving soldiers. The previously pale gray rocks were coated with the brushstrokes of blood from the colonial army's shoeless feet. The troops were cold, hungry and many not fit for duty at all in their condition.

A group was ordered to gather up every boat in the area and bring it to the Delaware River by where the men were gathered. They needed to use the boats to retreat across the river as they were being chased by the stronger force in numbers, better equipped British and Hessian army led by British Charles Cornwallis and the Hessian Johann Rall, roughly thirty miles behind them.

Washington sat atop his horse. He surveyed the chaotic scene, huffed in an offensively cold breath and looked toward the smattering of bare trees and snow-dusted hills in the distance. Among other vexations, he wondered, where, oh where, was General Lee and his army to reinforce and reinvigorate his ailing regiments?

Not a solitary word from Lee.

Washington drew in one more breath and rode off in the direction of his temporary quarters, a large home in Buckingham about ten miles from his troops. There was much work to be done. An unexpected blow to the enemy was so necessary, yet so impractical given the current state of the men. What choice had he? The time hath arrived.

42

Brunswick, New Jersey

December 6, 1776

The British Cornwallis and his men waited in Brunswick for eight days already, growing restless, recovering from sores. Kyle, among them, clutched the ribbon in his hand and smelled it inconspicuously on his walk over to the church. The foot long ivory ribbon had been balled up in his clenched fist so tight that none of the fellow red-coated soldiers surrounding him by the fire moments earlier, could see. Inhaling the aroma of windblown hair emanating from the ribbon hidden in the clutches of his fist was intoxicating perfume for Kyle. It generated in his mind's eye, the warmth of her smiling face, the eyes that encapsulated all of the beauty and mystery in the world, and invited him to share in it.

He arrived at the humble church and pocketed the ribbon in the bright white uniform trousers he currently donned. He pulled the large wooden handle before him.

The church was dark, having only two candles lit. Jeffrey stood alone by the priest's podium, his red coat, a flickering neon sign against the dimness. The tiny sea of brown liquid was choppy inside the clear glass bottle that greeted Kyle as he neared the podium.

Jeffrey had just swigged. He hid his grimace best he could but his pale face reddened nearly to the same swatch color number as his curly hair.

Jeffrey said, "Das fine English whiskey my lad. None of that peasantry grog rubbish." He held the tall dark bottle out and offered it to Kyle.

Kyle shook his head and smiled nervously.

"Aye?" Jeffrey said and looked at Kyle with indignation. "Tis admiral's orders. Twas conveyed that we are to tear up this countryside before delivering our decisive blow in the coming days." His voice raised higher with excitement and it reverberated off of the planks of the walls of the empty church in which they stood.

"You'll oblige me won't you?" Jeffrey said as he poked the bottle at Kyle once again.

The undertones were clear to Kyle. Jeffrey was more or less stating, *I saved your life and you better have a drink with me.*

It happened a few days back. Kyle was wearing a red coat uniform and came under fire by way of colonist musket balls. Kyle had flopped to the ground instinctively and lay paralyzed with fear. The two colonists who were on perimeter guard duty then came closer to Kyle to inspect his injuries and take him prisoner. Kyle's eyes met with the younger of the two Patriot soldiers, a boy who appeared to be even younger than Kyle. The young soldier jumped back unexpectedly and fell to the ground. The sound of the shot seeming to come seconds later, at least in Kyle's recollection. The other colonist looked over at his fallen comrade briefly and then came the animalistic battle cry bursting into the scene.

He saw flashes of silver, but it happened so fast. The force of the speeding bayonet wielded by Jeffrey was enough to send the colonist off his feet into the air before crashing down on his back. Jeffrey stabbed him repeatedly with the bayonet as he lay on the floor. Kyle had closed his eyes so solidly, trying to will himself out of this new reality.

So yes, Jeffrey had saved his life.

Kyle grabbed the bottle and said, "Bottoms up."

Jeffrey slapped his knee and said, "Aye."

Kyle felt the liquor fire-balling down his chest to his stomach, and then the acidic bodily juices rising back up. He gagged.

"Fine English scotch. For fine English gentleman," Jeffrey said and tore the bottle from Kyle's hand.

Jeffrey gulped greedily and took a deep breath once the harsh liquor rushed down his throat. His pale blue eyes were covered with a coat of lacquer and he smiled wide at Kyle. "Succeed," he said as he handed the bottle back to Kyle.

Kyle flipped the bottle up and took in a small amount of the whisky before clamping his upper lip down on the mouth of the bottle to stop any more from pouring into his mouth. He gulped down histrionically and winced again.

Jeffrey laughed. "Ha ha. You hear that?" He said and they both cocked their heads back to concentrate. They could hear faint screaming and laughter and then a banging sound and more laughter. "Night tis young. Let's hurry along."

He snatched the bottle from Kyle and began pouring it on the floor.

Kyle thought he must have really been stoned. Perhaps he started drinking long before he and Kyle met up.

Jeffrey walked over to the podium and placed the bottle down. He casually backhanded the half-melted burning candle.

Time slowed down for Kyle. The shimmering wax cascading down the melted candle stump, flickered. The reflection of the waving light of the flame atop and below, atop and below, the somersaulting torch. The flame increased in brightness, and decreased again to nearly extinguished. Kyle had time enough to observe all these details and to hope that the flame would be transformed into a smoking black wick by the time it joined the floor. It tumbled again and again and again. It was really only two times but Kyle remained stuck on its tumbling through the air despite the angry belch of the instant fire that ate up the dry planked floor insatiably.

"Regretful," Jeffrey said. "Ha ha," he then said jubilantly. His face was fully lit from the spreading flames below. He looked like a boy telling ghost stories in the campfire light.

Kyle's legs were heavy, his feet felt like cannonballs. He knew he had to move with the flames spreading. Jeffrey skirted around the fire and tapped Kyle's bicep playfully. This jarred Kyle from the mini-trance he'd fallen into and he followed Jeffrey quickly out of the front door of the church.

It was bedlam down the dirt road. The dark night was lit with flashes from the smattering of flames of burning hay fires and barns. Sounds of anarchy echoed through the cold night air. Hessians and Redcoats were wreaking havoc and destruction on New Jersey as they grew restless awaiting their orders to move on the fleeing rabble in arms.

Kyle walked swiftly, trying to keep up with Jeffrey. It all felt dreamlike. It felt as if he were on the intricately designed set of a major Hollywood production only no one was yelling cut. He looked over the red shoulder of his British infantry uniform at the church behind them. Pale light danced behind the glass windows and smoke floated upward out of every crack and imperfection in the wooden roof.

He thought of how many people had a hand in the construction of the church. How many hours did it take to build something so beautiful without the luxury of being able to utilize perfect machine cut boards and nail guns or even nails or proper saws to cut the wood? He marveled at how any of these amazing structures and creations came to be with such limiting technology - these same creations that these men were giddily burning and busting up with the colonist's own tools. How many children would wake up tomorrow and wonder why their church was burned to the ground, wonder why their houses were ransacked? They would wonder just the same as he wondered so many times as a young boy - why. Why? No good reason was available because there was no good reason.

The church roof was engulfed with fire now and Kyle felt his own fire growing inside him. He was angry, but what would he do? What *could* he do? He had little experience with physical confrontation. He'd been tested twice now within the past week and couldn't help feeling like an incredible failure. When those colonists' musket balls were firing at him, he was flopped on the ground, laying there like a dead fish. He knew how to operate the musket and bayonet. He experienced the complete training and deep stored that memory. He knew enough to infiltrate the ranks of the redcoats in the first place - to join the *right* team or so he thought.

Yes. He remembered now. This is ugly, but so is modern day America. Too much freedom, right? Too many guns. Britain had it right with their gun control laws and more socially liberal laws, didn't they?

Kyle surveyed the damage being done. He looked at the displaced residents being shuffled out of their homes in the cold and the Hessian and British forces gleefully plundering and destroying.

The end can justify the means, can't it?

He walked past two Hessians, easily distinguishable by the blue uniforms, threatening with death anyone who got in their way. Barrels of beer and wine and crops and anything inside the plantations were considered well deserved payment for their services.

Many occupants were fleeing. Some New Jersey loyalists led soldiers to the homes of their neighbors to steal their goods. A plump man in worn, drab pants and a cloudy ivory shirt beckoned Jeffrey and Kyle over. "I'll show you fine soldiers where they keep the fine spirits."

Jeffrey smiled and swatted Kyle's bicep. "Spoils of war."

They followed the plump man into a home lit inside with candlelight. A family was huddled in the small room, next to the fireplace. It was a man and a woman along with their teenage daughter of no more than fifteen and son of no more than six, Kyle estimated.

"We shan't leave. Tis our home," the woman said.

The plump man scoffed and batted the air down in the woman's direction. He walked over to the far wall and knelt down. There was a small square door fashioned in the wall, starting at the man's ankle height and ending at his knees. He bent down and pulled it open from the top. Inside were a half dozen bottles of booze.

The plump man said, "Ahh and there you have it."

Kyle was splitting his focus between the plump man and Jeffrey. Jeffrey was standing over by the teenage girl and eyeing her carnivorously.

Jeffrey said, "I fancy something else." He stared at the girl's chest.

Kyle was uncomfortable and felt his legs get immensely heavy again. He watched the girl's father watching Jeffrey with intense distress and fury.

Jeffrey grabbed the girl's breasts. He grabbed both of them simultaneously and then grumbled like a starting engine.

"There are other fine possessions here indeed," the plump man said.

Kyle was still a little unsure about his religion, but he thought pretty certainly, there must be a special place in hell for the neighbor that borrows salt one day and jollily walks assailants into their home the next, to pillage and sexually assault their family. Kyle was more angry than he'd been for some time yet his feet were glued. He could not move. His legs were going from heavy to numb.

Jeffrey became entranced with sexual desire and began aggressively groping the girl. He rubbed his greedy fingers all over her rear and then her front. Her plain dress was pulled up and most of her legs exposed to her family, as well as to Kyle and the plump man. The girl turned her head to look away and Jeffrey moved his face offensively close to hers. He was panting and rubbing her aggressively.

"Nay!" The girl's father yelled out suddenly. He shoved Jeffrey a few feet across the room, but Jeffrey only stumbled and didn't fall.

Jeffrey looked at the man incredulously. "You dare touch a British soldier. *Peasant*." Jeffrey eyed the entire family over and then quickly stomped out the front door. He returned moments later with two more British soldiers and two Hessians.

The father held his family tight together all at once. The Hessians marched to him and ripped his arms from his family. They threw him to the ground and kicked him. The young boy shoved one of the Hessian soldiers futilely and he was swatted to the ground as well. The mother was held by the remaining soldiers. They too started groping and laughing as they held the brunette woman against her will.

Jeffrey marched over to the teenage girl and wrestled her to the ground angrily. He pulled up her dress and tore at her under garment. Jeffrey fiddled with his belt as he slobbered the face of the girl.

What Kyle was witnessing was not historic, but rather prehistoric. It was barbaric in fact, and it sickened his soul, but he was frozen. Unspeakable acts happening right in front of him and no way to escape the sight. No way to look away.

The plump man looked on with voyeuristic curiosity.

Kyle was sick with rage, but he could not get his damn legs moving. He felt the intensity and love of this family unit being crushed out. He thought of Jennifer. This could be her. This *was* her. This was every young daughter, sister, friend - being ravaged, violated, *desecrated*.

He boiled over. He lifted one heavy leg, for what felt like his first time ever using it, and the other leg followed until he found himself marching over and tearing Jeffrey backward onto the wooden floor. Jeffrey sat foolishly on the floor, his belt undone and his trousers partially down exposing his under garment. He wore a shocked, disbelieving look.

"Leave these innocent people alone." Kyle yelled weakly.

Kyle wasn't sure if it was his unexpectedly pushing Jeffrey or the desperation in his voice, but all activities ceased. Everyone looked at Kyle. Kyle didn't care. He was feeling invincible with ire.

Jeffrey's face underwent an instantaneous color alteration turning crimson in the dim, candle-lit room.

"Bloody ingrate," Jeffrey said.

He rose to his feet, yanked up his trousers. He lunged at Kyle, tackling him easily. He was surprisingly strong and he speedily straddled Kyle's waist. He raised his fist and delivered blow after blow to Kyle's forehead, mouth, nose. The boards under his head were unforgiving and he felt his skull would crack open at any second.

He thought his only hope was if someone here would help him and break up the fight.

Another blow came hammering down, splitting his lip and swelling it like an overdone hot dog. Kyle felt around for something to whack him with to stun him for a moment - just long enough for him to run.

There was nothing.

He attempted feebly to push him off, but Jeffrey grabbed both of his hands and pinned them down at Kyle's sides. He let his hands go again and quickly resumed punching down at Kyle.

This time Kyle moved his face to the right to take the blow on the side. His ear was pounded and throbbed instantly.

One of the British soldiers attempted to stop Jeffrey now. He walked over and said, "Right," and grabbed at him, but Jeffrey pushed him away viciously.

Jeffrey was rabid.

He rained down another blow directly onto Kyle's forehead. He pounded with the strength and efficiency of an oil derrick, rearing back and busting Kyle's nose now.

Kyle thought he would pass out from the pain when he felt something. It was a very small, rectangular shape in his pocket. The last punch jostled his hand and his fingers brushed against it.

The slab.

It was wrong but he had no choice. He frantically wriggled his fingers inside his pocket.

Jeffrey's hand was cocked back when he heard the noise and stopped.

Doof doof doof-doof tss tss juwwwehhh. Doof doof doof-doof tss tss juwwwehh.

The music thumped loudly inside the colonial home. There were gasps, looks of confusion and then searchlight glances all around the room.

Kyle tore the tiny slab out from his pocket and projected a fully 4D video image into the center of the room. The voice of the beautiful woman dancing in her underwear said, *"Uh-huh. Yeah. You like that?"*

Jeffrey jumped off of Kyle and reverse-crab walked, his eyes fixed upward at the digital woman. He finally backed into the stone of the fireplace still locked on the unexplainable event to which he was bearing witness.

Kyle held his shaky hand as steady as possible as he sat up. He labored to his feet, using only his free hand to support him. The entire group was in a trance. Kyle felt like he was holding a fireball in front of a group of cavemen beholding such a sight for the first time.

His face was like bloody ground sirloin. It was puffy and swollen on every square inch. He slowly backed up toward the opened door as the high definition woman emerging from the slab, giggled and twerked in mid-air. The icy air on his back was welcoming.

He slid his thumb over the slab. It turned off.

He turned and ran.

He ran through the chaotic happenings; he was a bloody, bruised version of his former self. No one seemed to notice or care. He looked over his shoulder and saw Jeffrey and the others peering out the door at him, but they did not chase him. He ran past the blazing inferno that was once that nice church, and just kept on running.

43

Patriot Camp

Pennsylvania - Along the Delaware River

December 7, 1776

The retreat across the river from New Jersey had been chaotic and taxing. Washington had ordered his officers to have their soldiers destroy all local boats within fifty miles that were not being used for their escape across to Pennsylvania. Welly was among the party finding and hatcheting the local boats before boarding a boat and crossing the Delaware.

Washington suspected the British and Hessian forces would arrive at any moment to cross the river from Trenton and look to stomp out what remained of his army, and march on to Philadelphia. Washington reserved some hope knowing that General Charles Lee would soon be arriving with four thousand troops to reinforce the army and raise the spirits of the men.

With Lee and the reinforcements, Washington's army could make a semblance of a stand. Outside of that, it was difficult to imagine what might possibly stop the Redcoats and Hessians from crossing the river and delivering the final, decisive blow.

They were on the run. Welly hadn't time to think about the blisters on his feet from walking and the ones on his hands from hatcheting. He and the soldiers were weak and tired and hungry.

It was morning. The camp was cold, but not frigid for December. Everything was gray - the soldiers torn and tattered threads, the once ivory tents, the leafless trees surrounding the open field the men occupied, the frozen ground, the river. Even the glow of the spirits of the men were fading gray.

Lemus's once bright red boozed up face was graying too. He was thinner than he'd been when they first arrived and the skin on every one of his knuckles was cracked open as if sliced with the thick blade of a bayonet. His attitude remained cheerful, only the cheeriness was a bit more labored, but it still provided the only warmth for Welly.

The blackest sight Welly saw was the magical kettle he stared at now. The trio of flames lazily licked it's lower half, cooking the laughable amount of diced potato. Breakfast. One large potato, two men. The math was easy. The sum total equaled hungry men - hungry and cold.

The smell of the frying potatoes was intoxicating. No spices, just warming potato meat and skin. It reminded Welly of McDonald's fries and he closed his eyes to dare to dream of them. A gust of icy wind ripped him back after a few seconds as it had a way of doing since he'd been encamped here with the Colonial Army.

That ice wind pulled him back from more than just food fantasies. The cold hurried his body back up to a standing position from a squat last night after finishing his business in the festering trench. Then a frigid blast of wind had cut into him and restarted his mind from the temporary shock spell he fell into after seeing that young man's foot being amputated at the ankle on his way back from the trench.

He had stopped at that tent from which the screams were coming. He wished he never did. Lifting the flap, he saw first the young man's blue eyes bulging as he bit down on a dirty rag. His feral screams arose from somewhere deep down. Three soldiers stood around the young man, holding him down as a fourth steadily worked with a hacksaw on the young man's ankle. He stroked the wooden handle back and forth and the sound was of sawing soaked wood.

Welly had meant to look away immediately, but was fixed in a traumatic stupor watching the blood pool on the makeshift operating table composed of planks of wood. So much blood gathered below the man's blackened foot and his ankles. Welly gaped stupidly until that merciful blast of cold wind cut him. He perked up and let the tent flap go and tried to knock the memory from the front of his mind.

This was by far the hardest living Welly had ever done. The makeshift camp was barely holding it together and despite Welly's own knowledge of future events, he was scared. He wondered if the others there were as frightened as him. He didn't think so. Most had this ingrained resilience, an unspoken acceptance of all things, and a work ethic without limits.

Many spoke of the farms and shops they would soon be arriving back to once their enlistment expired in a few weeks, just after the new year. Welly did more listening than talking. He figured less was more here. Best to fly under the radar and besides, it was so cold at night when the work finally stopped, that he didn't trust his lips or vocal cords to work properly anyhow.

Even when his mind drifted to Kyle at night, and even with the intense stomach tightening worry it brought with it, he was only able to concentrate on not being frozen for a few seconds.

On cold nights, he and Lemus ritualistically sat facing the fire until their backs were numb from the cold and then spun to warm their backs until their faces were numb and on and on like a merry-go round in the cold section of Hell. Lemus told jokes to offer a distraction when they were not digging entrenchments or humping supplies and boats from point to point.

Welly glanced around the camp. He would have pinched himself repeatedly to be sure he was really here. His skin was so dry that a pinch may have caused him to bleed out and extinguish the small flame still putting along in front of him.

He looked over the messy men getting ready for the day of hard labor. Their torn up clothes, askew hair, unshaved faces. Some without shoes. This really was a rag tag bunch. Welly was proud to be part of it.

He took in a deep, naturally mentholated breath. There was a harmonious awful stench hovering throughout the camp. His eyes narrowed at the smell and all at once he realized something. Something came to him as clear as the road ahead once the windshield washer fluid and wipers worked their magic.

Physical appearance. Yes, physical appearance. That was it.

Physical appearance was a major factor in the outcome of this revolution. The Redcoats judged the Patriots like a hulking giant man rolling up his sleeves with pleasure, about to slug it out with a little boy. With a pshhh, and a figurative, dismissive shoulder brush.

It was an underestimation based on physical appearances. That was part of it - the part that sickened Welly. Welly now saw this clearly and he marveled at how stupid humans were on this matter, even still, hundreds of years later.

He and Kyle were just arguing about this recently. They were having an argument and Welly had told him he wanted to live in a world where physical appearances just don't matter anymore. Kyle informed him that was great, but he doesn't live in that world. Welly informed Kyle that it was finally proven beyond the shadow of a doubt that what matters most is in one's mind and that he, Welly, chooses his own world in which to live and the world he chose, invests not another single, solitary second on physical appearance.

On some level this was the cause of the squeezing of a major nerve when he was accused of being racist based on the ratio of ethnicities of new hires at his company. The utter idiocy of his fellow humans to be focusing energy on appearance. Especially in current time, when the mind was proven to be the source of human advancement. It was maddening. In fact, Welly changed nothing about his aptitude-based hiring procedure and the following year the ratio changed all by itself. It was proof that this all mattered zero, but no one had seemed to care much about this proof.

He had been sick of it all. He couldn't take anymore of the lunacy. People judging other people and deciding to hold them back or push them forward based upon their great grandmother's birth country or their gender or their shade of skin tone? Welly thought this was a special brand of insanity. He didn't deny its existence, but wanted those small remaining embers of it to just burn out by not acknowledging it. That's why he had written his scathing letter condemning all of it. That's why he pledged to shut the topic completely off. That's one of the many reasons Kyle was mad at him for life. He had known writing that letter would leave him open to being accused of hastiness or immaturity or both, but so be it. He would rather die than to feed one more miniscule morsel to such a reversing enterprise.

"Aye, Brack," Lemus said after ravenously swallowing a bite of potato. "A gentleman being in company with some ladies, who talked very amorously, felt an odd sort of motion in his breeches. So he whispered one of the ladies in the ear, and told her that his fusee was cocked. It is so, says she. Then you may fire at me if you please. I'll stand ye, I am not afraid of your flints, although there be two of them." With that Lemus slapped his knees. "Ha haaa!" he hooted.

Welly laughed at Lemus laughing, more than the joke. In fact, Welly was not quite sure he understood the joke. Were the flints testicles, he wondered.

"There be *two* of them," Lemus said and studied Welly to be certain he too was enjoying the punchline. Welly laughed more. It felt damn good. Laughter was the closest thing he had to a furnace out here.

"The Compleat Jester," Lemus said. "Aye. You've read it?"

Welly shook his head.

"Worry not, Brack. Lemus twill recite it for our entertainment."

Lemus was impossible not to enjoy being around and Welly was thankful to have someone close to a friend to help him pass this treacherous time.

Welly smiled amiably. He said, "Time to get to work."

"Brack," Lemus said. His face contorted from comedian to undertaker. "Remember. With you, she is always."

"As is your son."

"Amen," Lemus said.

"Amen," Welly repeated.

The night before, they had a long talk as they spun like dreidels by the fire. Welly opened up to Lemus about Christine. It had been years since he'd uttered those words. "She passed away."

He had been stunned at how quickly they fell out of his mouth and thinking about it later it shouldn't have been too surprising. He was trying to tell him with the speed of tearing off an adhesive bandage.

He said it. It was true. She was gone.

He knew it was real, but somehow saying it out loud made it more real, more final. His jaw and voice trembled as he tried to explain. "Terrible accident," was all he said and was all Lemus needed. He had no questions.

Lemus offered Welly his condolences verbally, but it was unnecessary. His eyes expressed everything Welly needed to hear. The eyes were pained and warm and inviting. His furrowed brow extended out and accepted Welly's grief - sheltered it somehow.

Lemus opened up about his son Liam. Liam left his earthly body at fifteen, a victim of smallpox. Lemus did not cry. His voice did not shake. It was a hardened grief. It was a grief that men of this time seemed to share. They had all seen death at one point or another in their lives.

Lemus had seen much before the war and more than twice that amount just at Bunker Hill, he'd expressed to Welly. But his life was dedicated to his only boy. Everything he did was for Liam. Every ear of corn he shucked, every straw of hay he baled. All for Liam. It was just he and Liam all of Liam's life. Liam's mother died giving birth.

He told Welly after Liam passed on, he didn't have much purpose. That was, until the revolution. He was fighting for the freedoms of all the good young lads, all of the Liams, that were still here. He was fighting for the grandchildren he would never meet and the children of those grandchildren and so on.

The two men had agreed in a pact-like fashion that their loved ones were still with them, always with them. The two men believed it as sure as they believed in God. Not because there was evidence to point to, but because they felt it, knew it, in the cavernous depths of their souls. There is not a chance that souls as good as Christine's and Liam's did not live ever on.

Now, about the souls of Lemus and Welly, well that's another story they joked to bring the lens back into focus. But they shared a moment spinning around by that fire and neither would ever forget it.

Lemus blinked and looked at Welly vacantly. Welly observed the whites of his eyes were yellowing - they were bright blue marbles floating in wonton soup.

Soup! Welly thought. *What I wouldn't do for some wonton soup right now or matzah ball. Stop it. Stop.*

The thought of soup was too much to bear. It was as far fetched as his home was far in space and time. The hunger was so vast it seemingly had no end nor beginning. He could not complain too much though. At least he had nourishment strips to ensure his good health.

The strips, like so many items of his day, were dissolvable postage stamp sized strips you pop on your tongue and are gone and working their magic in your bloodstream within seconds. Welly still had over one hundred strips in his matchbook sized stash and Lemus had none.

He thought about trying to slip one to Lemus, but rejected his own idea quickly. He liked Lemus, but he needed to do as little meddling as possible. Every move he made here could have big repercussions - ripples that grow into tidal waves over the ocean of years to come. He had to do what *had* to be done and nothing more.

Welly already acted without thinking when he rescued Lemus from imminent capture at Fort Lee. It was only later when he had more time to reflect that he kicked his own ass mentally for having committed such a blatant blunder. Selfishly though, he was glad. He felt like he had a true friend for the first time in some time.

Lemus slapped his knees with both hands and rose. "Aye," he said.

Welly rose slowly to his feet and winced. His back twinged.

Time to get to work.

44

The horse quaking the ground on the path between the rows of tents was a beauty. It's shining light gray coat and carefully brushed, bouncing gunmetal gray mane was the most well-manicured specimen in a five mile radius no doubt. It was a golden needle in a moldy haystack.

Welly noticed the man with great posture sitting atop the horse. The man seemed to be sitting on a skyscraper as Welly walked along carrying buckets of water. Welly observed his golden fringed blue coat. As his gaze lifted, it led him to the golden tassels on his shoulders and up further still, finally viewing the man's pale face, cheeks and nose reddened from the cold, and finally to man's dry white hair.

It was the general, George Washington. He was surveying the camp. Welly knew at once the horse was Blueskin and he immediately recalled several paintings of Washington and this horse. He now knew the paintings to be an accurate likeness. Somewhere buried deeply he thought that knowledge was interesting, but on the surface level he couldn't care less and he stood like an imbecile with a gaping mouth holding his heaving buckets, staring at the mythical man.

Washington moved his neck with purpose, almost robotically, his eyes scanning the activities of his men with the intensity of a soaring hawk seeking his supper. Washington pulled the reins and Blueskin stopped.

The brown horse following Washington's halted at once. The brown horse was being ridden by a dark skinned man. He was a stocky, neatly dressed man. His eyes remained fixed on the general.

Welly knew this to be Washington's assistant William "Billy" Lee.

Washington's deep-set eyes landed on Welly. He held his focus on this odd-looking man with the buckets of water. Washington tilted his head. Welly felt him browsing through his brain, feeling like his face was no more than a jewelry store window.

Washington bent his face forward and squinted. He then withdrew his stare quickly and Welly snapped back from his apparent daze. He began walking again.

After a few steps, he put the buckets down hastily. Freezing cold droplets splattered his dry knuckles. His shoulders burned. He wondered how long he'd been standing there. It felt like hours.

Washington and Billy Lee trotted off. Welly watched them. He rolled his shoulders attempting to wind out the soreness. At about a hundred yards away, Washington and Billy Lee stopped. They appeared to be talking to each other on the road.

Welly did one final shoulder roll and then lowered his knees, picked up the buckets of water once again.

A minute later, Washington galloped onward and Billy Lee was headed back to the camp. Shallow puffs of frozen earth dust coughed up behind his speeding horse. Billy Lee and his ride halted abruptly beside Welly. Billy Lee pointed down at Welly. Welly's mouth was stupidly agape once again. His eyebrows raised.

The other soldiers were creating the illusion of working now, but curiously watching on. Watching on curiously as well, was Brigadier General John Glover, the man in charge of Welly's entire camp. He made no illusion of working, but looked on concernedly.

"His excellency," Billy Lee bellowed. "Wishes to meet. Climb on."

Welly dropped his water buckets absently. One fell over, spilling most of its contents over the thinned, brown grass. He closed his mouth shut and picked up the fallen bucket.

He did as Billy Lee instructed. He only had one false start getting on the horse, falling back onto his feet. He played it off as if it was part of his horse boarding style and then willed himself, with every last bit of strength he could summon, up and onto the horse behind Billy Lee. He felt odd embracing a stranger as they rode and felt foolish not knowing the etiquette.

Once the horse burst into motion, Welly instinctively grabbed hold of Billy Lee, hugging him tightly. The two men bounced along stealthily; Welly wincing with every jackhammering hoof on the hard ground.

After ten minutes of trotting on the unforgiving solid dirt, the two men and the horse promenaded past a waist high stone wall. Beyond the stone wall stood a house about the size of Welly's current, historic home. The outer walls of the house were various sized smooth slate rocks stuck into a cement of sorts.

Welly knew the cement was more than likely some mixture of hardened clay and lime. Every rock surely hand picked and every small batch of makeshift cement, hand mixed. How long it must have taken. It gave added meaning to the term home-made.

Billy Lee pulled the horse up next to a small oak and quickly dismounted with the speed and agility of a world class gymnast. He wrapped a lead rope around the tree.

Welly tried his damndest to ignore the razor spikes burrowing into his lower back. He made a motion to lift his leg to initiate the process of dismounting.

"Ooofa," he said out loud.

Billy Lee stood patiently with his hands posed behind his back.

Welly decided against this initial de-boarding strategy and instead laid his stomach and chest down on the horse's back. From here he would fling and flop himself off the side - falling on the ground be damned.

That plan was a bust because once he laid flat, he couldn't so much as lift his neck, even slightly. His face was planted in the horse's mocha mane and he could taste the musty windblown blades of hair bristling over his mouth and up his nostrils. He looked like a Thanksgiving turkey on a brown serving dish and he felt as vulnerable. He prayed to God that his excellency was not watching from the window.

After a couple of unbearable minutes of Welly's feeble attempts, Billy Lee stepped up on a stirrup and grabbed Welly's plump, twenty first century mid-section, and pulled his body gently over the side. Welly slid off and landed on his feet.

He hunched and grabbed at his lower back. "Back," he said to Billy Lee, offering an explanation for what likely appeared as a ridiculous scene to the man. "Many thanks."

Billy Lee nodded and began to walk. Welly followed.

45

Welly and Billy Lee walked briskly through a small room with a round table occupied by a large, thick, white-haired man absent of neck. The man sipped tea and carefully eyed a map. The man did not look up. The man wore an ivory shirt, his round belly getting between him and the table. A navy coat with gold buttons and two stars on its shoulder's golden epaulet, hung behind him.

It was the famed Henry Knox. The man that led the impossible journey in the dead of winter, hundreds of miles, to retrieve giant cannons and haul the thousands of pounds of artillery over snow covered peaks and valleys and frozen lakes to get them to his Commander in Chief. A feat that inspired and made him a legend among men.

And there he sat.

The little boy in Welly wanted to run and gush and get an autograph or something, but the feeling quickly turned to smoke and exited his chimney as Billy Lee opened the large, white door which led them out of the room and into a small gateway room and then to another large white door that opened into a grand den.

The first thing Welly noticed was the high ceilings with ornate crown moulding that stretched into every corner. Hefty, royal moulding framed the large window on the far wall. Centered above the window was a carefully crafted peak with symmetrical wooden swirls like the end of an artist's hand-written signature. So neat and lovely.

Outside the window was Billy Lee's horse and Welly instantly thought if anyone was in this room they might have witnessed quite a horrifying spectacle a few moments earlier.

Billy Lee ushered Welly to the Gustavian sofa that rested upon the thick kaleidoscopic rug scribbled with tans and pinks. Welly knew it was a Gustavian sofa because he had one that was very similar. This one sat like an eight legged creature. Dark wood frame. Studded. Green and white plaid cushion. Billy Lee presented the sofa to Welly, gesturing with his hands that this was to be Welly's destination.

Welly sat. It was much more uncomfortable than his sofa. His, of course, had been reupholstered and offered a decidedly comfier stuffing.

Billy Lee exited the room through the same doors which they had just entered. He closed the large doors behind him.

Welly looked to his left. The fire roared inside its marble confines. He admired the taste applied in this house and made a mental note to come back and visit in two hundred and seventy six years or so.

Something flickered in the corner of his eye. He turned and startled when he saw George Washington standing but a few feet away, watching him intently. Washington smiled cordially, with his mouth closed.

Welly was angry at himself for getting caught up in the rapture of the home and not game planning what he should do when Washington entered. He jumped to his feet, back pain and all, and bowed awkwardly.

Welly said, "Tis a pleasure to make your acquaintance, your excellency."

Washington bowed in return. "Tis my pleasure."

He strode over to the large chair situated directly across from the sofa. He fixed his long coat and sat down gracefully.

Welly admired his gold sash and the shiny gold epaulets on his shoulders that featured three stars on each. There was a glow. It wasn't just the uniform with full regalia, but it was the man. Perhaps it was the backlighting from the large window behind him, but Welly could swear the man himself glowed.

"You are the lad who dropped the paper for me in New York. Are you not?"

Welly looked into his eyes; two clouds of imperial might, gripping Welly's courage like an eagle clutching a rabbit.

Washington continued, "The messages were received with great satisfaction. Your correspondence proved invaluable. In confidence I tell you, tis estimated half of our troops might have been captured had we retreated a night prior. Fog," he said and shook his head. "The merciful morning fog on that thirtieth of August sheltered our retreat, as you forewarned."

He paused and studied Welly's face. He said, "You have served our cause greatly and for that, I am most grateful."

Welly maintained his composure and resisted the urge to smile wide. "Tis my pleasure," he said humbly.

Washington nodded and said, "I would ask you how you came in possession of such yet unknown information as set forth therein, but I have an idea."

Washington studied Welly's face for evidence of his theory's validity. Welly cocked his head slightly to locate a clarifying connection, but found none.

"My reflection," Washington said, "has delivered me to only one plausible conclusion. You are aligned with the foreign visitors. Those I encountered in the forest. Are you not?"

Welly nodded.

"Indeed," Washington said. "How else would one come upon such information? Nary a man among us that could luck into such predictions of something so unpredictable as the weather."

Welly nodded again.

A flash beamed through Washington's eyes. "Information is of critical importance in this endeavor. As you know, my army is depleted, and we aim to deliver an unexpected blow upon our enemy. Have you any information which may aid us in this great work?"

Welly nodded again.

Washington stared at Welly for a few seconds and then spoke with a resolute chill. "Tell me everything. Omit nothing."

46

New Jersey

December 7, 1776

Kyle re-checked his mind's eye internal compass he had up-loaded a few years back. He was so far off course. He was ex-hausted. The night prior was spent mostly trading between sprinting, walking to catch his breath and sprinting again. He managed to sleep for a few hours in the morning when he found a small sun-soaked clearing. The sun was somewhat warm there and the surrounding trees blocked out most of the cold wind. He had awakened in a panic after a few hours and decided it best to keep moving away from Brunswick.

He knew he may be heading in the wrong direction to where he ultimately wanted to arrive, but he was putting distance be-tween him and the British and Hessian soldiers and that was good. All the movement kept his heart racing and kept him from fully realizing how cold his body was, inside and out.

His legs were buckling at about the twenty one mile marker. He stopped in the icy darkness and looked into the black. He listened. An animal wailed a desperate cry in the distance. Def-initely not a friggin moose.

He rubbed his temple and activated the night vision. He scanned the forest three hundred and sixty degrees around him. The bright green light illuminating the woods irritated his already swollen, blood burst eyes and he killed the night vision.

He considered just collapsing onto the cold ground come what may. He remembered a story of a seventeen year old kid that recently got drunk and fell asleep on a three degree night on the lawn outside his house and never woke up. He froze to death. Kyle didn't think it sounded so bad given his current situation, but a warm fire sounded better.

He gathered up some dry leaves, twigs and branches and sloppily threw them into a pile with the last of his energy. He dropped to his knees and brushed his pile of nature together like a child building a sand castle. He removed a metal cigarette sized object from his pocket. He gently rubbed his thumb in a circular motion over one side and a great flame was thrown out of the other end. The instant luminosity against the blackness felt like staring at the sun during an eclipse. He shielded his eyes with his left hand for a moment while they adjusted. He pointed the flame into the lower part of his brush bundle. He removed his hand from his eyes and watched the leaves light brightly and then wither.

There was something poetic here he thought, but he was too fatigued to capture it. The twigs caught and after a few seconds more there was a blaze before him. He dropped back onto his butt. He grabbed a chunky log next to him and heaved it on top of the fire.

He collapsed onto his side and curled up in the fetal position. He was dangerously close to the fire, practically spooning it.

He fell asleep.

When he woke up, it was bright. The fire was replaced with cold white ash. The spotlight sun shone intrusively through the barcode of leafless trees.

Kyle wiped the dirt and leaves off the side of his red coat and filthy white trousers. He then wiped out the unusual amount of discharge from his eyes and looked at it. There was the ordinary morning gunk coupled with puss and streaks of blood. He flung it from his fingers and started walking.

He was far from the vessel and far from his father who he knew, from their last conversation, was somewhere near Trenton with the Continental Army.

With the radiant clarity of daylight and some lucidity provided by sleep, he walked pointedly in the direction of civilization. Another night in this deadly cold forest was not an option. His body hurt everywhere.

There was supposed to be something of a town a couple of miles from his current location. A place called Bernards Township that had something of a village called Basking Ridge. If his inputted information that he accessed was accurate or, still accurate, there would be a tavern and some shelter.

The info seemed pretty certain so he followed his internal GPS, but so far there was nothing but unfriendly woods. He was uncertain if his body would carry him. Temperature had plummeted over night and his muscles and flesh and bones were freezing, shutting down.

Despite all the money his family possessed in modern day and all that technology, he was a still just a fragile human damn being - susceptible to frostbite, susceptible to organ failure as a result of sustained exposure to freezing temps, susceptible to throbbing battered gums and teeth, split and numb, dried-blood covered lips, cracked, stinging bridge of nose and inflated, half shut eyes, just the same as anyone else.

There is one positive, he thought. *No mirrors for miles.*

He stopped and leaned his hand on a tree. Looking ahead he saw the same seemingly infinite jail cell of trees that he observed to the left, right and rear. Gray trees and earth. Thin in parts and thick like an overcrowded party in others.

He stood. He stared. He watched the unmoving woods through the misty plumes of his exhalations and his blurred vision. There was no end.

Maybe there is though, he thought. *Maybe there really is.*

Sometimes your body just fails you. He was strong. He had things he wanted to do - needed to do - in his life, but his body was simply failing him. A thought slipped through his mind that if not for that fire he slept by, he would be dead already.

He nodded in approval with this thought and spun around, falling his back up against the tree he was leaning on. Better, stronger men than he had died throughout history. He was no different. He had an expiration date just like anyone else. He cupped his hands over his ears to shield them from the wind that was weaving in through trees. What he wouldn't do for a wool cap. He could feel every square centimeter of cartilage on his ear prickling with irritation.

He closed his eyes and thought of Jennifer for warmth. He re-lived the memory of the first time he saw her.

She had an instant hold on him. In a world where he already accessed, and experienced so many experiences, his own and countless others, to have a new and flare-bright experience such as this, was electrifying. It had been like someone putting paddles to his heart and he considered himself lucky for having met her.

She stuck to him. It was like, something. Like super glue creating an instant bond. No. It was more permanent. It was nuclear fusion. It was irreversible. She attached to his soul in a way never to be undone. She was *part* of his soul.

There she was.

The memory was whole and complete, but all he could see was her eyes. Those hazels filled the whole panorama of his memory. He thought about their brief time in the bedroom together. The feel of the course sheets on his palms and those hazels staring up at him from close range. Making love, to him, was a term from a foreign language prior to that moment.

All he could see was those eyes looking up at him; those hazels, lids blinking slowly, lashes locking and unlocking like the gates of heaven. He kissed her. If he had to choose one memory only to re-live for eternity, that would be it.

They barely knew one another and had nothing in common and yet there was nothing but comfort between them.

They had talked. And then when they didn't speak, that was okay. All was right for those far too fast, less than twenty fours they shared.

He bent his knees up and put his exposed hands between his thighs. His hands were purple and swollen everywhere. The skin on his knuckles was fat and burning with freeze.

His mind stole him away from Jennifer and delivered him to a memory of his father.

Welly was angry. He stood beside the breakfast table, talking at him while he crunched on an oversized bowl of cereal. His father was urging him, pleading with him - begging, really - for him to make the right decisions. It was a talk about Frummy and Kyle, uninterestedly glanced up from his yellowing milk and saw his father.

He froze the image in his mind.

For the first time he *saw* his father. He could see the raw pain behind his eyes. The pain fueled by love. The pain fueled by something he knew for a long time, but chose to ignore.

Now, weak and cold and alone, slumped up against that tree, something forced him to witness the reality. He was everything to his father. He was his father's whole world and he loved his father as much as his father loved him. It hurt. It hurt to feel that love. That love was too much. It's too strong. It's on the level with the infinite pain in his chest when he thought about his mother never coming home again.

Tears ran down his cheeks uncontrollably. He did not wipe them away.

He put his hands down on the solid earth and pushed. He rose to his feet.

He marched on.

In less than twenty minutes he reached what appeared to be civilization. He laughed at how stupid it would have been for him to give up, not knowing just how close he was to potential salvation.

Over the years, on those occasions when Kyle's attitude had been defeatist, Welly usually told him you never know what is waiting around the next bend for you. Once in a while, Kyle admitted, he said something half insightful to his son.

A white wall was visible about a hundred yards across the field past the tree line where Kyle was standing. Peering over an overgrown pine branch he saw it was a two story house wrapped in barn board. A dirt road in front. Several people neatly dressed padded along. It appeared to be two, maybe three families. Kyle scanned his mind for information.

Basking Ridge land was purchased from the Lenape Indians. It was originally settled in the 1720s by British Presbyterians. Presbyterian is part of the reform tradition within Protestantism. These Presbyterians were escaping religious persecution. Okay, got it. They're religious. Today's date here is December 8th, 1776. Day of the week - Sunday.

Church.

Satisfied with the knowledge and frozen, he stepped past the last tree in the line and onto the open dead straw grass. He took another step and then divine providence must have sought him. He remembered his current attire. He halted and looked up to see if any of the colonial pedestrians took notice of the tattered Redcoat emerging from the woods. They did not. He slowly walked backwards, sliding into the cover of the mixture of full pines and bare maples.

He breathed in a few quick hyperventilating breaths. He mulled. An obvious solution sprang forth. It might just kill two birds with one stone.

He removed the items from his pockets and set them on the ground. He wrestled his coat off, kicked off his shoes and stripped off his pants, leaving them on the ground. He left himself in only white undershorts, browning socks and a sweat stained long sleeve ivory shirt. He picked up the few small items from his pockets and stuffed them into his socks. He rubbed his hands feverishly together, took a deep breath and started to run.

He sprinted to the two story building, around to the front, up the wooden stairs and opened the closed door, directly past the outstretched wooden sign that read, White's Tavern.

47

Basking Ridge, New Jersey

December 13, 1776

Five days passed since the beat up, refrigerated and half naked Kyle arrived at White's Tavern, known to the locals of this place and time as Widow White's. The proprietor, Mary Brown, who was married to Ebeneezer White before he passed away, was the Widow White, Kyle read.

Oh, and blah blah blah, Kyle had thought, formulating his own custom ending to the historic tale.

He was wiped out. He needed to thaw for a good month. He had read enough history over the last few weeks to greatly exceed his personal quota.

Mary was a middle aged woman, pretty enough, under leathery skin that covered a tough interior that scared Kyle a bit if he was being honest.

She had studied him curiously when he arrived. He felt her looking over every bit of swelling, every open cut, bruise and dried red wax on his face. She said something about six pence and farthing or something to this effect. Kyle had pulled a couple of gold coins from his dirty socks and she showed him to a tiny room upstairs. He was not sure how much he gave her, but she seemed satisfied and told him when to expect to eat during the day.

He was convalescing and writing mostly. The more he fueled up on Mary's broth and bread and loads of fresh butter, the more his mind began to smooth. It was feeling like a field of freshly fallen snow, clear and full of possibility.

He penned, well, psyped his thoughts hastily, pouring them out like an open fire hydrant on a hot summer day in the streets of New York City. He wrote about the world as he saw it. He always had strong feelings and views, but now he had a little greater perspective and it was inspiring.

The room featured a small mirror along with a bed akin to a twin size, comfort akin to a sidewalk. Kyle checked the foggy mirror multiple times daily. On the morning of the thirteenth, the jaundice bruises were gone and his pale white skin moved back in their place. The gash on his lip was shrinking and whitening and the gash on the bridge of his nose was closed. Red, but closed. His nose was definitely off kilter, but all in all he considered himself lucky.

While inspecting his face, he remembered back to last night. He forgot how annoyed he was with all of the noise at the tavern below. Though, it was not unusual for nights at this place.

One night, Kyle had ventured to the bar out of sheer curiosity and was greeted by an eager woman in a strangling bustier. A man who had been unscathed by the deep cut of love would have been quite tempted to engage with her, Kyle had no doubt.

Night here always brought forth those unmistakable wall banging sounds for brief periods of time, but last night was especially raucous. There was singing and carrying on and he remembered how he just wanted to fall asleep.

The mornings were usually quiet. It was quiet now. Nice and quiet.

He studied his face for a moment longer and then thought, "*What the hell time is it?*"

11:34 a.m. according to the clock in his mind's eye.

His lunch would be ready soon. He threw on his new uniform - drab pants and long sleeve shirt that Mary brought him on his first night. Ebeneezer's no doubt, but beggars can't be choosey. He opened the heavy wooden door and it hissed loudly. It was a sound growing on Kyle. Growing on him too, the creaking planks, wining thoughtfully with every footfall on the narrow hallway. This place was starting to feel like home, but he knew it wouldn't last much longer.

He took the stairs down briskly, feeling the spunk returning a little more each day.

As he landed on the floor after the last step, everything felt different suddenly. The warm energy receded like the violent undertow from a crashed wave. It was an odd sensation and Kyle wondered what was this about. Immediately following this intuition he saw a soldier, a Patriot soldier, standing by the bar. Over the shoulders of the soldier he saw two more at the front door.

Mary was behind the bar. She looked at Kyle and raised her eyebrows just slightly and said, "Good morn."

Kyle nodded his response and looked over at the occupied table on the other side of the room. A disheveled man in a sleeping dress and wild gray streaked hair was face down and quilling something on paper at the small round table.

The soldier at the bar stood at attention, and looked at Kyle, his musket neatly at his side. "Do not disturb the general," he said.

Kyle looked perplexed and then it dawned on him. The general. That man at the table must be George Washington. Wow. Though he did not look like the painted images Kyle remembered seeing, or the guy on those old coins and antique paper money they passed around in class from time to time.

"Oh. Wow," Kyle said. "That's George Washington?"

The soldier looked annoyed. "Nay, lad," he said. "You know not who is this great man?"

Kyle raised his brows now feeling foolish.

The soldier shared a glance with Mary and then looked back at Kyle. He whispered now, "Tis General Charles Lee."

"Oh," Kyle said. "Of course." He tapped the side of his head to express his embarrassment. The name sounded vaguely familiar, but he could not place it.

Mary placed a tray on the counter. A plate with some kind of meat, bread, butter and a soup bowl filled with a fragrant brown broth.

Kyle said, "Many thanks," and grabbed the tray. He stole one last look at the scribbling General Lee before skulking back to the staircase.

He searched his memory files for anything about the general as he tore through the bread and gamey, burnt meat.

What was the General doing here on practically the eve of such major events in Trenton?

He tracked down some clippings from historical sources relevant to the name and dates.

General George Washington pleads with General Lee to hurry across New Jersey. Washington' expressed in plain terms he very much needed assistance reinforcing his position on the Delaware River.

More about Lee...Lee was nicknamed 'Boiling Water' by the Mohawk because of his notorious temper. Lee, finished military school at age twelve and entered into the British army. Twelve?

Kyle skimmed on.

Lee then served in North America during the Seven Years War. Sold his commission. Served briefly in the Polish Army. 1773, moved to North America. 1775, volunteered with the rebels.

Believed he should have been granted command of the Continental Army over Washington. He was angry and thought he had more experience than Washington. Reported to have overtly taken his time in getting to Washington, despite Washington's pleas.

Wow, Kyle thought.

It was a good thing he heeded the soldier's instructions not to interrupt this man, a general that apparently had some anger issues.

He read on.

Lee married a Mohawk woman and so he was an adopted tribesman. Despite this marriage, Lee was reported to still spend a great lot of time with prostitutes.

That explains a lot, Kyle thought.

He popped the last piece of buttered bread into his mouth and nearly choked on it as he read the next part.

General Lee is captured at Widow White's tavern in Basking Ridge, New Jersey and taken prisoner by the British.

What the?

Lee was at the tavern with a small guard. Banastre Tarleton and the Queen's Light Dragoons surrounded Widow White's and captured him around noon on December 13th, 1776.

Lee, a former British Army man, was now a captive of-

Wait. What?

Kyle's mind's eye bounced up to the previous line.

Banastre Tarleton and the Queen's Light Dragoons surrounded Widow White's and captured him around noon on December 13th, 1776.

If he was reading from a hard covered book, opposed to streaming text housed in the confines of his psyche, it would have tumbled from his hands absently and smashed onto the wooden floor boards with a thud. He checked today's date again.

December 13, 1776. Time - 11:56 a.m.

He read on.

Tarleton was reputed to have sworn in a London tavern that he would hunt down Lee, the traitor to the crown and relieve him of his head. Tarleton did keep his promise by hunting down Lee although Lee was not relieved of his head. Lee was taken prisoner, utterly humiliated as he was led from Widow White's tavern and delivered to New York City in his nightdress.

Kyle scrambled for another source about the topic.

December 12th - Lee stops at a tavern and is captured the next morning by the British as they shoot up his guards and he surrenders. He was at Basking Ridge and never made it to Washington to lend him his much needed support. Back at Brunswick, before transporting Lee to New York City, the elated British troops celebrated their new trophy. They drank and danced triumphantly before a band and were even reported to get Lee's horse drunk.

Kyle thought of Jeffrey and his cohorts, undoubtedly among the drinkers and celebrations at Brunswick.

The British troops exclaimed they caught the only rebel general they had cause to fear as Lee was the only one qualified, in their opinion, having his roots in the British Army.

Kyle lifted his head in thought. Just then was the sudden bang of a bad car accident. Kyle's body jolted as if impacted. Then there was another.

BANG!

Kyle quickly awoke from his shock and knew it must be, of course, gun fire. He tiptoed to his window which looked out onto the dirt road in front of the Tavern. He stood beside it like a spy and mustered enough courage to lean one eye over the cloudy glass just enough to see the half dozen horse mounted Redcoats surrounding the front door.

Kyle expected a musket ball to replace his right eye any second. He looked down and saw the unmoving bodies of two continental soldiers on the landing outside the front door. Another Patriot soldier ran down the dirt road.

The British soldier in the center - Tarleton - the one Kyle just read about it, started hollering.

"Fire! Fire into every door! Fire into every window!"

The British soldiers began firing. Their horses whinnying and lifting.

"Cut up as many a guard as you can. Fire!"

The shots were like sticks of dynamite detonating one after another. Some shots came from beneath his feet and the floor shook.

The firing stopped as the men reloaded. They quickly opened their musket pans, reached into their leather pouches and grabbed paper cartridges. They aggressively bit open the paper cartridges and spit the torn paper, poured some gunpowder into the open pan. They flipped the guns upright and poured the remaining powder in the gun's barrel. All so quickly and with great precision. At once they had their rods in hand and were ramming the powder down to fire again. But it was not gun fire that broke the momentary silence. It was Mary's voice shrieking.

Mary screamed, "Please. Lee is inside. Please! Mercy!"

Tarleton's eyes lit up.

"Lee! Surrender at once! Surrender and your life shall be spared. Lee! Surrender at once or it burns!"

A moment later Kyle could see Lee stepping over his fallen guards in his slippers. "I trust I will be treated as a gentleman," Lee said with his arms raised above his head.

The hatless Lee was flung over the back of a horse in his night dress and the battalion galloped off victoriously, hooting and howling. Kyle heard a trumpet sound from somewhere and bellowing cheers as they rode.

He moved his head away from the window and leaned it up against the wall.

He whispered to himself, "Holy shit. Holy shit."

A sudden flash glistened brilliantly in his mind and directed him at once to what he must do. He took a deep breath and worked on wrangling himself into calm so that he might make decisions that could save his life.

He looked out the window to be sure that the men were gone. He pocketed his things and ran downstairs and out the front door, crunching over the shards of broken glass and only glancing at Mary. His heart raced faster than the joyous Redcoats had just trotted away, leaving behind all of this destruction.

He grappled with one of the deceased soldiers on the stairs and removed his jacket quickly and without looking into the man's face. He was trying his best not to look into the dead man's open eyes, not to think at all, hoping to prevent future nightmares.

He yanked the soldiers pouch strap and snatched the musket that lay beside him. He started away and then turned and went back for the man's hat. He went and stood by one of the three horses left behind. He put on the coat and strapped on the pouch and musket. He bent and picked up his borrowed tricorne hat and put it atop his head. He untied the horse and mounted him.

Before he could process it all, he was moving rapidly, in an eastern direction. It was all clear where he had to go, what needed to be done.

A man exited the tavern behind him and started hollering. The man's voice was swallowed up by the mouth of Kyle's mission focus and digested by the melodic drum beat of the pounding hooves. Kyle's sight stayed fixed, straight ahead on the dirt path.

48

December 13, 1776

Evening

From his Trenton headquarters just across the river from Washington and his depleted army, William Howe made a major decision regarding the war. He suspended all military operations until the spring. He believed the weather had become too severe to keep the field of battle set and therefore would pause activities until the weather warmed.

Howe intended to spend the cold winter months in New York indulging himself in creature comforts such as fine spirits and fine women. The suspension of military operations due to wintry weather was not out of the ordinary for the time. However, with Washington's army severely weak and deficient and on their heels and, incredibly close to their location, many questioned the wisdom behind this decision.

A single, decisive blow was indeed within striking distance, but William Howe, Commander-In-Chief of British land forces, was the final decision maker and his orders stood.

If history could be restored to its original reality, many would look back on this key decision. People would discuss it, critics would criticize it, writers would write about it.

Sir William he,
snug as a flea,
Lay all this time a snoring,
Nor dreamed of harm,
as he lay warm,
In bed with Mrs. Loring.
    -Francis Hopkinson

49

Kyle arrived at his intended destination, having followed the compass coordinated with the vessel's directional pings he received on the slab. The red light from the overhead sky allowed a sleek glow on the otherwise camouflaged invisible silhouette of the vessel.

He actually made it. But what other choice was there? When destiny calls you that loudly you cannot ignore it. He just couldn't get Jennifer from his mind. She was unshakable. This must work. He had to see her again.

Besides, he checked his historical sources and word gets back to Washington about Lee's capture very quickly. And from multiple sources. Bad news travels fast.

He slid off the side of his horse and did what he saw in a movie once. He slapped the side of the horse's hind leg and yelled, "Yah!"

It worked. The horse galloped off into the woods. He hoped the horse would have a fighting chance out there.

Realizing he left his musket sack strapped to the back of the horse when he saw it bobbing up and down, he yelled "Hey, come back a sec."

The horse grew smaller and smaller eventually becoming brown vapor in the trees.

He climbed the steps and boarded the vessel and proceeded directly to the console. He accessed the pre-launch checklist and started to initiate each one mindfully. It was a combination series of mind's eye controlled program activations, physical controls to roll his fingers over - some visibly protruding and others embedded in various locations in a smooth surface beside the main console. Finally, the mental entrance of a long formulaic passcode to which only a small number of people had access.

The first couple of items on the pre-launch checklist were actually quite similar to beginning operations of many of the current day's higher end vehicles. Those were easy breezy for Kyle.

The part that made this vessel, Christine II, incredibly unique was the ratio of mind power necessary for its operation. Immense, deep concentration and focus needed to be accessed to put the vessel into motion and again at critical points along its journeys. It was accessing, unlocking a part of the brain unused by most humans. It had been discovered and utilized by Welly and for years he has worked with brains of all shapes and sizes to add to the number of people capable of this access.

Kyle dreaded this crucial step. The time had arrived. He felt confident though. It must be in him. He was the son of the man. So if anyone came equipped with this access, it must be him. Plus, the desire within him to see Jennifer. The attraction pulling at him, stronger than the strongest ocean's current, mightier than the mightiest winds from the mightiest storm, more unflinching than unstoppable time itself, must be enough to access that part of his psyche, to will it so.

He closed his eyes and relaxed his mind. He slid to the floor inside his mind.

His destination was several layers underneath.

He unfolded his hands and placed his fingertips on the metallic console and forgot about them. He was sliding through. Sliding through to her.

The ground was solid again.

He took in a deep, ever slow breath through his nostrils and exhaled even slower through his mouth.

He was sliding though the ground again. Feet and legs and hips and chest. He would be with her soon.

The ground was solid again and he stood atop it.

He knew he was breaking his own concentration and must focus deeply while letting all else drift. The focus must only be on this access and nothing else.

He worked at this for nearly an hour, employing every technique he had access to in his memory files, which to the best of his knowledge, was every technique.

It wasn't working.

He was drained. Heartbroken. Disappointed in himself. Disappointed in the universe for supplying him with a poison so potent as love without giving him an antidote. Disappointed in his father for not instilling this access into him somehow - through birth or blood or osmosis.

He thumped his forehead down onto the console and his new plan was to feel sorry for himself. His plan hardly got into motion when an idea entered his mind thunderously, affecting him like someone clapping cymbals together by his ear. His head raised.

Life vessels.

The main vessel came equipped with three smaller life vessels the way cruise ships carry smaller boats aboard in case of emergency. These smaller vessels are operational without the necessity of mind power. By law, they needed to be able to be operated by any of the historical tourists to give them a chance in hell if something should happen to their captain.

"Of course," Kyle said audibly.

He rushed past the galley and down the long corridor of guest quarters. A pocket door opened forcefully as he approached the end of the corridor. He walked through onto a catwalk. The door shut forcefully behind him. He took the twenty steps of the room lined with active lights of all colors zipping in and blinking seemingly without reason. This had been his favorite part of the vessel when he was smaller and less jaded.

Another pocket door opened to a small staircase. He climbed up and he was in the airy, sterile room that housed the smaller emergency vessels.

50

Pennsylvania

December 14, 1776

Cured meat. Welly's bones ached and his mouth watered. He chomped and swallowed bite after bite of the rations donated by the nearby Patriot farms. Camp fire roared and crackled a loud pop.

Lemus opened his blue eyes wide as dinner plates and he said, "Aye. The Redcoats," and chuckled. Welly chuckled too and then the smile was stripped from his face.

He felt an odd tingling sensation in his forehead. It was a low frequency buzzing sound. He rested the tin plate on his thigh and rubbed his forehead. He looked around the camp to see if anyone else was being affected by the humming. No one seemed to be.

A thought arrived and he wanted to slap himself in the forehead. He recognized this was a communication he was receiving. It was a slab communication, imperceptible to those not currently accessing a specific department in the mind that housed those receptors.

He had been accessing mostly the original wing of his mind for so many weeks now that he forgot the functions momentarily. Amazing how adaptable are humans - both in forward moving technology or primitive behaviors. Welly could easily see how the entire race could progress and make great strides, but just as easily, collectively regress and set themselves back hundreds of years with a few missteps. After all, humans are only as knowledgeable as the knowledge being passed along and then the new knowledge uncovered, added and passed along. A few breaks in the chain and who knows.

Of course, he thought. *An ultrasonic slab signal.*

It was like a dog whistle emitting ultrasonic sound that only animals, and trained humans can hear.

Wait.

A slab?

Now he did slap himself on the forehead.

"Thank God," he said out loud.

He looked off into the distance just above the edges of the swaying flames.

Lemus stared at him quizzically.

"Where are you, son?" he said.

He closed his eyes and focused on the steady high pitched sound. He was starting to triangulate the direction from which it was originating.

He opened his eyes and tuned back into the physical world around him. He looked at Lemus and shuffled to begin explaining.

"Aye," Lemus interrupted the words Welly hadn't yet verbalized. "Understood. Have me share of moments such as those." He reached over and swatted Welly's shoulder.

Welly nodded. "I need to go for a walk."

Lemus nodded. "And I need some rum."

Welly smiled and got up.

It was nearly full dark when Welly passed the three hundred yards mark, scoring himself three touchdowns. A shadowy

outline stood on the path just up ahead. Welly thought someone could line up a thousand similar silhouettes in the dark,
and somehow he would always know which was his boy.

His pace quickened and the outline grew larger and larger.
"Ky," he said and held out his arms.

"Hey Pop," Kyle said humbly. He kept his arms at his side
and allowed his father to squeeze him tightly.

Welly unclutched and stared at his son. "What's with your
face son? Did you get hurt?"

Kyle looked at the ground and then back up at his father.
"Look. I've been doing a lot of thinking and I want to be honest.
I want to be upfront with you. I think we should be more hon-
est and like, open. With each other."

"That sounds good to me. So what happened?"

"I broke off to join the British."

Welly controlled his reaction.

Kyle continued. "I thought. I don't know. I just thought
maybe that's the way it was supposed to be. You know looking
back through the lens smeared with I don't know, shit, I guess.
I thought maybe things would be different for people, maybe
better. Maybe I was right and you were wrong."

Welly tried to interject.

"Let me talk. Please Dad."

Welly nodded.

"Being here. Seeing this. It's different now. I've seen the op-
pression. I've seen it first hand. Maybe I was wrong. I'm not
saying I can get behind all modern day politics but I understand the spirit behind them now. Heh, I think I even have
some of the spirit now." He shook his head and stared at the
floor. "How corny. A damn cannonball should come knock my
head off for that."

"Son, don't forget you're talking to the king of corny," Welly
said and smiled. "I'm so proud of you. I'm just so damn proud
of you son." Welly went to hug him, but Kyle held his hand out.

"There's more. I gotta get this stuff out."

"Okay."

Kyle raised his hand and held a pale ribbon a few inches in front of Welly's eyes.

He said, "Jennifer Crowley. I met her in Lexington. That's the real story. I spent the day and night with her and I know I'm young, but I know what I know, and I *know* I'm in love with her. I know you see some young kid who doesn't know enough, but I know, okay. You can access parts of your subconscious that other people can't. You go layers down. And what I'm telling you."

Kyle stopped and huffed out a plume of vapor, and jetted out the rest of the breath like someone artistically exhaling cigarette smoke.

He said, "I'm saying that I just know from the lowest layer of *my* soul is all. I just know she's my love. I'm not saying I'm upset or mad or anything really. I'm just telling you. I'm just being honest."

Welly nodded a controlled nod, careful not to tread on Kyle's exposed emotions.

Kyle continued. "I took out a life vessel and went to her house to see her. I picked some English Primroses by her barn. It's this flower she told me about. It grows in the winter. Anyway, the house was empty. She was gone. I scanned all my available memory records for this month and even the upcoming months and there's no trace of her." He shook his head and looked off into the darkness. "Heh. Don't know what the hell the plan is if I did find her except just look at her some more. Once more even. I don't know. Ask her every question I could think of, you know. Spend just a little more time with her."

Welly exhaled slowly through his nose. "I understand. Sometimes we just know that more than anything else in the world we just want to spend a little more time with someone."

Kyle thought and then nodded. He said, "I *was* doing Frummy. You weren't wrong. I did it for a few months. I'll never touch the stuff again. I promise."

Welly nodded. "Okay. Good enough." He patted Kyle's shoulder much like Lemus had patted his, fifteen minutes earlier. "I know I'm a broken record and I know you don't know what the hell a record is, but I'm proud of you son. You're my greatest invention."

Kyle smiled. "You totally stole that line from Data's Dad in The Goonies."

"Doesn't mean it's not true," Welly said. "Let's get to the camp and get you in front of a fire."

They started padding back down the path, heading in the direction of the fluttering twinkles of campfire and muffled howls of the men.

"By the way, son. What did you do with the life vessel?"

"I buried it deep in the woods. It's under leaves and branches and it's in the middle of nowhere. We're good."

51

Manhattan, New York

December 16, 1776

Walton strode up to the corner Tavern with the stride only a man of great means could afford. Moreover, perhaps a stride only of a man currently palming something that would forever change the course of the world.

He was alone.

Livingston was assigned to wall watching duty in their tiny, ten pence a day, flat. He would have to report back on how many cracks were in the plaster of the second story two bedroom the two men shared. Walton must be alone. Livingston was too intimidating. He made people nervous. He enjoyed hurting people so bloody much and perhaps the other humans sensed it. Sensed it like animals sensed a storm approaching. Like rats.

The Manhattan roads were dotted with fire lights tangoing shyly in the dark night. Great torches flanked the entranceway and lit up the etched sign on the tavern that read, *Fraunce's*.

The great British General William Howe wasn't too difficult for anyone to find. Since he had called battle campaigning off for the winter, he was a man about town, having his fill of fine food and drink and lass.

Tonight he had Fraunces Tavern all too himself and his guest. The same tavern at which Washington *would* have made a farewell speech years later if savory, calculated destiny not been minutes away from intervening.

The restaurant was elegant, dimly-lit by aid of flickering candles encapsulated in table sconces. Polished floor. Shiny wooden table tops.

Toward the back of the room past the small bar on the right, two men were enjoying a meal in the corner. The table was nestled in beside an active fireplace. Walton's view was obscured by the red columns otherwise known as British soldiers, lined up like toys every three feet or so, a few tablespaces in front of the general.

Walton quickly surveyed the scene and marched with purpose directly toward the soldiers. The soldier on one end stepped forward and intercepted him. "Halt. His excellency, General Howe must not be disturbed," the soldier said.

Walton took in a deep, impatient breath. He said, "Tis urgent and he *must* be disturbed."

A blended look of puzzlement and disgust entered the soldier's face. "Oh?" he said.

"Inform him," Walton said. "The man with the Bunker Hill death toll is here."

The soldier offered his custom blend look once more and said, "Bunker Hill?"

He glanced over at the other soldiers. They offered no answers with their eyes. He looked back at Walton's unflinching white blue eyes. He looked Walton up and down and studied him for a moment more. He spun and marched over to Howe's table and began talking in a hushed voice.

Walton knew the message was successfully delivered when he viewed Howe's jaw suddenly cease chewing the gristly meat he was feasting upon. Howe looked curiously around his soldier and landed his gaze on Walton. He eyed him up and down. He began chewing again and looked up at his soldier. He nodded. The soldier turned and marched back to Walton.

"You may go," the soldier said.

Walton stepped forward on the wood floor. Every step reverberated so much noise in the open room. No music. No chatter. Walton's boots clapped on the wood floor and the two men dining stared openly at his approach.

Getting closer to the table he saw a few papers scattered about. One of the papers was a map. It was a working dinner no doubt. He eyed the man accompanying Howe. He had slightly rounded cheeks and graying hair. He looked a bit disheveled, under-rested perhaps.

Walton stepped to the edge of their table, as close as a waiter taking an order. "General," he said with a bow of his head.

Howe nodded solemnly.

Walton looked at the other man.

The other man offered, "Lee. Charles Lee."

"Ah. Of course," Walton said. "Presumably offering the great commander your advice on winning the war, are you?"

Lee raised his eyebrows and looked at Howe for support. Howe did not blink and cocked his head toward Walton.

Howe seemed to be just as history's research portrayed - a man reckoned sensible by silence. Though he was said to be so silent some did not quite know for sure. Nevertheless, he rose to the position of Commander-in-Chief of British forces during the American Revolution meaning, Walton knew, he was *the* man that could put a plan into motion.

"Your time is most valuable, General," Walton started. "It is my intention to be brief." Walton's hands were clasped in front of his pelvis, giving an ever-polite appearance. "Washington's rabble in arms is on their knees. The weakest thus far are they."

Howe's eyebrows raised and he tilted his head, gesturing across the table at Lee. The gentlest of smirks adjusted his thin lips and his large eyes became a little larger just for a moment.

"Indeed," Walton said. "Capturing Lee was a grand feat, but tis not enough. Washington will deliver a great and surprising blow to your army, reinvigorating the spirit of this cause. Tis a critical turning point that eventually leads to Britain's defeat and blemishes your great legacy, my lord."

The two men listened intently. Howe smiled. Lee looked at Howe and then smiled as well.

"Precisely, when and where might this *great and surprising blow* transpire?" Howe said.

Walton offered his own smirk and eyed the two leaders before him, furrowing each of their brows. He shook his head and said, "After my impossibly accurate prediction of Bunker Hill and still you believe not?"

Howe's jaw fell and clenched. His eyes darkened.

Walton said, "Forgive me, my lord. Why tell you when I can show you?" He unclasped his hands, revealing the white object, a slab, with dimensions akin to a single wall of a Tic Tac pack.

His hands were cupped like someone gathering rain drops. He dipped his thumb inside his palm and brushed the slab. A video beamed out directly in front of Walton's chest, set just large enough not to be visible from behind him. Walton checked the settings with his mind's eye, ensuring the picture was dim, illuminating the two men's faces only a slight bit more than the roaring fire behind them.

Both men gasped simultaneously and blinked multiple times to verify this impossible sight.

The reaction caused movement behind Walton. He sensed the soldiers approaching and knew he was about to be pummeled to the ground in a matter of seconds.

Howe raised his hands and the footfalls behind Walton ceased. He swatted at the air, brushing them back like flies, but not even looking in their direction. His gaze was still wholly fixed on the image in front of him. Walton surmised that a major battle could break out right there in Fraunce's and the great commander would remain paralyzed with curiosity as he was now.

The video started playing without volume. There were night time aerial drone shots of the Delaware river, icy in parts, snow covered on either bank. There was a timestamp displayed in the style of the day for Howe, on the upper right hand side of the beaming video - 26 December 1776. Underneath that displayed the words, *Wee Hours.*

The video panned in on the shore where there was great activity. Men were loading into flat boats and shoving off into the icy waters in the dark. Their faces looked a bit ghostly with the assistance of the night vision. A close-up shot of Henry Knox bellowing at the men. A shot of dozens of boats crossing. A quick zip down river at Washington himself crossing in a Durham boat.

Howe and Lee's heads jerked with the motion as if they were strapped to the drone as it flew over the river when gathering the footage. Their blinks were hurried as to not miss a second of this magnificent spectacle.

Washington was perched up, surveying the river ahead of him. He was flanked on one side by an African American Patriot named Prince Whipple, and on the other side, by a younger, pale-faced soldier - the would-be future U.S. president James Monroe, who held a flag, fluttering frantically like the wing of an injured bird.

The flag, however, was not the Betsy Ross edition portrayed in the famous painting of 1851 by Emanuel Leutze. The flag in the video was the Grand Union flag. It featured the British

Union Jack in the upper left corner nestled by thirteen white and red stripes, symbolizing the thirteen colonies.

The video jumped to an overhead, sweeping view of the army marching through the darkened forest, small bonfires dotting the sides of the path. Daylight started to break through. Views of the quiet barracks at Trenton, snow falling and swirling.

Howe broke his trancelike gape to study Walton's face. Walton gestured him back down to the video. The rabble in arms on the video were charging in ravenously. They raided building after building.

Partially dressed, Hessian soldiers exited the first building and began running. They were gunned down quickly. A small group of British and Hessian soldiers deeper into the camp ran to organize and were flanked by a group of hundred Patriots charging at them. They dropped their weapons and surrendered.

Within moments on the video, the carnage was over and the damage done. The entire camp of British and Hessian soldiers were surrounded and the Patriots were jubilant.

The video quickly cut to Washington addressing his men with a speech so thoughtful and heartfelt it was felt through the viewing of this silent movie. The Patriot men's faces were alive with elation.

The final quick cut was to 26 December 1776, *Evening*. It was Colonel Johann Rall, leader of the Hessian forces encamped at Trenton. His lifeless body laid in the bed. His jacket is searched by a Patriot soldier and a sealed, un-opened note is removed. The Patriot breaks the seal and the note is read. The video captured is zoomed in and enhanced and the written words viewable.

Urgent.

Imminent and surprise attack on Trenton by the Patriots is real and certain. Information obtained direct from Patriot camp. Password of the night - Victory or Death.

Be warned.

Be ready.

The video ended. The two men stared blankly at Walton's chest for a few moments and then blinked clarity back into their eyes. Howe looked up at Walton.

Walton looked down at Howe over the slope of his own narrow nose. He said, "Not yet hath this occurred."

Howe cocked his head back and thought with a statuesque posture for a few long seconds and then spoke. "Tis must be thwarted at all costs."

Walton stared into the great commander's eyes, enjoying his newly earned and most deserving power before saying, "Indeed."

52

Pennsylvania

December 19, 1776

Food was still scarce at camp. Welly should have lost twenty pounds in the week and a half he had been encamped there, just like the other men. He did not. With those retained fat cells came guilt. His compatriots were good and decent folks many, and had a work ethic such as Welly found to be superhuman.

Welly was the beneficiary of his coveted nourishing strips and half a dozen trips by request to Washington's headquarters. Washington had been beyond ravenous for information. The man had an innate sense for where to find information and for the great value of it.

The situation was bleak for the soldiers and for the cause. No one understand that better than Washington.

Kyle was doing incredibly well. He was working hard and complaining none.

Welly complained much, but to himself. He was so cold his skin burned and so hungry for substantial food that his whole body would ache throughout the day, but he drew inspiration from his son and the other men.

There was just more than five days until Christmas and one of the most bold and crucial attacks in the recorded history of the world. Though history *here* was still recording. These events that were happening now were becoming the new history. The history being manipulated by Walton, and undone by Welly and Kyle to the best of their abilities, slid over previously recorded events like a fresh coat of paint. The exact color and design of that paint yet to be determined.

Welly reflected it was only one month prior to this day at Fort Washington that Colonel Magaw was forced to surrender by General Howe. Twenty eight hundred thirty seven Patriots forced to lay down their arms and Welly now knew that the smug, little Walton watched on, surely grinning. He could feel his presence shrouding the pages as he read through much of his newly stored revised history. Yes, Walton was right there with Cornwallis and behind those four thousand Hessian troops as they began their attack on Fort Washington.

It was just too damned cold to think straight, let alone sleep. Everything wet and waterlogged. The canvas tent was a paper house to Welly. It let all of the cold in but somehow seemed to block all of the stink from seeping out. Another night laying in the otherwise unpolluted air next to a soldier named Franklin, Franklin the flatulent. Franklin snored away rhythmically.

Kyle was in the tent right next door, sharing with an amiable forty four year old man named Stephen from Hampden, Massachusetts. Stephen fought in the French and Indian War in his twenties. He had traveled and met up with this regiment during the Siege of Boston back in March and had been with them since.

Welly was getting used to sleeping with his secondary uniform shirt blanketed over his face, crudely acting as an air filter. Welly found his sense of humor waning and that was a bad sign for him. The mind can get you through most anything, but it needs to stay strong and it needs to whisk you away from the body at times.

Lemus was in a tent a few rows over. Welly and Kyle talked with him over breakfast and dinner, but during the day all were busy carrying out their assigned duties.

Welly stared into the darkness of the tent, still smelling the pungent odor of sweet rotting cabbage penetrating his shirt filter. He rolled on his side and shuffled his body an inch or two closer to the open flap of the tent. He stared out the partially open flap. A small light twinkled outside. His eyes barely peeked over the shirt covering his face. He felt like an old west bank robber.

No banks to rob yet, he thought and snickered gently to himself. *It'll be about fifteen years before the first bank opens its doors.*

He debated internally if he could hold it in or if he would have to get up and pee before trying to get back to sleep. It was inevitable and he knew it.

He rolled one more rotation onto his stomach and did a pushup. He winced and got his knees up and underneath him. From this dog stance, he lifted his right leg out and placed his foot on the floor. Before he had too much time to think and lock up, he pushed on his right foot and popped up and forward through the tent's flap.

Not too bad, he thought.

Outside the tent, the night air was crisp and completely still. It was dark, but not pitch black. He saw a fire light flickering, dancing among the rows of tents. Something about this light was calling him, summoning. A thought flashed by - perhaps it wasn't his blatter that motivated him to flop onto his belly and start the pushup process to stand up. Could it have been the beckoning firelight?

He walked toward the source of the light like a curious animal. As he crept closer he heard scratching. It was faint, but it was there. He padded gingerly on the solid ground, cloth tied around his feet for warmth. Beneath the cloth were blisters and he grimaced slightly with every step.

As he grew closer to the source of the light, he was drawn even stronger to it, alluringly, like a moth to light. He felt a slight temperature variation and sensed he was close. His view was obstructed by a tent. He stepped one foot over to his right and saw a man sitting before a fire.

He looked at him for a moment, feeling a familiarity he could not place. Feeling a little foolish for creeping around, he took a few more steps. He was within a few feet of the man and discovered the source of the scratching. The man was writing. So enthralled in his writing, in fact, he did not seem to notice Welly standing only a few feet behind him.

Welly saw the candle resting atop a marching drum in front of the man. The warm wax of the candle dripped down onto the drum head and glimmered only for a moment before the cold did its job, dulling and hardening it. They were tears of a musician beating a drum for the final time. Perhaps tears from the animal whose skin was used to stretch over the wooden base of the drum. Maybe they were the unseen tears Welly had shed every day in Kyle's absence. Possibly the tears of the scribbling man before him or those from George Washington, feeling the weight of this whole great cause collapsing on top of him.

It was a snapshot. An image burned into Welly the way the embers in that fire would burn into char and infuse with the ground and become one. Welly instantly knew he would never forget that silhouette of this man with his back to him, fire glinting just over the man's shoulder, snare drum, candle, wax with the tears of the world.

The man scribbled eagerly on parchment beneath the flicker of the melting flame.

Curiosity grabbed Welly, rattled him from his mental photograph. What would a soldier be so feverishly writing on such a bitter cold night? What could be so important? Then he had a sudden thought that perhaps the letter could be treacherous and he may have stumbled onto something that he should not have seen. A brief surge of panic raced through his body. He froze not knowing if he should go back or greet the mysterious scribbler.

He decided to take a half-step more and rise up on his blister covered toes attempting to sneak a peek at the man's paper.

The writer was so entranced in thought that he seemed not to have a care or clue of the presence of anyone around him. Welly took in as small and quiet a breath as possible and peered over the man's shoulder. He could make out the first few lines. He read them and a second later processed them. He placed that curious feeling of familiarity at once and chills scurried down his spine. He read the first line on the man's parchment.

These are the times that try men's souls.

The hairs on his arms stood at attention as he read on.

The summer soldier and the sunshine patriot will, in this crisis, shrink from the service of their country; but he that stands by it now, deserves the love and thanks of man and woman. Tyranny, like hell, is not easily conquered; yet we have this consolation with us, that the harder the conflict, the more glorious the triumph.

He felt these words resonating *in* him, in his core. The sentiment possessed a new and deeper meaning.

The lower part of the parchment was blocked, but he now knew undoubtedly, the man was Thomas Paine and he was penning a great work, *American Crisis*, working it out right there before his eyes.

Welly was filled with all-consuming pride and amazement and pure wonder. His eyes liquefied uncontrollably. There was also a sense of accomplishment knowing he helped this along, helped oil the great machine of history as it were. He had a passing thought that the great Thomas Paine would turn and see him weeping and he might throw the whole work into a tailspin and harm the course of history forever. He was struck with panic again.

The magnetic current that delivered him to this fire now felt like a repellent and the urge to urinate revealed its bloated face again.

He stepped back trying to be quiet. Every scrape of the cloth on the ground seemed amplified by a megaphone, but nothing seemed to distract the focused writer. After a few more reverse steps, he was back within the rows of tents heading for the trench.

After that, it was back to his piece of hard earth to try and get some sleep.

53

December 20, 1776

Welly woke with a spring in his eyelids. The sun shone through the thin fabric of the tent, but Welly only saw the scrambled and chaotic events behind his waking eyes.

December 26th, the great thwarting of the Patriot sneak attack. After weeks of thorough planning and much secrecy, the first of Washington's soldiers to board the flat boats to attempt the crossing of the icy Delaware River waters, were met with cannon fire from the opposite bank. A great wall of 10,000 British and Hessian forces had been established in the night on the New Jersey side of the Delaware. The Patriots shouted back to their comrades to warn them as their boats were struck and sunk. Washington's army retreated, this time deeper into Pennsylvania.

Welly blinked. Amazingly, he read the new account of altered events and knew it immediately to be a mod, but he also remembered first hand. He remembered the retreat. The mad scramble to disassemble the camp and load wagons with supplies and then marching briskly on into the peeking daylight and then bright day, feeling like a hunted rabbit. He remembered more.

No!

It was vivid.

The surrender. The capture of Washington. The unraveling cause.

Those nights on that rat infested ship.

Rat infested ship?

Welly could smell the putrefied, rotting corpses in his memory. The odor choked him. He felt the greedy tickle of the rats climbing on his ankles, nibbling at the exposed flesh on his leg.

Begging for death. That's right. Begging to be taken. Just take me already, but my immune system is too damn advanced to go briskly and then. Then. Finally.

Black.

But I'm still here. How is the war lost and I die on a prison ship and I'm still here? Impossible!

That word impossible triggered, as it had several other times, a flash to his ET friend imparting to him that *anything was possible.*

Suddenly his head throbbed. It throbbed in slow waving intervals. Each wave crashing down forcefully on his forehead.

Concentrate.

He sensed if he might get out past the breakers pounding his brain, there was something out there. Something missing. Something important. Something he needed to know.

A thought arrived. It shot into his brain as if from a great cannon and the notion was as heavy as a forty-two-pound cannon ball.

It hasn't happened yet.

That's it!

Only this can explain how I'm even still here to think these thoughts. Technically, scientifically, mathematically, it has not happened yet! We are not captured - yet. I am not on a rat infested ship - yet. I am still alive. Somehow.

Welly sprang up without thought of his back and did not feel the pain.

Holy shit.
The plan has to change. I have to speak to Washington.

54

Brunswick, New Jersey

December 22, 1776

Dawn

The new British and Hessian plans were mostly set. General Howe had done much of the heavy lifting with some input from the Hessian Colonel Johann Rall who was to be intimately involved with the attack. Eighty five hundred British and Hessian soldiers were scheduled to start their march from Brunswick to Trenton tomorrow morning, the twenty third. They would arrive at Trenton tomorrow evening and work with the fifteen hundred Hessians presently encamped there, to finalize preparations for the attack.

Last night after a fine meal, Walton met with and showed Howe the new version of the future video captured as a result of the new reality they constructed only on paper thus far. For the first, in the few moments leading up to the premiere of the footage not yet captured, Walton saw a child-like glee buried in Howe's steady eyes. He also noticed a hint of addiction tangled up with petulance and a smattering of desperation that he relished.

Walton had grinned wide and conspiratorially as he activated the images.

The drone cameras that captured the footage were small synthetic birds and bats and dragonflies. Some cameras preprogrammed, some programmed to follow certain unique images such as the one of a kind face of General Washington. The proper safe distance to record the footage was also preprogrammed, using the advanced, superior technology of Walton's time.

Howe had watched on with prodigious delight.

The two men had then toasted following Washington's capture and the night that followed was filled with glass and lass and debauchery which Walton relished even more.

Walton woke up momentarily excited, knowing he was scheduled for similar activities once this damned headache dissipated. He was in a tiny room at the end of a long hall in Howe's large and elegant Brunswick based headquarters. Next to Walton was a nude woman whose name he could not recall with this headache intensifying by the second. The auburn-haired young woman's bare breasts were both visible just outside of the reach of the comforter; one resting atop the other like scoops of ice cream.

Walton smirked.

The invisible hammer went to work on his brain again. He clutched his forehead. Ran a hand through his black, unkempt hair, flattening it a bit. He stood with purpose and drew the shades completely together thoughtfully, so to not let even a sliver of the evil daylight from raping into his room.

The headache intensified. Nausea arrived. He dropped to his knees to beg for forgiveness and vapidly promise to never consume alcohol again.

He clenched his eyes closed tightly.

The nausea strengthened, but vomit never came. Suddenly he opened his eyes and he was staring at wooden floor planks. A memory occurred to him. An impossible memory.

He remembered standing at the bank of the Delaware River eagerly awaiting the firsthand viewing of the new and virtuous history about to be created. Yes, he was about to watch history mould into its true and proper form. He remembered waiting for it and waiting longer, and assuring Cornwallis and then reassuring him. Then he was trying to explain to Howe, but Howe's admiration and adulation abandoned his eyes and were replaced by fury and disgust.

No!

No!

There had been a mod.

The rebels surprise attack on Trenton took place on January 1, 1777.

No!

Walton scanned through dozens of articles and documents.

Washington's brilliant and out-witting strategy marked as a turning point in the American Revolution.

He staggered to his feet and to the door. He opened it and dragged the heavy door closed behind him.

The nude woman turned over onto her other side, taking her scoops with her.

Walton walked, drunken with skull pain and torment, down the hall toward Howe's room.

He passed the door to Livingston's quarters. He would update him later. The big man had been even more withdrawn and quiet lately, spending most of his time in that little room alone. Walton never knew him to enjoy socializing in groups or one on one for that matter, but here, he'd been a hermit. Aside from pushups and situps, Walton wondered what in bloody hell he did to pass the time. Perhaps it was better he did not know.

With every step down the long corridor, Walton felt the new, *new* reality refine. The old crumbled and the dust blew off, revealing the new events, polished and glinting like glass. There was no doubt. It was fixed and certain.

He located the letter from Washington to Joseph Reed that confirms the date of the attack.

Camp above Trenton Falls, 23 December, 1776

Dear Sir,

The bearer is sent down to know whether your plan was attempted last night, and if not, to inform you, that New Year's Eve at night, one hour before day, is the time fixed upon for our attempt on Trenton. For Heaven's sake keep this to yourself, as the discovery of it may prove fatal to us, our numbers, sorry I am to say, being less than I had any conception of - but necessity, dire necessity, will, nay must, justify any attempt. Prepare, and, in concert with Griffin, attack as many of their posts as you possibly can with a prospect of success; the more we can attack at the same instant, the more confusion we shall spread, and greater good will result from it.

He would project it for the General.

He felt certain too that there was new drone footage already present in his slab. If so, he could show him drone footage from the upcoming, uneventful Christmas night that he was yet to coordinate and record, but knew he must and knew he *had*, if it was present in the slab's memory.

His mind was scrabbled. Everything was in disarray.

Howe would understand.

The plan *must* change.

55

Trenton, New Jersey

December 25, 1776

4:50 P.M.

Colonel Johann Rall, commander of the Hessian troops at Trenton sat at the table with his half drunk beer and re-read the letter from James Grant. Grant, who had been appointed command of the protective British and Hessian outposts dotted throughout New Jersey, was senior in rank to Rall.

The letter was dated 24 December and had just arrived from Brunswick.

Rall squinted down at the letter, fixing on those scratchy words he understood best.

Rebels - plan - attack.

He grabbed his beer and gulped down the remainder. He placed it back on the table. His eyes drifted down to that one line again.

Be on guard.

He looked out beyond the paned window at the freezing rain. The nor'easter out there seemed to be strengthening. He scoffed and tossed the letter on the table. He stood and walked over to the window for a better view.

Looking up, he saw the patches of icy rain being yanked harshly one way and then the other. The precipitation swirled and splashed on the glass in spurts.

Rall shook his head and then paused suddenly, listening.

It was a loud banging and then stomping footfalls.

One of his young soldiers was there, dripping all over the floorboards beside the table.

"The Rebels," the young soldier said, trying to catch his breath. "Colonel, sir," the young man gulped in a large breath. "The Rebels are attacking our guard on Pennington Road."

Rall grabbed his blue coat hung on a hook by the fire and followed the young soldier out of the house.

56

Upper Makefield Township, Pennsylvania

December 25, 1776

Dusk

The weather on this side of the Delaware River in Pennsylvania had been relatively cooperative most of the day. Now the whipping wind was flinging tiny pellets of frozen rain. But it was Christmas.

It was supposed to be cold and inclement, Welly thought. *Always had been on this particular Christmas night.*

Welly intensely thought about a lot of different topics over the last twelve hours following the morning mod. He implemented his mental training to deflect his thoughts far, far away from the thought he could not think. It was mission critical. No such thought can seep until the exact moment when it must pour. That time was soon approaching.

Welly and Kyle padded on the wet ground. They were fine gentlemen in their newly minted uniforms. The uniforms supplied by the great general himself, complete with strong navy jackets, gold buttons lining the breasts, clean ivory pants and shirts, black knee-high boots, black triangle hats. It felt good to be official. It felt better to be in clean clothes. Even the persistent flicks of rain felt kind of nice. Barring a warm shower, this was the closest to refreshed Welly had been in some time.

A gust of wind came on and Welly felt his hat lifting from his head, attempting to take flight. He grabbed the point of the brim and pulled it down.

They marched on in the darkness silently. Welly was quiet, focusing on the temperature drop that would occur shortly, focusing on the details of the New Year's Eve attack which was carefully constructed by Washington and his generals. Another welcomed thought suddenly occurred to Welly.

"Hey. Merry Christmas, Kyle," he said. He looked at his son and could scarcely make out his silhouette in pitch blackness.

"Thanks Pop. Merry Christmas."

"I can't believe I've forgotten to tell you that."

Kyle looked at his dad and didn't reply.

Welly could not be certain, but he could swear he somehow heard Kyle's eyebrows raise at this remark and the gentle swish of his eyes rolling.

"Are you okay?" Kyle said. "I mean the last few days you've been so." He paused to think. "So present. So in the right now. And it's been oak."

Welly could have done without the modern day slang, but the sentiment was right on.

"I know," Welly said. "I know. A lot on my mind. If we can get through all of this and successfully carry out the attack next week, I think I'll be able to get us home and relax my mind. Everything will pale in comparison to this son."

A silence fell between them.

Kyle said, "Yeah. I hope so, Pop."

Damn. Welly thought.

He knew he had earned that statement from his son. He never wanted that. He promised himself he would never let his best buddy down from the time when Kyle fit in the crook of his arm. He stopped walking. Kyle stopped walking as well.

He needed firm footing to deliver his thoughts. "Kyle, I know I've earned that. My priorities have been out of whack. I've justified it for years under the guise of saving the world or pushing it forward, partially because selfishly I needed a distraction. It's been so hard for me to look my life in the eyes. Now I know. This journey reminded me of what's important."

A gust of wind tore through them. Slushy, frozen rain pelted their faces.

He turned fully to his son now. "When we get back, things will be much different. I promise."

Kyle nodded and looked down.

"I know," Welly said. "You have good reason not to believe. I will get us back. In more ways than one. I will get *us* back."

Kyle remained fixed on the ground and nodded.

Welly gently shook his son's shoulders and said, "Okay, let's keep moving. Listen for moving water, a creek. We have to follow Jericho creek all the way up to Washington's quarters."

Kyle nodded. He said, "It's weird that he wanted us there for this Christmas party, but didn't send some guys on horses or something to get us."

Welly didn't reply.

They marched on in silence.

57

Brunswick, New Jersey

Walton remained in Howe's headquarters cordoned off in the room in the far end with the double scoop lass. In the den below, Howe sat stoically before the fire, deep in reflective thought.

Ambrose Serle entered noisily hoping to attract the attention of his lordship, but with no such luck. He adjusted his tiny neck tie and flipped aside the long curled locks of brown hair that cascaded down his forehead and tickled his brows.

Howe sat majestically, entranced in thought. Serle cleared his throat with purpose. Howe looked over lazily at Serle and nodded.

Serle said, "My lord, a rider dispatched a letter regarding the rabble across the river. Shall I?"

Howe dipped his head slightly, indicating an order for Serle to read the letter.

Serle read, "*An hour ago was I in attendance of a party at the headquarters of George Washington. Plentiful food, drink and dancing abound. Plans erected for attack on 31 Dec. Pass code for the night tis liberty. Long live the King. A. Fine Tory.*"

Serle looked up at Howe and said, "It appears as though your information is accurate, my lord. No attack appears imminent."

Howe dipped his head slightly once more, dismissing Serle.

"My lord," Serle said and turned to exit the room.

As he got to the door, it swung open and Walton was there. He was wide eyed and disheveled. His clothes were wrinkled and skewed.

Serle raised his eyebrows and looked Walton up and down.

Howe stared into the fire. His belly full. His eyelids heavy.

Walton shook his head and barreled past Serle, bumping him out of place.

"My lord," Walton said loudly.

Howe's eyes opened wide and he stared at Walton perplexedly. He blinked and examined the disheveled subject before him. He said nothing.

Walton said, "I've had a mod. What I meant, is there has been, um, yet another modification to events."

Howe lifted his head further back still and looked at Serle over Walton's shoulders. Serle stood neatly with his arms behind his back, eyebrows raised.

"They attack tonight," Walton said. "The rebels attack *tonight!* As they always have. Something changed. We must act *right now.*"

Howe tilted his head slightly, indicating to Serle.

Serle cleared his throat and said, "Francis, you've been most helpful with your." He paused briefly, considering his words. "Witchcraft," he said finally. "You forewarned the attack twenty six December and then, it appears, accurately predicted the amendment to this plan. The rabble movement commencing thirty one December. I am in possession of a letter penned not more than a few hours ago, dispatched to me directly with great haste from George Washington's headquarters, clearly indicating the rebel attack still remains as scheduled, thirty one December."

"It's a ruse," Walton said, almost shouting. "I *know* what now happens."

Serle raised his eyebrows. Walton spun to look at Howe. His expression was stone. He eyed Walton up and down and then turned his head back to the fire.

"Bloody arrogance," Walton whispered. "I haven't the time."

He turned and brushed past Serle again. He opened the door and said in his wake, "I'm borrowing a horse." He yelled, "Livingston. We're departing. Now. Let's go!"

Serle shook his head slightly and said, "My lord."

Serle bowed his head. He left the room and closed the door behind him.

Howe stared into the flames.

58

Keith House

Upper Makefield Township, Pennsylvania

Welly and Kyle ambled up the three slate steps and walked up to the great white door flanked with two etched white columns. The entrance appeared as a whimsical version of the gates of heaven, but this night Welly felt he was entering something closer to a black chasm. It was a displaced feeling, a feeling like everything was just plain wrong - because it *was* wrong.

Welly raised his hand to knock and the door opened, filling the outside air with the gentle sweet hum of a violin. The sound brushed back and forth riding out on the warm breeze from within the house.

Billy Lee nodded and smiled and gestured for them to walk down the short corridor. They stepped inside, shook off their clothes and removed their sopping wet hats. Billy Lee guided them into a grand den and they nodded their thanks. The melody grew louder as they entered.

The room was large and polished. Long tassel curtains. Wainscot walls. The furniture and rug were removed, leaving the center of the room open and bare.

Welly and Kyle were directed to an open spot along the wall as they entered. They bowed to the guests beside them.

Washington was across the room pollinating his guests with charm and injecting them with smiles. He bowed at each new person he approached, bringing him closer to their heights momentarily. Though there were two dozen people in the room, George remained the tallest of the lot.

He wore a long three quarters black dress coat and white neck tie that reminded Welly of a garter. His ivory leggings squeezed his thick calves tightly.

A plump young lady with hay colored hair, a pretty face and eyes blue enough to be unmistaken from far across the room, stood with hands clasped beside her mother and father. Her dress was long, the color of cream and formal with tufted shoulders. She wore white gloves that stretched up to her elbow. Washington stepped over to her and bowed. She curtsied. He said something to her and she extended her left hand. He took her hand gently with his right hand, his, white gloved as well.

They spun gracefully and then walked side by side to the center of the room still holding hands, raising them as they did so. Arriving at their destination, they broke off and faced one another. They ceremoniously walked past and around one another. Posture and form was magnificent. Welly marveled at the majesty and relished the attention to detail - the care. In his day, etiquette was a red diamond and most were perfectly okay with that. Most. Not Welly.

George and his dance partner twirled independently of one another and soon others were on the dance floor as well, gracefully weaving in and out of one another, twirling, bowing. This choreography takes forever in the future, but Welly knew this was simply behavior that was expected of those of this time so no direction was even necessary.

Washington made his way off the floor and greeted Welly and Kyle with a bow. He looked thoughtfully into both of their eyes. "I hope you are enjoying yourselves," he said.

Welly leaned into the general and said just loud enough for him and Kyle to hear. "General," he said and glanced at Kyle regretfully. "We have an emergency."

Kyle's brow furrowed.

Washington's white hair only lifted slightly and he indicated to the hall with his gloved hands. He bowed at the guests by the hall entrance and followed Welly and Kyle. They hadn't a clue where they were going, but banged a left and found a door. Welly opened it. The trio entered.

Washington's cordial expression washed away immediately as he closed the door behind him. A grave seriousness replaced it. "What has been discovered?" he said.

"The enemy knows our plan has changed. Their plans have changed likewise. We will have one chance to issue this all important surreptitious blow. Tonight. Right now."

Kyle issued his own blow. He huffed his disappointment into the air of the study in which they found themselves.

Welly had no choice but to withhold this from his son. He withheld it even from his own thoughts to be certain it was not put into motion or spilled into the ether where it could have been uncovered. Hopefully, it was not.

Washington gazed around the room for a moment, digesting the thought. "I knew it would be this night," he said finally. "A strong feeling seized me prior to the arrival of my guests. This night is written in the stars. Gentlemen," he said. He grabbed a shoulder of each man and looked into their eyes, one set at a time. "Victory or death."

59

Trenton, New Jersey

Walton and Livingston marched down the road from the small frame house that was Johann Rall's temporary quarters. The woman there said the Hessian commander was in attendance at a Christmas gathering down the lane and she had pointed out the house before closing the door and locking it behind her.

The hardened dirt road was blanketed with a thin sheet of accumulated ice crystals. The wind gusted and the two men crunched without speaking. The closer they got to the fingered house, the louder the chorus of singing grew. Male voices belted out something in German and loud enough to be heard from thirty yards in the midst of a nor'easter.

Two Hessian guards stood in front of the house in question. They watched the only other two men out in the nasty storm as they approached.

The single lantern sconce that hung beside the home's door contained a single candle and provided the only light. The guards were silhouettes with their backs to the weak flickering light, their faces appearing sculpted with cigar ash.

"Gentlemen," Walton said amiably and smiled.

His left hand darted out and upward. His glowing pointer finger flashed, leaving a trail of light hanging in its path. He pressed it against the young guard's neck. The guard opened his mouth as if to speak and then dropped to his knees, his face suspended with the animation. Walton stepped aside to let him fall without crashing into him. He flopped face down in the icy crust.

The other guard tried to process this three second sequence as Livingston casually raised his own glowing pointer finger and pressed it to his neck. The guard's eyes rolled back and he fell to his left, thudding onto the ground.

Livingston stepped up the three steps and pulled on the iron handle opening the door for Walton. Just off the small entrance area was an entryway to a living room area where a group of men, gripping elaborately detailed steins and silver mugs, were huddled together concluding their song with great hardiness. Johann Rall was in the center of the huddle.

He shouted, "Prost," at the conclusion of the song. He and the men raised their mugs high before drinking.

A young man with parted, neatly combed hair strode over to greet the two dripping strangers at the doorway to the room.

Walton assumed that it was Rall's servant.

The melted ice drops beaded on Livingston's short hair. Walton's soaked black hair was flat and stuck to his forehead in clumped pointy bunches like stalactites.

The man with neatly combed hair said, "Good eve," before Livingston flung him aside with great force. The man tumbled into a small round table in the corner of the room before hitting the floor.

The clatter gave pause to the men who looked at the two strangers with sober intensity.

Walton glared at Livingston before saying, "Halt." He raised his hands to buy a few seconds. "I come bearing orders from his excellency, General William Howe."

The group stopped and looked at Rall for direction. Rall stepped forward.

Walton continued, "The Rebels are planning to attack tonight. They shall be on the march heading here over the Delaware River in a short while. We must stop them."

The man with neatly combed hair stood and brushed his clothes into place. He padded over to the group of Hessian men and positioned himself behind them.

Rall said, "Received letter," but it sounded like lezzer with his thick accent. "Small skirmish. Pennington Road," he said and waved at the air. "Nought," he said. "The rebels not attack this," he paused to search for the word. "Weather," he said finally.

Walton thought and said, "Sneak attack *Schleichen attacke.*"

Rall laughed and the group of men followed in kind, laughing heartily.

Livingston stepped forward aggressively. Five Hessians stepped forward to meet him. Walton grabbed Livingston's arm.

Rall said, "Schleichen attack, nay," he shook his head. "Christmas," he said and smiled. He raised his stein and his eyebrows. "Happy Christmas," he said to Walton.

With that, the group of five Hessian men that had stepped moments earlier forward to receive Livingston, took another step forward to undoubtedly show the intruding strangers to the door. Time was up. Walton reached into his overcoat. He pulled out a neatly folded letter and tossed it to Rall. Rall caught it and stared down at it.

"Be sure to read that," Walton said as he stepped backward away from the encroaching men. "Else I shall see you perish in the fray," Walton shouted over the shoulders of the men.

Walton and Livingston spun and exited the house.

Rall placed the folded letter in his jacket pocket and raised his stein high once again. "Prost," he said loudly.

60

McConkey's Ferry, Pennsylvania

December 26th, 1776

12:30 A.M.

The scene at the side of the Delaware river was bedlam. Durham boats were loaded with cannon and with tired, obedient men, some with no shoes. The soldiers were incredibly quiet, following the orders of their officers. Officers wore a white piece of paper in their hat to help distinguish them from the others although visibility was quite poor.

The nor'easter was bearing down now with full might. Winds gusted. Snow and ice poured down and swirled angrily. The ground was covered in snow.

Kyle waited in line. He just could not take his eyes off of the freezing men silently loading others into the high sided flat boats and shoving them off into the blackness. They were machine-like, hungry, exhausted and seeming to be without a thought of slowing.

Sheets of ice, like panes from sliding glass doors, were plentiful in the river and collided with the boats as they floated on, creating a grading, cracking sound. The officers yelled at their men to remain quiet.

John Glover supervised the loading. He paced the hundred yards or so of river front real estate as the men loaded into the boats with their packs. Each carried pouches with rounds of ammo and food for a couple of days.

They climbed into the boats thirty to forty at a time - standing room only.

Washington had a force of only about twenty four hundred crossing here. But further up river, Washington knew he had Joseph Reed, John Sullivan and James Ewing with seven hundred militia to seize the bridge over the Assunpink Creek, blocking the retreat of the Hessians leaving Trenton. General John Cadwalalder with about nineteen hundred militia would flank the enemy after crossing up river as well. Welly and Kyle, with the advantage of hindsight, knew those crossings would be called off due to dangerous river conditions and Washington and his crew were on their own.

Kyle clutched her hair ribbon. He looked down at it poking out of his tightly closed, red, wet fist. That pale ivory ribbon was as vibrant a color as anything he could remember. He brought it to his nose and inhaled. It still smelled of wind-blown hair and was as fantastically fragrant as any smell from his childhood with the exception of mom's chocolate chip cookies baking after dinner.

Kyle looked left and saw horses being loaded into boats. He looked right and saw a cannon being loaded. The thick Henry Knox bellowed, "Stay with your officers! Move!"

Four men struggled with the cannon as they lifted it onto the boat.

Wind pummeled. Ice and snow pelted.

Suddenly Knox appeared and grabbed hold of the tilting rear of the cannon and the men heaved it into the boat.

"Another!" He boomed.

The men scrambled up to the shore and lifted another cannon in unison. Kyle stuffed the ribbon in his pants pocket and ran to the rear of the cannon to lend a hand. He grabbed hold of the soaked wood box that the cannon sat atop. He probably held about three pounds of it, but he was helping. They brought it to Knox waiting by the Durham boat and he provided the surge of strength needed to land it onto the boat. Kyle had a sneaking suspicion Knox could have lifted the cannon without the men, perhaps in one hand and held it over his head like a trophy, if he felt like it.

"In!" Knox yelled. The four cannon bearers and Kyle boarded the boat. Welly walked fast over to the boat and slumped himself over the side with Kyle's assistance. They were aboard with cannons.

The four other men took to the gigantic oars. They manned one each, two men standing on the left and two on the right. Kyle and Welly looked at one another, feeling uneasy, unsure what to do.

The water was extremely choppy. A large ice chunk slammed the side of the boat. The cannons slid.

Welly crouched up and made his way over to the cannon and grabbed hold of it. Kyle did the same.

Welly knew they may not be a match for a thousand pound cannon, but it sure beat feeling like freeloading assholes on a pleasure-filled gondola ride. They hugged those cannons, straddled them, leaned on them, shoved at them the whole way across. Anything to take their minds away from the numbing cold and the possibility of falling in that icy river.

Through the slanting, bombarding snowfall, they could see flames and then men gathered on the shore awaiting their arrival.

The rowing men made one final push with the oars and the boat slid into the ground, halting at the shore. A group of soldiers, swarmed the boat and started offloading the cannon. No one spoke a word.

Kyle and Welly climbed off the boat and made their way to the fire. Men stomped on parts of fences and twigs and threw it on top of the flames.

Welly felt like sticking his hands into the fire and browning them like marshmallows. It would have to feel better than the current throbbing sensation. He shivered all the way through. He folded his arms in and hunched. He tucked his neck and head in to shelter from the wind. He really was becoming a damn turtle.

Kyle looked more casual. Didn't seem as phased by the cold, standing there beside the flickering flame.

In one moment, the wind blew warm air from the fire their way, and at the next, it blasted it across the way toward the other men. It giveth and taketh.

Welly shivered bigly. Kyle reached his arm around his dad. He rubbed Welly's arm to provide him with some warming friction.

Welly would have smiled had his face not been frozen in place. He thought as we advance and progress and blanket ourselves with the latest technology, underneath it all, we are still just basic creatures. Animals. Animals that need love. Animals full of love to give.

It was over two hours until all the men arrived and gathered by the shore with Welly and Kyle and the others.

Washington appeared atop his horse, through the white cloud of swirling snow, and barked at the men, "Stay with your officers. For God's sake, stay by your officers!"

The men marched on without speaking. The darkness was dotted with small bonfires set by men up ahead. As they fell back in line they spoke three words in a hushed tone, "Victory or death."

Welly and Kyle droned on with the men. They lost themselves in the hypnotic repetition, placing one foot in front of the other and repeating.

Approximately halfway in their sloshy march to Trenton, Welly started to mimic the shushed sounds aloud, almost unconsciously.

"Poom. Poom. Poom. Psshh. Poom. Poom. Poom. Psshh. Poom. Poom. Poom. Psshh."

He continued on for a few minutes, imitating the sounds of the men's feet marching onward, loud enough only for Kyle to hear.

"Do you know what that is son?" he whispered to Kyle.

Kyle shook his head.

"That's the sound," Welly said. "Of America coming for your ass."

Kyle rubbed his hand over the hairs on the nape of his neck. He nodded in agreement.

They marched on for two and a half hours. Daylight began blending into the darkness. Black became deep royal purple and seemed to blue by the minute.

Sun was coming up. Visibility was low due to the swirling snow.

Washington continued riding beside his men toward the rear, keeping them focused. "Stay by your officers!" he commanded.

Another horse trotted up beside him, ridden by General Nathaniel Greene.

Greene leaned over and said to Washington, "Sir, many of the men's weapons are not in working order. Some wet. Some frozen."

Washington breathed in and looked out over the rows of marching men. This was a dark hour indeed for his army. With most of his enlistments set to expire in a few days at the turn of the year - the triumph of this attack was all the more crucial.

"Tell them to use the bayonets," Washington said.

"Yes sir," Greene said and yanked his reins to u-turn his horse.

61

Despite the relentless snow following and blinding them, Welly and Kyle both knew they were out of the woods now. Out of the shaded cover of flanking trees and close to civilization. In fact, when the snow broke for just a moment, Kyle could make out the silhouettes of rooftops of small buildings and then he heard it. Muffled mouse traps snapping. One after another.

Suddenly, men were yelling. The men marching directly in front of Welly and Kyle began to run, charging. All the men began to yell and run. Kyle and Welly were packed in and being pulled forward with the current, like two fish in the middle of a school.

"Stay close son," Welly said, jogging along as fast as his legs could carry him.

The snapping mouse traps grew louder into thunderbombs and then sounded more like dynamite blasts as the men around them fired their weapons. The wind was now graciously at their backs and whipping snow into the faces of the retreating Hessians as they volleyed fire intermittently and haphazardly between the row of small wooden buildings.

A burst of a dozen sprinting men barreled through Kyle and Welly heading toward the action. Kyle picked up the pace to keep up with them and to keep from being knocked to the ground. He ran. He ran fast and yelled along with the men.

Soon he was at the front of the pack and the strangest feeling swept over him. The feeling of oneness, fearlessness. The feelings were one and the same. All of this was bigger than he and worth fighting for; it was worth dying for and he was ready. He was ready to die *because* he was ready to die.

This certainty seemed to spackle over all the many cracks, heal over all wounds somehow. He felt the spirit of his mother with him. He felt Bobby's spirit with him. He felt the spirit of the love of his life that never would be. He felt the spirit of the men he ran beside. He was them. They him.

They were running into harm's way for him, for their sons and their daughters and their grandchildren and great grandchildren. Together they were lighting a torch. A torch that they would not carry, but pass on. The base of the torch, the victory of this war and the flame burning was *this*; this feeling, this American spirit.

Just up ahead, Hessian soldiers were spilling out of open doors on either side and attempting to congeal into something worthy of a counter attack against the on-rushing Patriots. One group finally formed. It was a mob of Hessian soldiers of forty or so. They charged toward Kyle and the charging Patriots. Kyle and a few others fired. Two of the Hessians fell and soon they were intertwined.

Three thoughts swept quickly through Kyle's mind.

These guys are big.

This could be it.

Live!

Welly ran as fast as he could. He slushed through, but could not keep up. He saw Kyle motoring off. The boy always could run like a weimaraner.

Welly got another thirty feet and then felt a vice-like tightening on his neck. His feet were lifting on the ground. His eyes filled with water. His vision blurred.

A loud boom erupted and seemed to echo for minutes.

Welly's light receptors dimmed and then turned off entirely.

Kyle looked down at his soaked musket and sharp edge of the bayonet. He fired at the group of enemy men without much thought, but stabbing someone? He grabbed the barrel of the gun and jumped aside as a Hessian charged at him. He swung his gun like a baseball bat and cracked the enemy upon the ear and side of his head. The Hessian thudded to the ground.

Kyle was admiring his work when a blood-thirsty Hessian provided him a two second warning with a battle cry sounding like a prehistoric carnivorous creature securing dinner. Kyle's grip on his weapon slipped and there was no time to swing at the man. Instinct grabbed the steering wheel and he flung himself onto the smashed, snow covered ground, flat. He threw his legs out and sent the enemy tumbling down beside him.

Kyle grabbed his weapon and sprang up. He gripped it with both hands and had the bayonet positioned like a sword to stab through the man who lay belly up holding his weapon on the ground. This was it. Moment of truth.

He looked down at the blood-thirsty animal and the animal was gone. What remained was a young man, not much older than Kyle. Fear coursed through the young man's green eyes. The young man heaved his weapon over his head onto the ground and lifted his arms up. Kyle halted. He looked behind him and all the remaining mob of Hessian soldiers had their hands up as well. This small battle was over. Kyle helped the young man to his feet to join his gathered compatriots and to be added to the prisoner tally.

Welly blinked back consciousness and his first thought was of the bitter cold slush on the back of his neck.

Damn cold! He thought and then he flashed back to when Kyle was little and they would bundle up in their snowsuits and go out to do their manly work - making snowballs and snow angels. No matter how bundled he was, when he laid on the ground to design his snow angel, inevitably some snow would sneak through to the back of his neck and it was damn cold.

The fuzzy image materializing above him was a man way up high. Must be hundreds if not thousands of feet up.

Heaven?

Upon a few more blinks it was clear the man was much closer and it was George Washington. He held a smoking flintlock pistol. The pistol's polished wood and silver etched trim, gleamed even through the constant snow.

Welly looked beside him and saw the large body and bloody face of Walton's henchman, John Livingston. He stared back up at Washington who only nodded, holstered his weapon and galloped off.

Welly clutched at his neck and rubbed it gently.

Kyle!

He crooked his head the opposite direction of the deceased Livingston and saw Kyle raising his bayonet above an enemy soldier. The enemy surrendered and got to his feet with Kyle's help.

Emerging from the snow behind Kyle was a shadow, a black figure. Between bouts of thick snow, Welly saw it was Walton. He went to roll over and jump up to run and be with his son, but the pain in his lower back ripped through him like a lion through flesh.

"Ehhh!" he cried out. "Kyle!"

Kyle heard something familiar carrying dully through the wind. "Kyyyy. Kyyyy." He spun in the wrong direction of the calling wind and was face to face with Francis Walton.

"A good morning to you, Kyle," Walton said casually, putting on an American accent.

Kyle's face was frozen with shock and fear. His heart thudded heavily both from the peak adrenaline of battle and terror, but the words came easy.

He shouted over the abusive wind and snow. "You thought you could change the outcome of the world by winning a battle. But you can't kill the spirit by killing the heartbeat. Win this battle. Go ahead. Kill everyone here. They will rise up later and kick the *shit* out of you. Every time."

Walton raised his eyebrows and gawked pityingly at the boy. "Fine profundity. You might have a future if you were not about to become part of history."

Walton raised his futuristic flintlock.

Kyle started in motion. He attempted to dodge. The weapon fired and entered the center mass of Kyle's white uniform shirt and exited through the back of his coat.

Walton's face took on a look of shock even more pronounced than Kyle's expression only seconds earlier. His body jerked and his face lifted as the bayonet stabbed through his heart.

The soldier behind him removed the bayonet and Walton tumbled to the ground. The soldier stepped forward and looked down at the gasping man, Walton. The soldier used the blade of the bayonet to slice Walton's throat. The blood ran down both sides of Walton's neck and his eyes remained open, fixed on the snowy sky eternally.

Welly lay on the floor wrestling with the pain. He grabbed the black pouch in his pants pocket, opened it, grabbed out a small translucent strip and popped it in his mouth without thinking. He closed his eyes tightly and gathered everything he could muster and rolled over. He hoisted himself to his feet with a loud grunt and ran toward the body of his only son.

62

The entrance to Jekyll and Hyde's NYC restaurant brought a tingling excitement to Kyle. The squared windows, nestled in the deeply stained wood along the front, glimmered like colorful mirrors filled with reflections of vanishing cars and pedestrians. He just couldn't wait to use the bathroom hidden behind the bookshelf.

Entering through the heavy wooden doors, the smell of roasting onions and garlic greeted the trio like old friends. The red table tops seemed to hover and the monsters on the wall all but jumped right off and hissed and howled. Kyle smiled nervously when he saw the skeleton in the suit and hat. The bubbly hostess girl pointed to a booth with the hand not holding the menus. Kyle quickly scooched into the maroon leather booth.

Climbing inside that booth meant so much. Being here to have this meal meant so much. Kyle grinned ear to ear as he perused the menu and salivated. He had a good feeling that Mom and Dad wouldn't deny him a tall glass of chocolate milk on this day. He couldn't explain why, but he just had a feeling - a thought that entered him and bounced around inside like a brightly glowing pinball.

This was going to be a good day.

The meals were devoured and Kyle was full, but the chocolate lava cake the waitress laid on the table was divinely decadent.

Welly grabbed up one of the three spoons and said in a silly voice, "Now who will be joining me in eating this fresh pile of p-"

Christine glared at Welly, cutting him off.

Kyle was mid-sip and started laughing hysterically. He laughed so hard that chocolate milk spilled out of his nose.

Christine handed Kyle a napkin and threw Welly a dirty look and a firm whack on his forearm. "There are so many things wrong with that, Well."

"What?" Welly said in poor defense of himself. He knew this might get Kyle giggling and he just scored himself a belly laugh. He said, "I always wondered how chocolate milk would taste mixed with boogers."

Kyle laughed.

Welly took a bite of the cake. He and Kyle locked eyes and thoughts. The two giggled. "Mmm," Welly said. "It really is quite delightful though." He started laughing again. Kyle started laughing again.

Christine shook her head. "My God," she said. "Help me out with these children."

Welly swallowed his bite of cake and raised his eyebrows to Christine. "Oh yeah," he said. "So how about now?"

"Now?" Christine said.

Kyle sensed the uneasiness enter his mother.

Christine said, "Okay, sure. Why not. It's as good a time as ever."

The voices were getting distant. They sounded like they were yelling down to him as he sat at the bottom of a hundred foot well. Echoed. Muffled.

"Son," Welly said. "We have something to tell you."

Kyle's eyes opened on a shimmery dark object with a piercing light above it that shown directly into his waking cornea. He squinted and focused. It was a shiny surface. He realized his sense of feel now and noted the ground was remarkably soft. He knew with impossible certainty he was in his bedroom in Brooklyn. It was restored to the way it had been, down to the mess of products atop his dresser like a sloppy city skyline complete with the rising sun from the large mirror reflection behind.

He felt something else. A heaviness was by his feet. Something was tightening the comforter down there. He shifted his weighted head and startled.

Welly sat at the foot of his bed, quietly staring, grinning.

"Jesus," Kyle said.

Welly looked at him to remind him of the lord's name and then said, "Hey son."

"Pop! You're here. *I'm* here. At *home*." Kyle blinked and tried to focus his eyes. He shook his head. He was scrambled. He said, "Last thing I remember. I remember Walton. He pulled the trigger. I tried to jump, but he pulled the trigger."

He flipped the covers up and grabbed at his chest, here and there, feeling around like a doctor with a stethoscope.

Welly raised his hand and said, "I ran over and all I could think was how I just wanted. I only just wanted a little of the one thing I couldn't have. Time. I said I'd do anything just to make the things you wanted in your short life be true. I could do that. I *could* have done that. It wasn't asking too much. You were worth it. All of it. No matter how small or big. No matter the historical consequences. All of it and more I would have told you. You're my best buddy. You're my best buddy in the whole world, I would have told you."

Welly gulped and continued. "Then it hit me. If I can get to the vessel I could get back and I could change this. But as I got closer to you all the thoughts vanished like smoke being sucked through a fan. You weren't there. You were over *there*. You were on the ground. You were naked and laying on the snow. Your uniform, all your clothes were balled up next to you. Pants, shirt, underwear, socks, shoes, everything. Some of the men helped me carry you into a house."

"Wait," Kyle said. "So everyone saw my junk, Pop?"

Welly laughed. "I'm afraid so, son. So we wrapped you up in blankets. I had my healer in the pouch I brought. You know the one-"

"The one I bought you at my school fair in third grade," Kyle said.

"One and the same. I actually took some ibuprofen when I was stuck in pain on the ground in Trenton."

Kyle said, "And you lived to tell about it."

Welly said, "So I got the healer out to apply to your wound, but there was none."

Kyle lifted his shirt and felt his chest.

"It's been almost three days son, that you've been out. I've been feeding you macrobiotic strips, keeping you nourished."

"Thanks," Kyle said. "I appreciate that."

Kyle's mind was speed racing. Faces and names whizzed by at full tilt. He pit-stopped on Stewart, Head of Janitorial at the Forward Facility.

"Stewart!" he blurted. "What about Stewart? We left him with those zoot suit guys."

"He's fine. They knocked him out with a Crystalline Luma." He held up his index finger for Kyle and made it glow on and then off.

Kyle said, "Good, good." He rubbed his temples with both hands. "Damn I have a monster headache"

"Ibuprofen strip?" Welly said and smiled.

Kyle laughed dully and said, "Yeah, if you got one."

Welly reached into the pocket of his khaki pants and pulled out the black pouch, removed a strip, handed it to Kyle.

"Never leave home without my medi-pouch," Welly said.

Kyle placed the strip on his tongue and it disappeared. He swallowed and then said, "It's weird." He shook his head slowly. "I can't remember Bobby at all, but then again I can, like from forever ago. Everything is so damn...fuzzy."

"I know the feeling," Welly said. "Look, Kyle, you never really hung out with Bobby in this new event path. You didn't go to public schools so everything changed. Bobby's alive and well, but I'm not sure he knows who you are."

Kyle squinted and rubbed his temples. "What new event path?"

Welly said, "I assume the memory of it hasn't fixed in place yet, but I do believe that argument you made in your letter to the governor started that massive boulder rolling toward gun control reform. And *that* may have inadvertently helped to save your old pal's life."

Kyle thought about this, trying to recall and sort through all of this simultaneously.

Welly said, "You *are* a hell of a writer, son. Turns out maybe you just needed to feel comfortable sharing your thoughts. That was my fault."

The two sat in silence for a moment.

Kyle looked at the ceiling and nodded, registering a thought.

"Uh huh. Damn, I am a pretty great writer, aren't I?" He smiled and said, "So, can I ask? What in the hell are we talking about? What the hell happened? I mean to me. Why am I alive? Why was I naked? What's going on?"

"When I first saw what I thought I saw. Kyle, I thought for sure it was over. I saw the bullet blast right through you. And it did. But it didn't really. When I recalled the memory and analyzed it closely I saw you set yourself in motion just as Walton is about to pull the trigger and right at the moment he does pull the trigger, you're gone. All that remains is a pale blue vapor for just an instant and it's gone."

"What? So. What are you saying? I was vaporized and then reconfigured back together or something."

"Son, you traveled interdimensionally. I happen to know this is real. Meaning. It's possible and other beings can do it. Conforming your molecular structure for weaving in and out of different dimensions. Not capturing energy or exerting it, but actually *being* it."

"That sounds amazing," Kyle said, his eyebrows frozen in a raised position. "Truly amazing, but why the hell would I be doing that?"

Welly rubbed his forehead trying to cook down the long explanations into something quicker, more palatable.

"I was visited," he said. "When I was a boy. At the house I grew up in. A being from another planet visited me and imparted a vast knowledge unto me, into me. This is how. This is *why* I've come so far so fast."

He took a deep breath and peeked up at his son who was motionless. He didn't seem to not believe him, so he continued.

"I have so much more to tell you, but right now it's important to know that *you* were visited. It might sound creepy and crazy, but it wasn't at the time. I promise." He huffed in and then exhaled a large, dense breath. "Mom was pregnant with you. I was a nervous wreck. I was worried about every possible thing someone can worry about as it relates to a pregnancy, birth, bringing up a child. The works. I woke up one night and saw a cloaked being sitting by your mother. He focused on her big belly. Didn't care that I saw him or her or it. I don't know what it was doing, but something with her belly, and I was unafraid. Any other time I would have jumped up and strangled the thing and went crazy but I was overcome with this overwhelming feeling that everything was going to be alright. I still remember it washing over me right then and there. That feeling never left me the whole rest of the pregnancy and even in the delivery room. I never knew what it meant and I'm still not to-tally sure really, but I think it's all starting to make more sense. After what happened."

Kyle blinked. He rubbed his hand over his mouth and chin. He blinked a few more times. "So. Am I like, a friggin alien, Pop?"

Welly laughed. "You are mine and your mom's son. There is no denying that. But maybe. Maybe you are something more as well."

Kyle smiled uncomfortably. A shocked look swept over his face. "Oh my God. I just thought of something. What about Stephen? What about Lemus?"

Welly looked down at the fluffy white comforter. He looked back up at Kyle. "Stephen made it through the battle. I looked up his relatives, his ascendants, and he's got a bunch of family in New York actually, out on Long Island. There were only two American casualties by way of the battle of Trenton. Same as there always were. Both perished as a result of the cold. They froze. Lemus was one of those two men."

Kyle grinded his jaw and looked up, his eyes dampening.

Something clanged in the house. Kyle eyed Welly curiously. Welly held up a hand informing Kyle not to worry.

"It's important for you to know that Lemus died a noble death on his terms. By getting him out of that fort, he missed out on spending his last days on one of those British prison ships. On a prison ship he would have been packed in with thousands of others to die among the vermin, the decaying bodies and disease. We helped him. He's reunited with his son."

Kyle continued to bounce his eyes around, studying the edges of the ceiling.

"We did some good and you know what else?"

"What?"

"Son, look at me. There's something else I have to tell you."

Kyle looked at Welly.

"Son, you were tested in battle and you were more brave than I could ever hope to be. Hey, I would have been proud of you even if you rolled around like a flipped turtle like your old man, but Kyle, I can't tell you how proud you make me." This time the tears could not be gulped away. They staggered down his cheeks.

Kyle's eyes shined with wetness in the glow from the lamp atop his nightstand. He blinked a few more times to stifle the tears.

"What about Walton and-"

"All dead," Welly said.

"So," Kyle said. "We changed everything back?"

Welly sniffed vigorously and said, "Eh. Apparently it's close enough. The Boston Massacre still stands as the Boston Witch Hunt. It looks like history from this point on will have to include all that just happened, including what *we* did, if it's to be portrayed accurately. I am going to have a talk with my old pal President Denny, and see if he's open to a planned historical modification mission to change it back. Don't feel too good about the odds though."

Kyle nodded and said, "Like I always say, there is no perfection."

"Smart kid," Welly said and smiled. The smile left his face and he said, "Look. There is something important I need. Can I ask you an important question?"

Kyle Shrugged yes.

"I'm still really curious," Welly began. "How does chocolate milk mixed with boogers taste?"

Kyle processed this for a moment and then his head sprung up.

Welly grinned with the tears streaming down. "Wait." Kyle said. "I never. Wait." Kyle said again.

"That's your cue Chrissy," Welly said. .

The bedroom door opened. Kyle's mom, Christine, was there. Kyle's vocal cords quivered and his eyes filled with water. A puff rose up the back of his throat and he coughed. The cough was a pull cord violently starting the engine of tears that was dormant for so long. He felt like an angel was pressing his cheeks together trying to squeeze out tears of joy. He knew he wasn't dreaming this time and he had to remember how to move his body. He did. He swung his legs out and stood up and staggered to his mother. He hugged her tightly. He never wanted to let her go. He longed for this hug for so many days, so many hours, so many lonely minutes. He hugged her long and tight and wept. "I missed you so muuu," he mumbled.

"Oh. I love you so much Kyle," Christine said, now crying as well.

Kyle opened his eyes and looked over his mother's shoulder. He saw the kitchen table with a centerpiece of sloppily stacked pancakes. Right beside the pancake platter, there was a bottle of syrup featuring a little maple leaf logo and the words, Delhi Syrup Co.

"Oooo," another voice said. Kyle let go of his Mom and stumbled back a step. He grabbed onto the door jam on both sides of him to stop himself from falling down. He was woozy. Intensely woozy. His knees weakened and trembled.

His eyes closed.

He was back in the restaurant. Jekyll & Hyde's. They were leaving. Kyle was walking behind his parents and smiling.

Then he was in a large truck with dark tinted windows. He was taken out of school early.

He was being escorted into a hospital by a strange man in a suit. No. Not strange man. No. It was Cecil. Yes, it was Dad's assistant. Doors flew open. Kyle was jog-stepping to keep up. He was scared but happy to be out of school.

They arrived at the room. He was afraid to look in. He peered slowly around the banana colored molding and scanned the cold, speckled gray floor. The gray speckles led his eyeline to the metal wheel of the hospital bed and then upward. He could see his mom lying in the bed, a plastic bin that looked like a fish tank next to her.

"Meet your baby sister," his dad said, handing the baby gently into his waiting arms as he sat in the large reclining chair in the hospital room.

His eyes opened.

He was back in his bedroom. He clutched his forehead and grabbed at the golden door handle for support.

A shrill and youthful voice said sarcastically "Oooo, I missed you so much Kyle."

The voice was both familiar and foreign. "Sis," Kyle said, gently looking up, trying desperately to not shift the plates or fault lines in his head.

A blonde haired girl as tall as his chest walked over to him. She wore an oversized green t-shirt with the Forward logo, the pencil sketched Leyland Cypress, embroidered on the breast pocket. She hugged him. He patted her back absently.

She stepped back and looked up at him. "They said you would be out of it. Guess so. What a weirdo," she said and laughed.

Kyle laughed moronically. He stared vacantly at his sister. "Kaitlin," he said finally.

"Is he a zombie?" she said.

"He's remembering," Welly said in a wondrous tone.

Kaitlin made her way over to Welly. Welly reached down and picked her up, lifting her over his head, careful not to knock her on the ceiling.

Kyle looked on in awe. He held the expression of a tourist beholding the grandeur of the grand canyon for the first time or that of a landlocked dweller viewing the ocean for the first time. It was all the warmth and beauty in the world and processing it, didn't come easy.

Kyle was trying to place what was happening. It was off somehow. "Your back!" he said finally. "What about your back?"

Welly smiled. "All good. The mind is a powerful thing. Turns out."

"I don't get all this. Isn't there supposed to be like an apocalyptic, cataclysmic paradox that kills us all instantly?"

"Well," Welly said. "I really don't friggin know, son." He smirked and said, "Best I could tell you is sometimes you need to look up and other times you need to look down. Most times, I think you just need to look straight ahead and see what's right in front of you."

Kyle nodded and ran a hand through his hair. He looked at the floor trying to focus and absorb his father's beautiful sentiment. Everything was so different. He felt a tingling in both sides of his jaw and he gently massaged his cheeks with his hands.

Welly said, "Now would be a good time to look up, son."

Kyle lifted his head and looked up blankly. He tilted his head and blinked. His head jerked back and he blinked again.

Jennifer said, "Kyle Brackford." She smiled and grabbed hold of Kyle, clutching him tightly.

Kyle reached his arms around her and closed his eyes, inhaling the sweet fragrance of her windblown hair.

He said, "Jennifer Crowley."

THE END

Thank You!

Thank you to my family, friends and co-workers, for all of the support along the way. It means more than you know.

Thank you to everyone who produced any form of media on the subject of the American Revolution. I ferociously consumed all I could get my hands on and I thoroughly enjoyed the research part of this project. My favorite, an outstanding book titled 1776, by David McCullough, which I read and re-read and referenced many times. If you are curious on the topic and want to read up on it, I highly recommend this masterpiece.

Thank you, Reader, for spending your valuable reading time on my book. There are so many great books out there. You invested your time in this one and it is very much appreciated!

I hope you enjoyed it.

Sincerely,

Derrick Bliss